When I heard the commotion, I was certain
that bounty hunters were on our riverbank.
Oh, such a night! Shouts, gunfire, tragedy
beyond description. My dear neighbors' lives
are irreparably altered by the skirmish that
took place during the cover of darkness...

November 30, 1856

SECRETS OF WAYFARERS INN

Family Secrets
River of Life
All That Remains
Greater than Gold
A Flame in the Night
Never the Twain Shall Meet
The Innkeepers' Conundrum

The Innkeepers' Conundrum

KIM VOGEL SAWYER

Guideposts

New York

Not that I speak in respect of want:
for I have learned, in whatsoever state I am,
therewith to be content.
Philippians 4:11 KJV

For *Don,*
my "coin collector"

CHAPTER ONE

LuAnn gently twisted the glittering gold ribbons cascading from the bow at the top of the Christmas tree and directed them toward the thick bottom branches. She'd considered draping the tree in threads of tinsel, but when she spotted the gold topper with its array of four-inch-wide ribbons in the holiday section of a specialty shop in Canton, she'd changed her mind. Now she was glad for the choice. The half-dozen falls of ribbon finished the tree perfectly.

Such a lovely tree, a towering ten feet tall and covered from top to bottom in ornaments similar to the ones her mother had hung when she was a child, including antique multicolored reflector balls and mercury glass Santa Clauses, birds, pinecones, and stars. Of course, she couldn't cover a ten-foot-tall tree with antique ornaments. Not without breaking the bank. But reproductions, purchased at a fraction of the price of genuine antiques, interspersed with shatterproof balls, teardrops, and onion-shaped ornaments, gave the old-world appearance she wanted.

Tess descended the stairs, her arms full of linens, and peeked over the railing at the tree. She whistled. "Wow, Lu, it looks fantastic. The prettiest of all of them."

"Thanks." LuAnn had insisted on putting seven-foot-tall trees at the ends of the hallways on all levels, one in the café, and one in the library. Pint-sized trees decorated mantels, bathroom shelves, and the corner of the bar next to the antique cash register. But this one was definitely the *pièce de résistance*. It needed to be special, since it was the one guests would see when they stepped through the front doors.

LuAnn eased backward several feet, perusing the tree with a critical eye. Ribbons evenly spaced. Ornaments strategically placed both at the branches' tips and closer to the tree's trunk, giving a 3-D effect. No empty gaps, except—

She darted forward, removed one teardrop-shaped ornament, and reaffixed it a scant half inch to the right. She angled her head, scowling, then nodded. The painted snowflake on a blue background now complemented rather than competed with a striped, oversized ball.

Tess came the rest of the way down the stairs and stopped next to LuAnn. "You really have outdone yourself with the decorating. Thanks for taking it on. I can't imagine the inn being any more festive."

Their first Christmas at Wayfarers Inn. Shouldn't it be extra special? LuAnn fluffed one of the gold ribbons. "I still need to clip on the bubble lights and the LED candles on the tips of some of the branches, but now that I see the tree with the ornaments in place, I'm no longer disappointed about going with artificial." She tossed a grin over her shoulder. "I like being able to bend the branches to put the ornaments where I want them."

Tess shook her head. "You are such a perfectionist. Really, you need counseling." Her smile let LuAnn know she was teasing. She bounced the rumpled bundle spilling over her arms. "I better get these to the laundry room before Janice comes looking for me. You know she doesn't like being down there by herself too long." She ambled through the foyer to the café and disappeared from view.

LuAnn pulled a string of liquid-filled bubble lights from the box next to the stairs and untangled them. Christmas...a time of peace and goodwill to men. A time when families gathered to celebrate Christ's birth, partake of traditional recipes, and exchange gifts. It should be a joyful time. So why did sadness pinch her chest? She didn't have to ponder long. For as far back as she could remember, Christmas meant being with Mom. Until this year.

The passage of months hadn't erased the dull ache of grief, but at least she wouldn't be alone, thanks to Tess and Janice and the scheduled guests. In fact, she'd be less alone than she'd ever been before. With no husband or children, her holiday gatherings had always been quiet and largely uneventful. With the exception of the year an ice storm brought down a tree limb on the power line to their house and they spent Christmas Day without electricity. Cold sandwiches made a poor holiday dinner, but they'd bundled up in blankets and played checkers and Parcheesi by candlelight. A smile tugged at her lips. Funny how a day that had seemed so awful then now lingered as a precious memory.

She hummed "O Christmas Tree" while clipping on the strings of bubble lights and the individual LED candles. When she finished, she knelt and plugged in the outlet strip. The tree lit up like ... well, like a Christmas tree. Smiling, she stood with her hands on her hips and admired her handiwork. As soon as she put the Victorian crazy-quilt tree skirt into place and added a few empty boxes dressed in holiday paper and oversized bows, her decorating would be complete. She tapped her chin. Now, where had she put that tree skirt?

The lights on the tree flickered, the overhead chandelier strobed in offbeats, and then with a *pop!* the area went dark. LuAnn blinked in surprise. She almost ran to the window to see if a tree limb had taken out the power line, but the pendant lights in the café and the upstairs hallway lights hadn't gone out, so she must have tripped a circuit breaker. She huffed. Hadn't the electrician assured them the new wiring would handle the needs of the inn?

The front door opened, allowing in a chilly breeze, and their Realtor and friend, Brad Grimes, blew in with it. He pushed the door closed with his foot while balancing a sizable box against his stomach. He looked around, confusion marring his face. "Why's it so dark in here?"

LuAnn huffed again. "I blew a breaker. And I only plugged in one power strip." She plunked her fist on her hip. "That shouldn't happen with our new wiring, should it?"

He crossed to the bar-turned-reception desk and slid the box onto the top. "Hmm, that depends. How much amperage did you put on the power strip?"

She'd taught English and American History to hundreds of students. She was not a stupid woman. But she had no idea how to answer his question. She flapped her hand at the tree. "Only what's on this."

Brad frowned at the tree, his gaze drifting from the fluffy gold ball of ribbon at the top all the way to the lowest branches. He fingered one of the now non-bubbling bubble lights. "How many of the little incandescent strings did you wind onto this tree?"

She shrugged. "Sixteen, I think." She peeked in the box with the empty light containers and then nodded. "Yes, sixteen."

"Did you put them all in one long cord, end to end?"

"No. I did half and half, so eight strung into one. Then I ran an extension cord up the trunk for the bubble lights and candles. I couldn't connect them together, because they didn't have a receptacle end, only a prong end." LuAnn smiled smugly, proud of herself for knowing that much about electrical cords.

He frowned. "Well, it looks to me like you're pulling too much power from a single outlet. You'll either need to take the extension cord you used for the bubble lights and candles around a corner to another outlet that happens to be on a different circuit, or remove a couple of strings of lights."

She was not going to remove any of the light strings. Not after the hours she'd spent winding them around branches and then hanging ornaments over the top of them. And she wouldn't take off the bubble lights or candles, either. "All right. I'll run an extension cord under the door to our office."

He frowned again. "Well..."

LuAnn rolled her eyes. "Don't tell me. That outlet is on the same breaker as this one."

"Most likely."

Tears threatened. Such a silly reason to cry. But she wanted this Christmas to be perfect. The best ever. Blown circuit breakers and cords strung from one end of the inn to the other did not fit her perception of *perfect*.

Brad folded his arms and gave the tree a good look from top to bottom. "Tell you what, I'll check the breaker box. The electrician put a whole-house diagram next to the box. Every room and outlet is marked with a specific breaker. The office might have its own separate breaker."

She sniffled. "All right. Thanks."

"Now..." His million-dollar smile briefly lit the space. "Come see what I have for you." He led her to the box and lifted it to the floor. "My aunts insisted you needed these things. Don't feel obligated to keep them, but since Aunt Thelma and Aunt Irene intend to pop in for soup on Saturday, I suggest having at least one out where they can see it."

LuAnn looked in the box and gasped with delight. "Oh, those dear ladies." His elderly aunts had become good friends to the new owners of Wayfarers Inn after a rocky start. But this gift was enough to erase any memory of ill-will. She reached into the jumble of wadded old newspapers and withdrew one of six brass candelabra. The weight startled her, and she gripped it with both hands.

Even in the dim light flowing through the front windows on this cloudy day, the candelabrum shone with a fresh polishing.

She turned a disbelieving look on Brad. "Are they sure they don't want to use these themselves?"

"They aren't even putting up a tree this year. They said it's too much fuss and bother." He glanced around the spacious café and lounge space. "But obviously the thought of decorating isn't a 'fuss and bother' to you. It looks like the North Pole exploded."

She chose to ignore his last comment. "If they're sure they won't want to display them at their house, I'll gladly put them to use here. I can put one on the grand piano in the middle of the pine garland, another on the corner of the coffee bar, and—"

A tremendous crash sounded from overhead. Both Brad and LuAnn looked up to the long, railed landing, then looked at each other. She put the candelabrum on the bar and, without a word, dashed up the stairs. Brad thundered up behind her. They reached the second-floor landing and were met by the newly hired part-time housekeeper, Constance Wright.

Constance's hazel eyes were as round as a pair of full moons. "Did you hear that?"

LuAnn nodded, releasing a nervous laugh. "I imagine the neighbors heard it."

Brad pointed to Maple and Mum, the room at the end of the hall. "I think it came from over there."

LuAnn's heart raced as if she'd just finished a marathon. She'd run up and down the stairs so many times in the past few months, she knew the heavy *pound-pound-pound* wasn't from exertion. Real concern gripped her. With the Thanksgiving rush done and the Christmas rush yet to begin, only one guest resided under the inn's roof—Alice Busby, a self-proclaimed wannabe novelist who claimed she intended to stay in the Honeymoon Suite until she'd completed her very first whodunit. She was probably bent over a spiral notebook, scrawling red herrings with her pencil. If Constance hadn't created the noise, then who had?

Brad touched LuAnn's arm. "Is the room locked?"

LuAnn thought for a moment. "It shouldn't be. We've been cleaning and doing laundry the last couple of days, and with only the one guest, we haven't been as vigilant as we are with a full house."

"Stay here." He tiptoed to Maple and Mum and pressed his back against the wall next to the doorjamb. He pushed the door open slowly, his head cocked at an angle as if fearful something might leap out at him. Then his tense frame relaxed. He crossed the threshold. "Oh, boy..."

LuAnn darted to the room and looked in. The large, ornate mirror that had been hanging on the wall across from the bed lay shattered on the floor, its frame bent into a rhombus. She crouched and touched one shard of thick beveled glass. "Did the hanger come loose?" Their handyman, Tory "Thorn" Thornton, was so careful about securing heavy paintings and mirrors to studs, but maybe the hanger hadn't been strong enough to hold the mirror. She remembered struggling to carry it to the car after buying it at Harry's antique store.

Brad scowled at the wall. "No. Thorn used two hangers instead of one, and both are secure on the wall."

"Then the wire we put on the back of the mirror must have come loose."

He picked up the misshapen frame. Even LuAnn could see that the eyebolts were still screwed into the thick wood and the wire remained stretched across the back of the frame. Brad looked from the frame to the wall to the frame again. He frowned. "This didn't fall, LuAnn. It had to have been lifted from the hangers and dropped."

CHAPTER TWO

LuAnn gazed sadly at the shattered mirror. The pieces reflected various surfaces and created a bizarre mosaic that reminded her of the confusing scenes from *Alice in Wonderland*.

Constance had stayed in the doorway. She now stepped in and touched LuAnn's arm. "I'll get the broom and dustpan and clean this up." She scurried out before LuAnn could thank her.

Brad propped the broken frame against the wall. "I didn't realize you'd hired Constance."

LuAnn toed a shard of glass. "She's here temporarily—only through the holiday season. Taylor asked to take off the month of December to focus on semester exams, so Tess is pretty much fulfilling his duties waiting tables. We needed someone to help with the housekeeping chores. Already Constance has been a blessing. She completely freed me up to decorate the place for Christmas."

Constance returned, broom in hand, and Brad escorted LuAnn to the hallway. When they were well away from Maple and Mum's open door, he leaned close and whispered, "Is Constance the only one on this floor besides us?"

She shot him a startled look. "Well, Alice is in the Honeymoon Suite, but other than that, yes."

He followed her down the stairs. "You might want to ask Alice if she saw or heard anything."

LuAnn ran her fingers along the railing, touching the looped garlands of greenery attached with gold ribbon. "I'll be sure to do that. But I can't believe either of them had anything to do with the mirror coming off the wall."

They reached the lobby, and he headed for the front door. "Be sure to have those candlesticks where they're visible before my aunts arrive, or they'll scour the place looking for them."

LuAnn laughed. "Do you think they would have some time to tell me about the original owner of the inn? I've been wanting to gather as complete a history of the inn as I can to share with the guests." Another project she'd undertaken to keep her mind off missing her mother.

Brad nodded. "I think they can be persuaded to tell you everything they know. And what they don't know they'll make up." He tossed her a grin. "I need to run."

She waved goodbye, then sent a puzzled look toward the second-floor railed landing. Constance seemed like a very nice, conscientious young woman. Surely if she'd broken the mirror, she would own up to it, wouldn't she?

Saturday dawned with strong winds and snowflakes swirling like confetti. Although there were three different soups simmering, LuAnn wondered if anyone would venture in. She tried not to worry, but they'd invested so much in Wayfarers

Inn. If it failed, how would they—at their ages—recover the losses?

Despite the unpleasant weather, a dozen people found a seat at one of the round tables or clustered around the recently added farmhouse table and ordered peanut soup, loaded baked potato soup, or clam chowder. The aroma of savory soups and the mouthwatering scent of fresh-baked biscuits permeated the entire first floor and stirred LuAnn's appetite while she carried a plate of biscuits from table to table, offering guests another serving. She'd already sneaked a cup of chowder, but she might need a second serving before the lunch rush ended.

At a quarter of one, the dear older ladies Brad called Aunt Irene and Aunt Thelma entered the inn. Janice set the coffee-pot on an empty table, bustled over, and gave them each a hug. Then she pulled back and shivered.

"*Brrrrr.* You're cold! Come over here, and I'll pour you a cup of coffee. It'll warm you up in a hurry." She ushered the women to the café the way a mother duck urged her ducklings into a pond.

"I'd rather have a cup of tea," Thelma said, unwrapping her scarf.

Irene popped the knitted cap from her head. Her soft gray hair stood up in staticky puffs, reminding LuAnn of a gone-to-seed dandelion. "Shame on you, Thelma. Why not accept the coffee instead of requesting something else? You aren't being polite to our hostess."

Thelma snorted. "There's not one thing wrong with asking for tea if I'd rather drink tea. I'd only waste the coffee. How polite would that be?" The two of them settled across from each other at a round table and continued to bicker.

LuAnn chuckled and nudged Janice. "That'll probably be us someday."

Janice rolled her eyes. "Are you kidding? That's us already." Affection softened her smile, and she laughed. She moved next to the table and put her hands on the ladies' rounded shoulders. "All right, what will you have?"

"Peanut soup," they said in unison.

"Coming right up." Janice hustled for the kitchen.

LuAnn started after her, intending to refill the biscuit plate, but Thelma beckoned her with an arthritic finger. She changed direction and approached the table.

Thelma pointed to one of the empty chairs. "Sit down for a minute. Bradley said you were curious about the original owner of the Riverfront House."

She had things to do, but LuAnn couldn't resist slipping onto the chair's round wooden seat. Her canvas cobbler's apron—embroidered with *Wayfarers Inn* in arching letters over her name, an early Christmas gift from Winnie—bunched up around her neck. She shifted it into place and smiled at Thelma as Janice delivered their beverages. "I'm very curious. I'm gathering information to put together a history-of-the-inn book to keep in the library for guests to read. Since Alfred Dawes was the original owner, his story should come first."

"It's a sad one..." Irene clucked her tongue on her teeth and shook her head. "Fraught with tragedy and heartache."

Thelma pursed her lips. "Really, Irene, there's no need to be so melodramatic." She patted LuAnn's hand. "It's sad, but no more than many others' stories from that rough and turbulent time."

Irene glared at her older sister, and LuAnn hid her smile behind her hand. She waited for one of them to continue.

Thelma took the lead. "Alfred Dawes was an evil man, well-known for his fervent pro-slavery views. He provided lodging for bounty hunters, and there are even accounts of him giving false testimony against free black men and women who were captured and 'returned to their owners.'" She shook her head. "I'm sorry that the inn has to acknowledge such a person in its history, but we can't whitewash what he was."

LuAnn was sorry too. "What eventually happened to him? I know he sold the inn in 1857."

Irene took up the tale. "He got restless and went west to Kansas territory, part of a movement that sought 'free-soil for whites only.' He was a supporter of the Kansas Bogus Legislature, so called because its pro-slavery members were elected by widespread and flagrant voter fraud. They stuffed the ballot boxes so badly that the victors won by almost twice as many votes as there were registered voters in the entire state. Of course, that was before Alfred got there."

Thelma reached for the cream. "The violence that erupted between the two sides during the settling of the territory is where the term "Bleeding Kansas" came from. Alfred Dawes was hit by a stray bullet in a shootout between a bounty hunter and a free black man. The bounty hunter and the black man survived. Alfred did not. Some people would say it was poetic justice."

November 30, 1856,
a quarter hour before midnight

Prudence tiptoed into the kitchen of the Riverfront House, note in hand. She couldn't leave without informing the Stanfills about the two packages she'd taken to her house, but then she needed to hurry home before Jason started to worry. The only reason he'd allowed her to make the visit was the hotel caretaker's assurance that the pro-slavery owner of the hotel was out of town.

The room was as dark as a cloud-covered night sky but, familiar with the kitchen's layout, she felt her way to Elswyth Gardener Stanfill's work counter. She slipped the small square of paper on which she'd written *2 chickens roosting*—their code for two packages safely hidden— beneath the edge of the sugar crock and then turned to go. A vicious thump-thump-thump on the back door froze her in place, her entire frame prickling with gooseflesh despite the chilly night.

Elswyth's sleepy voice carried from the room behind the kitchen. "A guest? At this hour?"

A low-pitched groan, no doubt Elswyth's husband coming awake, followed. "I'll see to it. Stay here, my love." The sound of his slippers scuffing across the floorboards alerted Prudence to his approach.

She pawed on the corner of the counter for the tin matchbox. She withdrew a match and struck it against the rough countertop. It flared and she winced, then touched the tiny flame to the charred wick of a candle standing at the ready in its little pewter holder. She puffed out the match, picked up the holder, and held it high. Only a moment later, Frederick Stanfill entered the kitchen.

His gaze whisked in the direction of the candle, his eyes reflecting shock, but at once his expression relaxed. "Ah, Prudence, was it you at the—" Another flurry of demanding thuds shook the door in its frame. Frowning, he took a step in its direction.

Prudence handed him the candle and flattened herself against the wall behind a standing cupboard. She wanted to see the face of whoever knocked on the door with such insistence. She wanted Frederick to see too. She'd learned over the course of their shared work that he was a good judge of character. If he viewed the individual as trustworthy, she would set all worry aside.

Frederick reached the back door and swung it open. He thrust the candle forward. She received only a glimpse of the fright-filled face of one of the inn's closest neighbors before a gust of chilly wind extinguished the tiny flame.

The man grabbed Frederick's arm. "They're comin'."

Frederick shook loose. "Who's coming? You're not making sense, man."

"The marauders. They're in our town."

A gasp came from the kitchen doorway. Elswyth staggered forward and clung to her husband's hand. She rasped, "The band of riverboat pirates that has been terrorizing towns up and down the Ohio River is in Marietta?"

"Yes'm." The man's face contorted into a horrible grimace. "I'm warnin' ever'body. Hide your valuables an' load your revolver." He leaped from the porch. "Gotta tell the others." He disappeared into the shadows.

Frederick snapped the door closed and whirled on the women, his gaze settling on his wife. "Fetch the box."

Elswyth shivered, but Prudence suspected it was fear rather than cold rattling her slight frame. A bitter taste, the flavor of terror, filled Prudence's mouth. She took the candle from Frederick, relit the flame, and placed it in on the trestle table in the center of the room.

Elswyth remained near the door, as if her feet had sent down roots. She wrung her hands. "Where will you put it that they won't find it? They've ransacked homes and businesses from Toronto to Newport. Nothing is safe."

"Don't fret." Frederick spoke as calmly as Prudence had heard him address his little son. "I'll put it under the hay in the stable. Isn't that where Prudence hides packages? Who would look for valuables there?" His hand raised and cupped his wife's cheek. "I won't let robbers take the gold doubloons. They're to be Reggie's someday."

Tenderness welled in Prudence's breast at the mention of the Stanfills' four-year-old son, who must be blessedly asleep in his little trundle. She prayed he would stay asleep rather than be terrorized on this night.

Frederick leaned down and placed a quick kiss on Elswyth's lips. "Hurry, Elswyth. Fetch the box while I load my flintlock."

Elswyth scurried across the floor and disappeared behind the bedroom door. Prudence held to the edge of the table, her heart pounding in both fear and anguish. Months ago, Elswyth had confided that her father gave Frederick three gold doubloons in a carved wooden box as her dowry. Frederick, the proud man, had sworn no dowry was needed, for he would always provide for his beloved Elswyth, but her father, also a man of pride, had refused to send his only daughter into marriage without honoring the ancient custom.

Unexpectedly, tears stung Prudence's eyes, and a prayer lifted from her heart. *The coins are a symbol of her dear father's love for her. Keep them safe from the robbers, please.*

Elswyth returned and carried the box to the kitchen table, where the candle illuminated Frederick's sturdy night-shirt-covered frame and the gleaming barrel of the pistol in his hand. Elswyth held out the box, but then she paused and a frown creased her face.

"Have you tobacco tucked in your jaw? You promised to give up the vile habit that is blackening your teeth and fouling your breath. You've gone weeks without it."

Prudence touched Elswyth's cold hand and whispered, "He must be as frightened as we to have dipped into snuff for bolstering. Do not scold him, dear friend."

Elswyth nodded and fell silent.

Frederick took the box from her and placed it on the table. He opened it, removed the three coins, and clinked them into a nearly empty snuffbox. His grin wobbled as he placed the snuffbox inside the carved wooden box. "An extra precaution, yes? Nothing valuable to be found in a snuffbox." The jewelry box under his arm, he picked up his pistol and moved stealthily to the back door. He aimed a stern look over his shoulder, made ludicrous by the telltale lump in his cheek. "Stay here. No matter what happens, you stay here." Then he slipped outside.

CHAPTER THREE

Something brushed LuAnn's arm, and she yelped. She spun and glared at Janice. "Gracious sakes, you nearly frightened me out of my wits."

Janice nodded to the tray in her hands which held two steaming bowls of peanut soup and a plate of biscuits. "I'm sorry. I bumped you by accident trying to get out of the way of the people leaving."

LuAnn hadn't realized how caught up in Alfred Dawes's tale she'd become. Several patrons had departed, new ones had arrived, and a couple now waited to pay. She bolted from the chair. "Excuse me, ladies."

She accepted payment and compliments from the couple at the register and wished them a pleasant day, then hurried back to the table. But Irene and Thelma were eating, and their soup would get cold if she interrupted. So she went to the kitchen instead.

Tess was removing a fresh batch of biscuits from the massive range they'd dubbed Big Red, and Winnie was stirring one of the kettles. For a moment, jealousy struck. LuAnn had envisioned herself doing much of the cooking and baking, but Winnie had proved so competent, most of the time they all just got out of her way.

LuAnn snagged a bowl from a stack on the counter and crossed to the kettles. "Peanut soup, please—half a bowl will be enough."

Winnie shrugged. "Sorry, Miss LuAnn, the peanut soup's all gone. Nearly every person who came in today wanted it, and I gave the last bit to Marcus." She nodded at her sixteen-year-old grandson, who sat at the kitchen table with his usual sullen countenance. LuAnn had never met a more taciturn teenager. She smiled at him, but he bent over the bowl and acted as if he hadn't noticed. Winnie's expression turned smug. "Might have to start making double batches now that cold weather's here to stay. Nothing warms your innards better than a bowl of my good peanut soup."

"Unless it's these biscuits." Tess dipped low over the pan of fluffy discs and inhaled. "I think this is what heaven must smell like."

Winnie laughed. "Miss LuAnn, you want some more of the chowder? There's the most left of it."

LuAnn set the bowl aside. "No, thank you. I'll just have a biscuit instead."

Winnie waved a wooden spoon. "Oh, no, you don't. Those're for the paying guests."

Tess handed LuAnn a plate of biscuits and a pair of tongs. "Here you go. Share these with the paying guests."

LuAnn took the plate and glanced at Winnie, who stirred the chowder and hummed. "She's pretty comfortable around here," LuAnn whispered, "ordering around her employers."

Tess nodded. "She's not the only one getting comfortable. I caught Constance coming out of our office yesterday afternoon."

LuAnn frowned. "I thought we told her she wouldn't need to clean in there—that we'd see to everything in the office."

"We did."

Their safe where guests entrusted them to place valuables, as well as their personal locked cabinet, was in the office. No one but the owners should have access to anything in the small room. "Did you remind her that the office is off-limits?"

"No."

"Why not?"

Tess shrugged. "I looked, and nothing seemed disturbed, so I didn't think it was that important. Maybe she's super conscientious. She's been doing a great job on the rooms and common areas. I'd hate to scare her off by being too nitpicky."

"Well, I—"

"Why are you still standing there with those biscuits?" Winnie's voice cut in. "They'll get cold and hard as bricks. I didn't spend my morning locked up in this kitchen rollin', cuttin', and bakin' those things so they could turn to bricks. Take 'em to the customers, Miss LuAnn."

LuAnn was too startled not to obey. She made the rounds again, and nearly everyone wanted an extra biscuit. Only two remained on the plate when she reached the last table, where their most recent check-ins, Mike and Julie Rollings, who'd confided they'd never before left their children for an entire weekend and were a little nervous about it, were finishing bowls of potato soup. LuAnn offered them the biscuits.

Mike patted his belly. "No, thank you, ma'am. I've already had three. Do you sell recipe books here?"

"No, I'm afraid we don't." LuAnn filed away the idea for future consideration. "But I'm sure our cook would write out the recipe for you."

"That would be great! They're the best I've ever had."

LuAnn smiled. "That's music to our ears. Is there anything else I can get you? More water, coffee, maybe a piece of pie?" She'd helped Winnie bake several cherry, apple, and butter-milk pies yesterday evening for today's guests.

"No, thanks. We don't need anything else," Julie answered, shooting her husband a meaningful look. "Except..."

LuAnn's scalp prickled. "Is something wrong?"

"Not *wrong* exactly, but..." The woman's expression became intent as she stared at her husband.

Mike cleared his throat. "The thing is—now, this isn't a complaint, because everyone's been real nice to us—but we caught the maid in the closet in our room on her hands and knees."

First Constance was in the office where she didn't belong, and now in a guest room closet? "You did? Did she say why she was there?"

The man used his spoon and scraped at the remnants of thick broth on the sides of his bowl. "She said she'd dropped something."

"But she didn't say what she'd dropped," Julie added, "and after she left, we noticed a floorboard was sticking up at one end, like she'd been prying at it."

"Now, honey, that board might have been loose before, and we just didn't notice." Mike set the spoon in the bowl. "Nothing was missing from our room and, like I said, everyone's been real nice. But we thought we should mention it. It seemed... strange."

Yes, it did. LuAnn forced a smile. "Thank you for telling me. I'll have our handyman check the board and make sure it isn't a hazard for the two of you."

"Thank you." Julie rose. "I assume you'll let us know when he intends to go in our room?"

"Of course."

"And I think it would be best if you asked the maid to leave our room untouched for the remainder of our stay." She scribbled her name on the tab lying on the table and picked up her purse. "Let's go, Mike."

Her husband trailed her, offering LuAnn an apologetic smile as he passed her. LuAnn, frowning, gazed after them. They'd better have a talk with Constance. As much as they needed the extra help during the busy season, they couldn't afford for her to run off guests.

After church Sunday, Janice and Tess left straight from the service to spend a few hours with family. Both of them invited

LuAnn to join them, but she declined. She always felt like an intruder at family gatherings. Besides, they'd left the inn untended for almost two hours already. Ordinarily one of them stayed behind on Sunday mornings in case a guest needed something, but all but one—Alice Busby—had checked out that morning. Alice had assured them she'd be fine on her own, so they'd enjoyed attending service together. But now LuAnn needed some time to herself to think about Christmas gifts. The day would sneak up on her before she knew it, and she was only half ready.

As she walked to the inn, head low against the cold, damp wind, she searched her mind for ideas to finish her Christmas list. She'd ordered lovely silk scarves in bold floral prints for Tess and Janice from a boutique she'd visited in France several years ago, and she'd picked up a coffee table book at a flea market for Brad. A whopping four pounds, the book was full of photographs of vintage houses and buildings with extraordinary architecture. Since he sold real estate and seemed enamored with historical properties, she thought he would like the book.

She needed to shop for Irene, Thelma, Winnie, and Pastor Ben and his wife, Paige, plus a few other friends. She hadn't come up with ideas yet, but she knew she didn't want to settle for boxes of chocolate-covered cherries or Christmas-themed mugs stuffed with packets of cocoa or teabags. She wanted something personal. Special. Chosen specifically for each of them so they'd know they were important to her. Even more important now that she had no family of her own with whom to celebrate.

She waited at the corner for traffic to clear, then trotted across the street. As she stepped up on the curb, another name came to mind—Constance. Even though the young woman was temporary help, she shouldn't be neglected. LuAnn would give some thought to an appropriate gift for her too.

The inn waited ahead, and she sped her steps, eager to get out of the sharp wind, heat a bowl of leftover chowder, and maybe curl up in one of the reading chairs in the library with a good book. As she approached, the front door of the inn opened and a woman exited. She scurried in the opposite direction and darted between buildings. Although LuAnn only got a glance, she was almost certain the woman was Constance. Why would she be at Wayfarers today, on her day off? Had she needed to talk to them?

LuAnn entered the inn. While removing her coat and scarf, she scanned the foyer and café dining room. The Christmas tree and garland lights twinkled, casting a cheery glow that adequately lit the area. Everything looked exactly as they'd left it earlier that day. She crossed to the office tucked behind the stairs, checked the door, and found it locked tight. She breathed a sigh of relief and then gave herself a mental kick. What did she suspect Constance of doing, random dusting and unsolicited tidying?

There was the question about Constance pawing around a guest room closet. Thorn had told them the loose board in the closet was simply warped from age, so at least they could rest assured she hadn't been prying up floorboards. But she had been caught on her hands and knees in a guest's private space. Peculiar…

LuAnn carried her coat and purse up the flights of stairs, forcing herself to keep her gaze straight head rather than searching for signs of sabotage, and deposited her belongings in her private living quarters. She changed out of her church clothes into a bold pink jogging suit, then brushed her hair up into a ponytail. Comfortable, she headed back down the three flights and to the check-in desk. As she opened the register, a startled gasp sounded from behind her. She turned and found Alice standing in the hidden doorway that led to the basement. LuAnn had never seen a more guilty-looking face.

"You're back." The woman pushed her old-fashioned-looking wire spectacles up her nose and clutched a spiral notebook to her bosom. A pencil seemed to hover over her right ear, jammed into the thick strands of gray hair pulled back into a fuzzy bun. "I…didn't expect you."

LuAnn choked back a chortle. That much was clear. Although they'd already gone over the inn's regulations, LuAnn suspected Alice was somewhat scatterbrained. She might have forgotten the "no guests allowed in the basement" rule. Winnie's grandson, Marcus, was a frequent visitor to the basement, but since he used the loading dock to deliver their weekly groceries, they'd made him the one exception to the rule. LuAnn formed a gracious reminder. "Alice, we—"

"I know guests aren't supposed to be in the basement. But I heard a noise."

LuAnn raised her eyebrows. "What kind of noise?"

"I was writing. In the library"—Alice flapped the notebook in the direction of the designated reading area—"when I heard something suspicious. Somebody shuffling around. From beneath my feet." Her brown eyes narrowed. "I knew you three ladies had gone to church. Since I was the only one here, I felt it my duty to protect this fine establishment from intruders."

Had the woman not heard about 911? "So you went downstairs to confront a potential intruder?"

"Of course!" She smiled, holding the notebook aloft. "What better research than firsthand experience? It could have been such an exciting scene for my novel."

"Yes, but—"

"This door was standing wide open, inviting me in, so I had to go." Her eyes sparkled, her plump body quivering. "I called out—'Who's there?'—but no one answered. So I started checking all the little rooms down there. When I was in the second room, I heard somebody run up the stairs." She sighed, her lower lip poking out. "Alas, the intruder escaped me. Then I figured, as long as I'm down here, I might as well look around a little bit. So I peeked in all the rooms. I hope you don't mind."

LuAnn did mind, but she couldn't say so without seeming ungracious. After all, Alice's motives sounded good even if it was foolish to go after an intruder by herself. This time the intruder was most likely Constance—although why she was snooping around the inn, and especially in the basement, on her day off, LuAnn couldn't imagine—but next time it could be someone dangerous.

She drew a deep breath. "I appreciate your attempt to protect the inn from an intruder, but what if the person had pointed a gun at you?"

Alice's mouth formed a perfect *O*. "I didn't think about that. But what a good thing for my heroine to remember." She flopped open the notebook, plucked the pencil from its spot above her ear, and scribbled something. Then she sent a beaming smile at LuAnn. "Thank you very much. If I use your idea, I will be sure to credit you when my book is published."

LuAnn couldn't hold back a smile. The woman might be scatterbrained, but her apparent sincerity was touching. "Thank you." She took a gentle hold on Alice's elbow and guided her from behind the desk. "Now that the inn is secure, let's—"

Alice came to a stop. "Oh! Before I forget… The nice young woman who cleans my room—what is her name again?"

"Constance?"

"Yes, Constance. She stopped in and picked up your biscuit recipe. She said she had company coming for supper and wanted to make them, and the cook had written out the recipe for her on a card, but she'd forgotten to take it with her yesterday. So she came to get it. She asked me to tell you ladies, since none of you were here when she came by."

A funny prickle crept up LuAnn's spine. "When was this?"

The woman tapped her lips with the pencil eraser, her brow puckering. Then she brightened. "Before I heard the intruder in the basement. She'd just walked out the door when I heard the thump and bump downstairs." She stepped free of LuAnn's hold. "You go ahead and get your lunch now. I have writing to do."

CHAPTER FOUR

Since Alice had taken up residence in the library even though she was renting the most spacious guest room in the entire inn, LuAnn decided to close herself in the little office. With all the getting-ready-for-Christmas busyness, she'd neglected her personal notebook recently, but while the inn was quiet, she could catch up.

She retrieved her turquoise notebook and jeweled pen from the center drawer in the desk and opened to a fresh sheet. She recorded the odd happenings over the past few days. *Mirror dropped from wall—Constance only person close by; Constance snooping in closet of guest room—why?*

She paused. Had Constance actually been snooping, or had the guests misinterpreted her actions? If she was snooping, what did she think she'd find on the closet floor? LuAnn shook her head and returned her attention to the notebook.

Constance at inn when she knew all of us were away; Unknown person in basement.

LuAnn frowned at the list. Only one of her notations didn't include Constance's name. If Alice heard someone downstairs immediately after Constance left, she couldn't have been in the basement. Unless she'd run around and sneaked in the back door. Which she couldn't have done without a key. The only people who had keys to the back door were Winnie, Tess, Janice, and LuAnn. LuAnn didn't suspect Winnie of coming in and prowling around in the basement. If she wanted to go down there, she'd announce herself. But what about Marcus? When he came to the loading dock to deliver groceries, someone with a key always opened that door for him. But he had access to his grandmother's house and could borrow her key. She wrote behind the last notation *(maybe Marcus? But why would he be in the basement when he doesn't have a delivery?)*.

Then again, was there any proof that someone had been in the basement? Alice Busby admitted to writing a mystery novel and using happenings at the inn as inspiration. Maybe she'd decided to explore and made up an excuse to keep LuAnn from being upset about her entering a part of the inn not available to guests. A troubling thought struck. Alice claimed the door was open, inviting her entrance. When the door was closed, it would be very difficult for someone not familiar with it to find it. And they kept it locked when they weren't using it. LuAnn had gone down to the laundry room after breakfast for a sweater she'd left draped over a drying rack. Had she secured the door when she came up? She pressed her memory, but she couldn't remember.

Growling under her breath, she put her pen on the page and wrote *Alice could have imagined or made up an intruder in the basement.* She stared at the sentence, wishing she could be sure whether she'd closed the basement door or not.

The bell on the front door jingled, derailing her thoughts.

November 30, 1856, just before midnight

Frederick had told them to stay inside, and Prudence intended to follow his instruction. But when a rumble of voices came from the yard and the glow of torches flashed on the windowpanes on the west side of the kitchen, Elswyth darted to the window overlooking the porch and peered out, and Prudence couldn't resist joining her.

Frederick was at the bottom of the porch steps, holding his pistol low against his thigh, the carved jewelry box tucked in the bend of his arm. A group of men—five or six, as best Prudence could tell—stopped a few yards from him, their torches held high and illuminating their whiskered, scowling faces. A tall, broad-shouldered man with a knitted cap drooping over his ear pointed at Frederick.

"You there, what's that you're holdin'?"

Frederick's head dipped briefly, and Prudence imagined him searching for a believable reason to be standing in his backyard with a jewelry box under his arm. "This?" A nervous laugh filtered to her ears. "Nothing important."

"I'll be judgin' that. Give it over." The entire group surged forward a few inches, their stances menacing.

Frederick seemed to freeze for a moment, then he threw the box at the men. It hit the hard ground and bounced, and the lid popped open. One of the men bent over and snatched it up. He looked in it, shook it, then held it out to his gang. "There ain't nothin' here!"

The man in the cap shook his fist at Frederick. "Where're the contents, man? What've you done with the jewels?"

Frederick turned for the house, and at the same time Elswyth darted for the back door.

Prudence lunged after her. "Elswyth, no. We must stay inside. Thy husband—"

A pistol shot blasted, then three more. With a scream, Elswyth threw open the door. The gang of men turned and disappeared into the night. Elswyth darted onto the porch, and Prudence hurried after her. She nearly tripped over Frederick's prone form, lying on the porch.

"Frederick! Frederick!" Elswyth dropped to her knees beside him and rolled him over. A dark stain marred the chest of his nightshirt. Prudence gaped in horror at the growing spot. Elswyth cupped her husband's face in her hands. "Frederick!"

His eyes fluttered open. He lifted one hand and pressed it weakly to her cheek. "My love…the light…the light…" His arm flopped down. His eyes closed, and his body went limp.

Neighbors came running. Prudence lifted Elswyth from Frederick's lifeless frame and helped her inside. Others carried in Frederick's body and placed it on the kitchen trestle table. The constable came, fetched by a neighbor. Elswyth seemed to be in shock, so Prudence did her best to explain the night's happenings. But there was much she didn't know.

Who had shot Frederick? Had he shot any of the thieves? Had the marauders stolen away with the doubloons, or were they lying out there somewhere in the dried grass?

"Did he say somethin'—anything—before he passed?" Although the constable spoke kindly, his words stabbed. How could it be that Frederick was dead? Poor Elswyth, who must now face life without her beloved husband and father of her child. And poor little Reggie.

Prudence swallowed a knot of agony and nodded. "He said, 'the light.'"

One of the neighbors released a heavy sigh. "Prob'ly saw heavenly angels comin' to get him."

She wished the angels had left him. Surely Elswyth needed him on earth more than anyone could need him in heaven.

The constable left with a promise to fetch the doctor, although what the doctor could do for Frederick escaped Prudence. One by one those who'd come to offer support, or came out of curiosity, left, and only Prudence remained. Should she go? Jason would be sick with worry if she wasn't in their bed when the sun came up. But how could she leave Elswyth at such a time? In a few hours, guests would expect breakfast. Someone should stoke the stove, gather the eggs, all the things necessary to start the day. Elswyth, slumping on a bench and clinging to her husband's lifeless hand, wouldn't be able to see to the chores.

Although Prudence hated the idea of worrying Jason, she could not leave. She would lend a hand to her dear friend who needed her. Before she started morning chores, though, she must search the yard. If the pewter snuffbox in which

Frederick had placed the gold doubloons was still on the property, she needed to find it. Little Reggie would have to grow up without his papa. At the very least, he should have his inheritance.

LuAnn slapped the notebook closed, dropped the pen, and hurried to the foyer. Thelma Bickerton Martin toddled toward her, a smile lighting her wrinkled face. LuAnn gave the sparrowlike woman a hug. "Hello. What brings you in on a Sunday afternoon?"

Thelma pulled back and released a little snort. "Irene and I took lunch at Jeremiah's Coffee House, and she's still finishing a chicken salad sandwich. She'd be done by now if she wasn't stopping every bite to pick out the walnuts. Why order something with walnuts and then pick them out? I decided I'd rather come sit here than sit there and watch her tear her sandwich apart bit by bit. Do you mind having a visitor who isn't a paying guest?"

LuAnn laughed. "Not at all." She escorted Thelma to the sitting area overlooking the river and they settled onto one of the sofas. While Irene was picking at walnuts, LuAnn could pick Thelma's brain for Christmas gift ideas. "Thank you again for the loan of your lovely candlesticks. They add such a nice touch to the holiday greenery."

Thelma examined the arrangement at the end of the bar. "You sure knew what to do with them. Chose the perfect spots." She sighed and faced LuAnn again. "At our ages, having so much bric-a-brac around is almost distracting. I keep telling Irene we need to—what do they call it these days?—downsize. Or minimize. You know, get rid of stuff. But she isn't ready. That's why she told Bradley those candelabrum were a loan." Her eyes glittered with mischief. "But I'd rather you considered them a gift. By the time Christmas is over, she'll have forgotten about them. So just tuck them away with your other Christmas decorations, and think of us when you set them out again next year."

LuAnn's eyes misted. She squeezed Thelma's hand. "That's so sweet of you. Thank you."

"You're welcome." The older woman pushed a throw pillow behind her back and wriggled a bit. "I must confess, I also wanted to stop by and ask you how you intend to handle the information we gave you about Alfred Dawes. How much of the story will you tell your guests?"

"As much as I'd like to leave him out of our timeline, I'm afraid we can't take the good without the bad. And we already know a bit about him because of Prudence's journal." She snapped her fingers as realization dawned. "You know, I remember reading something about him . . . " She bounced up. "Let me get my copy." She retrieved the stack of printed pages from the office and returned to the sitting area. Placing the stack on the coffee table, she grinned at Thelma. "The history teacher in me enjoys these forays into previous centuries more than the average individual would."

Thelma chuckled. "All the more reason why it's right that you have ownership of this historical building. I know you'll honor its history."

LuAnn gave the older woman a warm smile and began turning pages. She scanned the lines of penned text, and she found what she wanted in the entry for December 3, 1856. "Here it is. Listen." She bent over the page. "'Oh, such a solemn ceremony today, bidding farewell to the caretaker of the River-front House. My heart aches for his dear wife, who must forever live with the horror of losing her husband to murderous thieves, and for the poor little boy who wailed for his papa through the entire service. How will Elswyth care for her small child and take care of the inn without a husband's assistance? I fear the hateful owner of the hotel will relieve her of her position and, in so doing, her home. I had the opportunity to speak a few words to her after the ceremony, words I prayed would give her comfort, but she comforted me by reminding me of her husband's final words. He spoke of the light. Does that not indicate he received a glimpse of heaven's gates opening wide? Surely he is now in the presence of his Savior, and in that we take great hope.'"

She looked up to speak to Thelma and discovered Alice Busby standing at the end of the sofa, open notebook and poised pencil in hand. Her eyes gleamed. She glanced at the diary pages and then pinned LuAnn with an intense look.

"A man was murdered in this very inn? Perhaps his soul still haunts the grounds. Maybe it was the murdered caretaker I heard prowling in the basement earlier today."

CHAPTER FIVE

O f course it's ridiculous." LuAnn cupped her hands around the mug of steaming cocoa and sent a tart look across the small dining table at Tess. "Despite the legend about the inn being haunted, there's no such thing as ghosts. There might not even have been an intruder. Other than Alice, that is." LuAnn had insisted on using the common area of their fourth-floor apartment for a private chat to avoid the possibility of the aspiring mystery writer listening in. The woman had seemed to pop up everywhere LuAnn went during the afternoon and evening.

Tess took a sip of her cocoa and held it under her chin, her expression turning contemplative. "She seems a little eccentric—"

"And nosy," LuAnn said with a light laugh.

Tess grinned. "And nosy. But she doesn't strike me as conniving. She was alone in the inn. The size of the place and the quiet probably started feeling overwhelming, and her imagination played a trick on her."

"That makes sense, I suppose." Janice tipped her head, puzzlement pinching her face. "But how did she get in the basement?"

LuAnn grimaced. "She said the hidden door was wide open and 'invited' her in."

Janice gaped at LuAnn. "Wide open? Then somebody had to have been down there after me. I closed the door and locked it when I came up from putting my dirty clothes basket down there."

LuAnn touched her hand. "When was that?"

"Right before we left for church."

LuAnn shuddered. "That's a creepy thought. With the tunnel and ladders in the closets sealed, the only way into the basement is through the loading dock, the outside tunnel door, or through the hidden door. We always keep the loading door's deadbolt locked unless we're using it, and Janice, you locked the hidden door. Surely no one could come in through the tunnel door."

The three women sat in silence for several seconds. LuAnn set her cocoa aside and reached for her notebook. "I made a list of—"

Tess burst out laughing. "Of course you did."

LuAnn shot her a mock look of annoyance. "—anyone who has a key or has had a key to any of the three entrances to the basement. All of us, Brad, Winnie, Thorn, the various workers who were in and out during renovations, and Constance." She tapped the page. "So out of these names, who seems the most likely to have been sneaking around in the basement while we were at church?"

"Maybe..." Tess pinned a thoughtful look on LuAnn. "Lu, you said Alice eavesdropped on your conversation with Thelma today. Is it possible she's eavesdropped at other times and heard someone say where they keep a key to one of the basement doors? Or maybe she convinced someone to open a door for her. Maybe she asked Constance to let her see the basement and Constance gave in. And now Constance is afraid to tell us."

Janice nodded. "I like that idea a lot better than thinking that an unknown someone got in through a locked door and was sneaking around in the basement."

LuAnn set her notebook aside. "For my peace of mind, I'm going to ask Constance if she let Alice in the basement." She needed to remember to ask why the housekeeper was on her knees in a guest's closet too. "If she didn't, then I think we'd better be more diligent about making sure that door is always secure. Maybe nobody was in the basement and Alice only imagined it, but it's better to be safe than sorry, don't you agree?"

"Agreed." Tess and Janice immediately chorused the response, which should have given LuAnn encouragement. But their approval only increased her apprehension. Because it meant they, too, were nervous about the possibility of some unknown person prowling the inn in their absence.

"No, Miss Sherrill, I didn't let Ms. Busby go in the basement."

Constance twisted her dustrag in a knot, and her gaze seemed aimed at LuAnn's chin, making her seem much younger than her twenty-five years. And untruthful.

"The only thing I told her is please let you ladies know I'd come by for the recipe Winnie wrote out for me. I . . . I hope you don't mind me picking it up when you weren't here." She finally looked LuAnn in the eyes.

LuAnn smiled and squeezed the younger woman's arm. "It's fine that you came for the recipe, although it's probably best not to make a habit of being here unless we're here or you're on duty. And I'm glad you didn't let Alice into the basement. It's important to keep guests out of the basement, for their protection and to keep us out of trouble with the insurance company."

"Of course, ma'am." Constance nodded, making her brown ponytail bounce. "I'll not let anyone go where they're not supposed to."

"Thank you." What else did she want to ask Constance? "Oh! Constance, one of the weekend guests mentioned they'd seen you on your hands and knees in their closet."

Constance dropped her gaze to the dustrag again. "I…um…lost a contact lens and was trying to find it."

Constance wore contacts? LuAnn hadn't noticed, but then, why should she have? "Were you successful?"

"No, ma'am." She took a sideways step. "May I go now? Alice likes to have her room gone over every morning, and the reservation book shows guests coming to fill all six rooms on the third floor this afternoon. Even though I cleaned those rooms after the last guests checked out, I want to scrub the bathrooms again so everything smells fresh and clean."

"Of course. Go ahead."

Constance scurried off. LuAnn couldn't fault Constance for her diligence. Sometimes it seemed she was more on top of the guests' comings and goings than were the owners of the inn. LuAnn only wished she could shake the uneasy feeling that she'd just been fibbed to.

The bell on the front door jangled, and LuAnn turned in that direction. Brad strode in, his cheeks and nose red and a huge smile lighting his face. LuAnn shoved the troubling thought about Constance aside and moved to greet him.

"Good morning. You're too late for breakfast and too early for lunch, but there are a few leftover cinnamon rolls if you'd like one with a cup of coffee."

He unzipped his jacket. "That sounds great. While I enjoy it, can I bend your ear?"

She quirked her fingers and took off for the dining area. "Follow me."

Tess and Winnie were busy in the kitchen, chopping vegetables for the day's soups, and Winnie raised her eyebrows when LuAnn took a cinnamon roll from the tray on the counter and put it and a fork on a dessert plate.

"You havin' another one of those, Miss Lu?"

Amusement fluttered through LuAnn's chest. Even though Winnie was the youngest of the four women at the inn, she was the one most likely to play the mother hen. "Brad's here. He wants one. And a cup of coffee. Is there coffee left in the pot?"

"Isn't there always coffee in the pot?"

Tess snickered. She and LuAnn exchanged grins, and LuAnn removed a chunky mug from the cupboard. She filled it with the hot aromatic brew and carried the cup and plate to the dining area. Brad had chosen one of the small round tables near the windows overlooking the river.

She set the items in front of him, then took the seat across from him. "Okay, my ears are ready. What did you need?"

He stabbed the fork into the cinnamon roll and grinned at her. "Actually, this concerns what you need."

"Me?"

"Yep. You said you needed gift ideas for Aunt Thelma and Aunt Irene." He put a chunk of roll in his mouth. While he chewed, he groaned. "Even cold and hours old, these things are amazing. Winnie could put the bakery out of business if you all started selling them by the dozen."

LuAnn ignored the suggestion. Winnie would pitch a fit if they asked her to make more than the customary five dozen each morning for the breakfast crowd. "What's your idea for Thelma and Irene?"

He took another bite and chased it with coffee. "They're in the habit of stopping by Jeremiah's Coffee House at least once a week. What if you bought a slice-of-pie certificate for each of them—one slice a month for every month of the new year?"

LuAnn considered the proposition while he enjoyed his cinnamon roll. Although slices of pie weren't terribly personal, Thelma had indicated they had more than enough bric-a-brac in their house. And at their age, things they didn't already own were hard to find. Giving them the opportunity to enjoy a piece of pie at Jeremiah's once a month as her treat was better than anything she'd come up with.

She smiled. "I like it. I didn't know Jeremiah's did slice-of-pie certificates."

"It's kind of a new thing. Most people do it for somebody's birthday month, but I don't see why the certificate couldn't be tweaked to cover a full year." He ate the last piece of cinnamon roll and drained his coffee mug. Then he patted his stomach. "That was good, thanks. I'd love to make a habit of a treat like that every morning."

"You're welcome anytime." LuAnn rose. "Maybe I'll run over to Jeremiah's now, while things are quiet in here. Thanks for the great idea."

"No problem." He stood and pushed in the chair, then zipped his jacket. "My car's out front if you'd like me to drive you over there. I know it's only a short walk, but the air's pretty cold this morning."

She'd surmised so by his reddened face. "Let me put these dishes in the kitchen and get my coat. Then I'd appreciate the ride."

"Sure thing. I'll wait by the front door."

LuAnn dropped the dishes in the sink, told Tess her intentions, then retrieved her coat from the rack in the office. Brad held open the door for her, and then he opened the passenger door on his sleek car. She slid in with a self-conscious smile.

He drove the single block to Jeremiah's and pulled up to the curb. "There you are. Do you want me to stick around and take you back to the inn? I don't mind."

She appreciated his kindness, but he had other duties besides being her taxi service. "Thanks, but don't worry about it. I don't mind the walk." She hopped out of the car, waved, and hurried into Jeremiah's.

The wonderful aromas of the coffeehouse were almost intoxicating. She inhaled the unique potpourri of coffee, pastries, and fresh bread as she crossed to the counter. No wonder Thelma and Irene enjoyed coming here. It was worth a trip if all a person did was sniff.

LuAnn explained what she wanted, and the perky young woman behind the counter modified two slice-of-pie certificates to encompass a full year, then wrote Thelma's and Irene's names in a flowing calligraphic script. She put them in Christmas-themed envelopes and handed them over with a flourish. "There you are."

"Thank you. I appreciate it."

She grinned. "You're welcome. It'll be fun to see the ladies enjoy their pie. I bet Thelma always orders coconut cream and Irene, pecan. Then they'll sit and argue about whose has more calories in it."

LuAnn laughed. Obviously the elderly sisters' reputations were well known. She tucked the envelopes under her arm, waved, and set out for the inn. A cold gust attempted to steal the envelopes, but she held tight. The wind managed to bend them a bit, but LuAnn thought she could flatten them out if she put them beneath something weighty, like Brad's coffee table book. Once in the inn, she headed for the office.

She opened the door and crossed to the console-type cabinet along the back wall. She opened one set of doors and reached in to pick up Brad's Christmas book. As her fingers closed around it, her gaze was drawn to the empty spot on the other half of the shelf. That spot had not been empty earlier. But what should be there?

She gasped. She slammed the cabinet doors, left the envelopes behind, and raced for the kitchen. "Tess! Janice! My copy of Prudence's diary is missing!"

CHAPTER SIX

C alm down." Janice patted LuAnn's back. "You're going to scare off our customers."

LuAnn shrugged her hand away. "We don't have any yet." They wouldn't open for lunch for another half hour.

"Then you'll scare Alice," Janice said. "She was in the library the last time I walked through there."

LuAnn hadn't peeked in that corner, but if Alice heard anything remotely suspicious, she would come running. "All right, I'm calm. Now please tell me one of you moved the diary."

Tess turned from rolling out biscuit dough. "I moved the diary."

LuAnn spun to face her. "You did?"

"No, but you asked so nicely, I had to honor your request."

LuAnn groaned, and Winnie clicked her tongue on her teeth. "Miss Tess, that's not nice at all. Miss Lu's all worked up. Don't tease her."

LuAnn almost said, "Thanks, Mom." She cleared her throat. "Seriously, have either of you taken the diary out of the office?"

"I didn't take it." Janice picked up the biscuit cutter and pushed it through the layer of dough.

Tess returned to the cutting board. "Neither did I. Who had it last?"

LuAnn pointed to herself. "I did. I got it out yesterday when I was visiting with Thelma. We found an entry that mentions the inn's original owner. I put it in its spot in the cabinet afterward." Or had she? Gracious sakes, why was she getting so forgetful? Had old age set in? "It is definitely not there now. Oh!" She lowered her voice to a whisper. "Alice was there too. She seemed pretty interested in it. You don't suppose...?"

Tess raised her eyebrows. "How? We keep the office locked."

LuAnn shook her head. "Apparently we don't. Because it was unlocked just now when I went to put Thelma's and Irene's Christmas gifts under Brad's coffee table book."

The others gawked at her, and she realized how ridiculous that must have sounded. She quickly explained her purchase and the reason for wanting the envelopes under a weight. Then she held her hands wide. "So...who all's been in the office this morning?"

"Not me," Janice said.

"Nor I," Tess added.

They looked at Winnie. She snorted. "Don't be lookin' at me. I have no reason to go in there even if I do have a key that would let me."

LuAnn covered her eyes with her hand. "Then I did it. I must not have locked it behind me when I left with Brad." How could she have been so careless? At least there weren't any valuables in the office right now. They could get another copy of the diary made—Maybelline at the Marietta Underground Railroad Museum would run one. For a fee. But she still wanted to know who'd gone into the office and taken her copy.

The front-door bells jangled. The first lunch customers were arriving. Her investigation would have to wait until everyone cleared out. She headed to the dining room to greet the new arrivals.

After lunch, several members of the Jenkins family checked in. The matriarch was celebrating her ninety-fifth birthday, and the few family members who lived in town couldn't accommodate everyone in their homes. The families were delighted to take possession of the entire third floor, and the Inn Crowd was delighted to host them even though they'd had to haul hideaway beds into every one of the six rooms so the children had places to sleep. But the family was cared for, and Wayfarers Inn received a good profit. What Tess called a win-win.

LuAnn checked them in, and she and Constance kept the elevator busy for nearly a half hour transporting guests and luggage to the appropriate rooms. It did her heart good to hear the compliments on the decor, and she couldn't help but notice how clean the rooms were. Not a speck of dust on any piece of furniture, quilts hanging just so on the beds, and not so much as a single dust bunny on the planked floors. Constance did a great job, and LuAnn told her so as they trudged down the stairs together when everyone was finally settled.

Constance's cheeks blazed red. "Thank you, Miss Sherrill. My mom always said, 'If you're going to do a job, do it right.'"

LuAnn smiled. "My mother said something similar. Must be a piece of advice from the book of mom-isms." Loneliness for her mother struck anew, and she blinked rapidly to chase away the threat of tears. "Does your mother live here in Marietta?"

An odd look crossed Constance's face. "No." But she didn't elaborate, leaving LuAnn hanging.

They reached the lobby, and Constance took a step in the direction of the reading area. "I haven't cleaned the public bathrooms yet today. I'll do that now."

"Before you do..." LuAnn waited until Constance turned around. "Did you happen to go into the office for something today?"

Constance's eyebrows descended. "No, ma'am. You all said for me to stay out of there."

LuAnn's scalp prickled. Yes, they'd told her, but she had gone in before. Tess had seen her. She chose her next words carefully. "I was curious because some papers are missing from the cabinet." She examined Constance's face for signs of guilt. She saw none.

"I didn't go in there, but..." Constance inched closer to LuAnn. "It's funny you say things are missing from a cabinet. There are some things missing from the linen armoire too."

They'd recently put an antique wardrobe on the third floor to hold linens. Tess had feared the musty basement smell would seep into the sheets and towels, and having them closer to the rooms made sense.

"What's missing?" LuAnn folded her arms and prepared herself for bad news.

"Two of the white Egyptian cotton flat sheets. I wondered if one of you ladies needed them for something. Maybe to cover something?"

LuAnn hadn't taken sheets from the linen armoire, and she doubted either Janice or Tess had. Those sheets were for the guest rooms. They had their own sheets for the beds in their apartment. "Hmm, I'll check with Tess and Janice. Maybe they're in the wash."

Constance shrugged. "Maybe. But they were in the closet last Friday, and today they're gone. I don't know why they'd need to be washed when they hadn't even been used yet."

LuAnn couldn't think of another explanation. "Don't worry about it. I'm sure they'll turn up." The way she hoped the diary would turn up. She waved Constance on and then hurried to the kitchen. She'd intended to help with cleanup, but the dishes were already in the drying rack, and every counter sparkled with a fresh scrubbing.

Winnie was hanging her apron on a hook by the back door. She spotted LuAnn. "You get the guests all settled in?"

"Yes." LuAnn glanced around the clean kitchen. "Where are Tess and Janice?"

"Janice left to meet Paige for their weekly get-together. Tess is downstairs tossing the tablecloths, napkins, and dish towels in the wash."

LuAnn paused before leaving the kitchen. "Thanks again for everything you do, Winnie. We couldn't do it without you."

Winnie released a deep, throaty chuckle. "It doesn't hardly seem like a job, I enjoy it so much." She tugged her coat on. "I'll see you tomorrow morning, Miss Lu. Bye now."

After Winnie departed, LuAnn trotted down the basement stairs and found Tess at the washing machines, measuring detergent into a cup. Tess put the items down and grabbed LuAnn's elbow. "Come here." She drew her to the door leading to the loading area and pointed to the deadbolt. "Notice anything?"

LuAnn looked, then she drew back and gaped at Tess. "Why is the deadbolt unlocked?"

Tess's lips formed a grim line. "I don't know. It takes a key to unlock it. We haven't used this door in a couple of weeks at least, so it should be locked. Yet it isn't. That means the inn's been basically open to whoever wanted to come through this door for who knows how long."

LuAnn's mind raced through the names of those who had a key for the deadbolt. It was a short race. Each of the Inn Crowd ladies, Winnie, and Constance, since she carried a ring with keys to all the guest rooms in the inn.

Tess squeezed LuAnn's elbow. "Now that you've seen it, I'm going to lock it again." She pulled her keys from her jeans pocket and turned the lock. "Don't say anything to Janice about this. It'll only spook her."

LuAnn chewed her lip. "Should we keep it from her, though? We agreed…no secrets."

Tess grimaced. "All right, we'll tell her, but she might not come down here again for a good long while. You know how goosey she is about the basement anyway, and—"

A strange sound intruded. A *clank-clank*, followed by a *whoosh* and spatter. Both women spun in the direction of the sound. Water gushed from the ceiling near the stairs. Tess gave LuAnn a push. "Go turn off the main water line!"

LuAnn darted for the master lever that shut off water flow to the entire inn, and Tess raced up the stairs. Flipping the lever brought the gush to a trickle. Her heart pounding, LuAnn pattered up the stairs in pursuit of Tess. Tess and Constance were in the dining room, and Constance's face was as white as the missing Egyptian cotton sheets.

"I'm so sorry. I don't know what happened. I turned the spigot in the men's bathroom to rinse my cleaning cloth, and something underneath the sink popped. Then I heard running water."

Tess put her arm around the younger woman's shoulders. "I'm sure you didn't do anything wrong. The public bathrooms are new to the inn. Maybe the plumber didn't seal one of the joints well enough. We'll get someone over here right away to check it out. In the meantime, you can just carry on with your other duties."

Constance nodded and scuffed through the kitchen doorway.

Tess turned to LuAnn. "I hope no one was in the shower when we shut the water line off. Call Thorn. If he can't come, ask him who he recommends for emergencies. I'll go up and let the guests know what happened. I hope they don't all decide to go to another hotel. We need the revenue, especially since that man who booked for a three-month stay didn't show last week." She pursed her lips. "I think we ought to establish a policy about no-show with no-notice—your credit card gets billed anyway. We can't afford this lost income."

Lost diary, lost sheets, and lost income. What would turn up missing next?

CHAPTER SEVEN

L uAnn and Tess stood in the doorway of the men's public bathroom. Thorn lay on his back on the floor and messed with something under the sink. LuAnn sent up a prayer of gratitude that the handyman had known which line fed to the two bathrooms on the main floor and was able to turn it off. She'd opened the main line, so water was available to the rest of the inn.

He slid out from under the sink and sat up. The grim set of his lips sent a prickle of worry up LuAnn's spine.

"Well?" Tess put her hands on her hips. "What's the verdict?"

"Somebody fiddled with the plumbing under here, that's the verdict."

LuAnn and Tess exchanged a frown. Tess said, "What do you mean, somebody fiddled with it? It wasn't a line break from a pipe freezing or something?"

Thorn pushed to his feet and started clanking tools into his metal toolbox. "These bathrooms were plumbed with flexible PEX piping. They're run through interior walls, so the chance of freezing—or of breaking even if they did freeze—is minimal. But it looks to me like someone pulled the line from the wall under the sink, made about a six-inch slit with a pocketknife or some other sharp object, then pushed it back into the wall. When Constance ran water, the force split the tubing open, and water went where it isn't supposed to."

LuAnn's head began to throb. "Deliberate sabotage? Why would someone do something like that?"

"No idea." Thorn snapped his toolbox shut and turned to face them. "Be grateful it was a ground-floor pipe and not one from your apartment, which would've sent water down four stories. At least this one only poured into the basement."

LuAnn tried, but she couldn't conjure up much gratitude. It hurt her heart to think the broken water line was an intentional act.

Thorn headed for the front door, and the women followed. "I'll give Tom at Davis Plumbing a call, let him know what I found. I'm sure he'll get over here as quick as he can to replace the pipe. In the meantime, leave the valve to the bathroom off and put up an Out-of-Service sign. You could also make the women's bathroom unisex until the men's room is operational again."

"I'll do that." Tess took off for the office with a determined stride, arms swinging.

Thorn gave LuAnn an apologetic grimace. "Sure am sorry that happened. Too bad you don't know who was in there last. Besides Constance, I mean. Whoever went in right before her is most likely the one who slit the line."

She thanked him for his help and closed the door behind him, then hurried to the office. Tess was at the desk, marker in hand, crafting a simple sign.

"Tess?" LuAnn hated to ask the question, but she needed an answer if for nothing more than her own peace of mind. "You don't suppose Constance split the pipe, do you?"

Tess jerked her attention from the sign. "Constance? Why would she do that?"

LuAnn shrugged. "I have no idea. But Thorn said it had to have been recently—right before Constance turned on the water in the sink. You caught her coming out of our office, and a guest caught her in one of the closets. Is it possible she's trying to make trouble here?"

Tess chewed the cap on the marker, her brow puckering. "I don't guess anything is outside the realm of possibility. But if she wanted to make trouble, wouldn't it be a lot easier to just leave the rooms dirty or something? So guests wouldn't be happy here?"

"If she did that, we'd fire her."

A self-conscious snort emerged from Tess's throat. "You're right. So she can't be obvious." She bent over the page again. "Let me finish the sign and get it up on the men's room before somebody goes in there."

LuAnn retrieved her notebook. She needed to write the recent events down while they were fresh in her mind. She jotted, *Missing diary, missing sheets, deliberately damaged water line. Who? Why?* She stared at the page for a long time, forcing her brain to think, think. But no answers came.

Tom Davis arrived Tuesday morning in the middle of the breakfast rush. Terrible timing. He needed to access both ends of the flexible piping, which meant he needed to go into the basement. They couldn't have him traipsing back and forth through the dining room while people were eating, so LuAnn unlocked the loading area door and instructed him to go around the outside of the building. She felt bad for making him use the outside basement access. The temperature had dropped to its lowest numbers since the onset of cold weather, and it was quite a trek from the front door to the loading area door. But he didn't complain.

Pastor Ben and his wife Paige came in midmorning. They sat at a little table next to Alice, whose bright eyes seemed to examine them as if she had them under a microscope, and ordered tea and a cinnamon roll. As LuAnn brought their items to the table, Pastor Ben rose.

"I'm gonna wash my hands before we eat. I rearranged some dusty old songbooks this morning at the church."

"Oh," LuAnn said, "you'll need to use the sink in the women's bathroom. The men's is out of order at the moment."

His eyebrows rose. "Uh-oh. Anything I can help with?"

LuAnn noted Alice leaning slightly toward them, and she forced a nonchalance she didn't feel. "No, it's just a little water line issue."

"That's too bad. Everything seemed fine when I went in there yesterday." He smiled at his wife. "I came looking for Paige, and all the while she and Janice were having fun at the parsonage planning a baby shower."

"What time was that?"

"Hmm…" He looked at Paige. "Three thirty? Four, maybe?"

She nodded. "Probably closer to four. You got home around four fifteen."

"That's right." He aimed his bright smile at LuAnn. "You might ask Marcus if he noticed anything, though. He went in when I came out."

"Marcus?" An unpleasant thought entered LuAnn's mind. "I wonder why he was here. He makes his deliveries on Fridays."

Alice yanked the pencil from behind her ear and aimed it at the pad she always carried.

Pastor Ben glanced at the aspiring writer. "He said he'd come to pick up Winnie. He was all excited because he had just gotten his provisional license and wanted to give his grandma a ride, but she'd already left." Alice started scribbling something. He planted a kiss on the top of his wife's head. "Go ahead and start without me, honey. I'll be right back."

He strode off, and LuAnn darted to the kitchen. She crossed directly to Janice, who was filling a trio of glasses with orange juice, and leaned close. "Did you see Marcus in the inn yesterday afternoon?"

Janice paused, her forehead scrunching in concentration. "Um, no, I don't think so. Why?"

LuAnn repeated what Pastor Ben had told her. "Marcus might have been the last person to go into the men's bathroom before Constance went to clean it. Which means—"

"What're you two whispering about over there?" Winnie's tart voice intruded. She waved a spatula at them. "Janice, get that orange juice out there. LuAnn, I'm ready to serve up the french toast. Hand me some plates, would you?"

LuAnn held a plate out to Winnie and watched her arrange triangles of crisp, cinnamon-scented french toast like a fan. "Winnie, may I ask you a question?"

"Sure. I reserve the right not to answer, though, if it has to do with my age or dress size."

LuAnn swallowed a smile. "Actually, it has to do with Marcus. Although I've seen him nearly every Friday for several weeks, I don't think I've ever seen him smile. Is he always so somber?"

Winnie chuckled. She pointed to a second plate, and LuAnn held it out. "No. Of all my grandsons, he's the most likely to cut up and make everybody laugh. He doesn't smile here, 'cause he's not happy about me taking this job."

"He's not?" LuAnn set the second plate aside and offered the third and final one. "Why?"

Winnie poked out her lips. "Well, I guess maybe he thinks I'm too old." She pointed at LuAnn with the spatula. "But that's nonsense. A body's only as old as she feels, and I feel spry as I did when I was thirty. Well"—she chuckled—"most days. Get the fruit on those plates and take 'em out before the toast is cold."

LuAnn scooped a spoonful of strawberries, blueberries, raspberries, and blackberries onto each plate, hoping the colorful mix would be seen as more than an embellishment. Out-of-season fruit was too expensive to toss down the garbage disposal.

She passed Janice, who was returning, as she left the kitchen. She rasped, "We need to talk about Mar—"

"There you are whispering again. It's not the most polite thing a person could do." Winnie's indignant voice rang out again. "Save your chitchat for when breakfast is over."

LuAnn placed the plates of fruit and french toast on the table, asked the guests if they needed anything else, and then turned for the kitchen. But the plumber gestured to her from the foyer. She hurried over to him. "Yes? Did you get the line fixed?"

"Yes, ma'am. I turned the water on to the bathroom too."

LuAnn raised her eyebrows. "Already? Doesn't the glue need to dry?"

He shook his head. "The PEX lines get crimped, not glued, so they're good to go in minutes. The hardest part was stringing a new line through the walls. But you can take the signs down now and let people use the room."

LuAnn surmised it would need some cleaning first. Thorn had mucked things up yesterday with his toolbox, and even though she hadn't looked, she imagined the plumber's dirty boots had trekked mud and dried grass into the bathroom. A trail stretched from the front door and around the corner, showing the path he'd taken. "Thank you. If you'd like to leave an invoice—"

His hand whipped forward so fast the yellow paper pinched between his fingers seemed to blur. "Here you go. Mailing address at the top. My phone number's there too. Call if you need anything else."

LuAnn sincerely hoped they wouldn't need to call him, but she appreciated having the information. "Thanks. We'll get this sent out tomorrow morning."

He tipped the brim of his baseball cap and departed.

As he left, Constance came down the stairs. LuAnn waved her over. "The plumber is finished in the men's bathroom. I imagine it'll need some cleaning up before we can let guests in there. Would you mind checking on it?"

"Not at all." Constance shifted from foot to foot, her expression apprehensive.

LuAnn touched the younger woman's arm. "Is something wrong?"

"Um..." Constance swallowed. "There's something I need to tell you. And I don't think you're going to like it."

LuAnn bit the inside of her lip, bracing herself.

"I found the missing sheets. But they're all torn up."

CHAPTER EIGHT

Since the inn was well-manned—Constance was finishing her cleaning duties, and Winnie was in the kitchen baking tomorrow's pies—LuAnn had suggested they take their conversation to Jeremiah's Coffee House to avoid being overheard by Alice. No doubt the woman didn't intend to be intrusive, but her constant presence and scribbling who-knows-what in the notebook she always carried set LuAnn's teeth on edge. She now thought she understood how it felt to be under a private eye's surveillance. Although other customers sat at nearby tables or in the reading chairs, no one seemed to pay a bit of attention to them here. But LuAnn still couldn't relax. This was supposed to be the season of peace and goodwill, not suspicion and foul deeds. Where had her picture-perfect Christmas gone?

"I agree," Tess said as she ran her finger down the list of notes LuAnn had made in her notebook, "that we should give more thought to whether or not Marcus is wreaking havoc at the inn out of some misplaced concern about his grandmother, but we can't rule out Constance."

Janice sighed. "I have to agree with Tess. Even if Marcus was in the bathroom, that doesn't mean Constance didn't cut the line when she went to clean in there. We know for sure she was in the men's room when the water starting pouring into the basement."

Tess nodded. "And it would be pretty easy for her to find the lost sheets if she was the one who took them in the first place."

LuAnn pushed aside the rest of her peach pie, her appetite gone. How strange to have the tangled wad of sheets show up in the armoire again. "But why tear perfectly good sheets into strips and then tie them into a rope? What purpose does it serve?"

Janice tipped her head and tapped her chin with her finger. "I read a book once where a person stole things, then pretended to find them to make himself look good in front of his peers. Could Constance be doing that? Trying to win our favor, so we'll keep her on even after the holiday season?"

LuAnn gulped. "She does seem awfully eager to please."

"And she tends to be wherever the mishaps occur." Tess moved her empty plate to the side and leaned her elbows on the table. "I mean, doesn't it seem odd she was so close when the mirror fell and broke?"

"Brad said it didn't fall but that someone took it off the hook and dropped it." LuAnn searched her memory. Where had Constance been when the mirror crashed? It seemed she'd come from the third floor, but she could have had time to get to the staircase, maybe intending to hide, before LuAnn and Brad made it to the second-floor balcony.

LuAnn reached for her notebook. "I don't think we can eliminate Alice Busby, either."

Both Tess and Janice gawked at LuAnn. They chorused, "Alice?"

LuAnn envisioned the unpretentious woman with messy gray curls, frumpy Grandma-style dresses, and glasses that always seemed to slide to the end of her nose. The image didn't paint a picture of guilt, but how many times did the least suspicious-looking person end up being the guilty party in murder mysteries? "You've seen how closely she watches everything that goes on. What's not to say she's stirring the pot and gauging our reactions so she can give the characters in her book realism?"

Tess laughed, but she pointed at the notebook. "Go ahead and write her down if it'll make you feel better. I'll be honest, though. Blaming Alice Busby makes about as much sense to me as blaming...well, Winnie. I'm leaning toward Marcus. That young man seems to have an ax to grind."

"And I think Constance is our mess-maker," Janice said. "I think she's doing it to get our attention. She seems extra needy to me."

LuAnn wasn't ready to choose a perpetrator. Not yet. But neither was she ready to rule anyone out. Somebody broke the mirror. Somebody took the sheets and the diary. Somebody cut the water line. So somebody wanted to cause trouble. Her cell phone rang, and she dug in her purse. Brad's face showed on the screen. She ignored Tess's and Janice's smirks as she pressed the accept button and put the phone to her ear.

"Hello?"

"LuAnn, I hope I'm not bothering you. Constance said you and the others were taking a break at Jeremiah's."

"That's right. Are you at the inn?"

"Yes. A couple who want to do some house-hunting here in Marietta need a place to spend tonight and maybe tomorrow night. I stopped by to see if you had a room available."

LuAnn pinched the phone between her chin and shoulder and gathered up her things, gesturing for Janice and Tess to do the same. "Yes. The whole third floor is filled, and the Honeymoon Suite is already occupied, but either Maple and Mum or Lily and Lace are available. Let them choose which they prefer, and Constance can check them in. We'll be right over."

"Sounds great. See you in a few." The connection ended.

Tess arched one eyebrow. "Did you say, 'Let Constance check them in'? After all we just said about her being our saboteur?"

LuAnn dropped her phone into her purse. "Well, if she is our saboteur, she might start feeling guilty if we heap coals of kindness on her head. Giving her extra responsibility shows her we trust her, doesn't it?"

"Or proves we're stupid enough to be tricked."

LuAnn didn't want to consider that possibility. She buttoned her coat. "If you don't want Constance checking the guests in, we'd better hurry."

Dean and Kay Pankratz, the couple Brad had brought over, were so friendly, LuAnn hoped they would find a house and stay in Marietta forever. She especially enjoyed visiting with them because she learned Kay was a watercolor artist. An idea struck as if from heaven above.

She slid into one of the open chairs at the couple's table where they were enjoying rolls and coffee. "Kay, did you bring a portfolio with you that I could look at?"

"I did," Kay said. "Let me run up to the room and get it."

While Kay was gone, LuAnn got herself a cup of coffee and chitchatted with Dean until his wife came back, a large flat case under her arm. She opened it on a nearby table, and LuAnn got up to view the paintings Kay spread across the tabletop. Several of them were of famous landmarks, each remarkably detailed and gorgeous.

"Do you do paintings on commission?" she asked Kay.

Kay's expression brightened. "Sometimes. What did you have in mind?"

LuAnn gestured to the room in general. "The inn. A painting of Wayfarers that we could hang in the foyer to welcome guests."

The woman clapped her hands. "Oh, I love the idea!" She touched her husband's wrist. "Dean, take lots of pictures of the outside while we're here for me to use as my model."

Another thought zinged through LuAnn's brain. "What if I gave you copies of the earliest pictures of the inn? There are some fuzzy black-and-white images at the Marietta Underground Railroad Museum. I could get them from the curator, and you could use them as your model."

"Even better!" Kay laughed. "Such fun... I can't wait to see the historical pictures. Is the museum open this morning?"

Dean checked his cell phone. "It'll have to wait, hon, because we're due to meet Brad in fifteen minutes. We'd better go."

They dropped their napkins beside their plates and rose. LuAnn bid them a good day and returned to work. She couldn't erase the smile from her face. What a perfect way to commemorate the inn's history. Maybe they could have small prints made from the painting for notecards. Or even zero in on one part of the painting and have it printed on Christmas ornaments. She envisioned the image of the inn on a creamy glass disc with a decorative gold hook.

Excitement swelled in her chest. Such a welcome emotion after yesterday's worries. Surely this guest's special ability and willingness to use her talent for the inn was a sign that things were looking up. She spent the morning sending up thankyous to God and planning the perfect location for the painting when it was finished.

When the breakfast rush ended, LuAnn cornered Tess and Janice and told them about the painting. Their faces lit.

"Oh, watercolor paintings always seem so romantic. What a great idea." Janice turned to Winnie. "Did you hear what Lu said?"

"'Course I heard. For once you weren't whispering." Winnie aimed a tart look at the trio of women. They laughed.

Janice sighed. "It really is a marvelous idea. Too bad we didn't think of it earlier. It would have been a great addition to our grand opening weekend."

Tess clanked clean silverware into a drawer. "Too late for that now. But I really like the idea of using the image for notecards and so forth if the painting comes out okay and she approves us duplicating it."

Winnie frowned. "Bet you'll have to pay her a commission for every sale. It'll cut into your profit."

LuAnn refused to let anyone rain on her parade today. "We'll work that out when the time comes. In the meantime, I'm going to make a list of possible uses for a painted image of the inn." She charged out of the kitchen and nearly plowed into Alice Busby. Both women yelped.

Alice put her hand to her chest. "Gracious, you nearly frightened me out of a year's growth."

Apparently the woman had been frightened many times before, because she barely topped five feet tall. LuAnn swallowed the humorous thought. "I'm sorry. I didn't see you there." Suspicion prickled. Was the woman listening at the door again? "Did you need something?"

"Yes. Clean towels."

"Didn't Constance put fresh ones in your room yesterday?"

Alice waved her hand. "She put towels in my room, but they weren't fresh. They have a foul odor on them." She wrinkled her nose, making her glasses jiggle. "Like spoiled milk."

"Spoiled milk?"

Alice nodded. "The towels look clean enough, but they stink. I'd rather have some new ones."

"I'll make sure you get some."

"Thank you." Alice hurried off in the direction of the library, which she'd apparently decided was her office, and LuAnn rode the elevator to the third floor. The linen closet stood sentry between the elevator and the door to Apples and Cinnamon. LuAnn pulled the armoire's mirror doors open. Constance had done a great job organizing the shelves. Cleaning supplies on the top, toilet paper and tissue boxes on the second, towels on the third, and sheets at the bottom. LuAnn reached for the stack of neatly folded towels. An unpleasant aroma tickled her nose.

LuAnn frowned. She leaned close. The stench was even stronger when she put her nose next to the linens. They would need to be washed before they could be used. She trotted up the stairs to the fourth floor, retrieved her laundry basket and carried it to the armoire, then began filling it with the sheets and towels from the shelves.

Constance approached, her little sectioned tote with cleaning supplies in hand. "What are you doing?"

LuAnn barely glanced at her. "Taking these things down to be washed. They smell bad."

Constance put her cubby down and grabbed a stack of hand towels. She lifted them to her nose and made a horrible face. "Phew. What is that?"

"Alice said her towels smelled like spoiled milk. I'm inclined to agree with her, although I can't figure out why they smell that way." LuAnn knelt and pulled out the last stack of sheets. She released a huff. "But now I know. Look."

A half-pint milk carton sat in the far corner of the bottom shelf.

CHAPTER NINE

Constance bent over and peeked into the armoire. Her jaw dropped. "What's that doing in there?"

LuAnn took it out. Curdled milk stuck to the edges of the opened top and yellowish chunks filled the bottom third of the carton. "Yuck." She tucked in the lip on the opening.

Constance wrung her hands. "I'm sorry, Miss Sherrill. I had no idea that was in there."

LuAnn wouldn't have seen it if she hadn't gotten on her knees to empty the bottom shelf. From a standing angle, the back of the lower shelves was out of view. But hadn't Constance smelled it? The odor had been obvious the moment LuAnn opened the doors. "It was well hidden visually, that's for sure."

Constance cringed. "I admit, I thought I smelled something funny yesterday when I put the towels away, but this is an old building. I blamed it on old-building smell."

LuAnn wouldn't have considered spoiled milk a normal "old building" smell, but Constance seemed honestly distraught. She decided not to push the issue. She handed her the carton. "Would you throw this away, please? I'll take the sheets and towels to the laundry room."

"Yes, ma'am." Constance scurried for the stairs, and LuAnn took the elevator, returning to the kitchen. She dropped the basket onto the counter with a thud. "I'm on my way to the basement to wash these linens."

Winnie gaped at the stacks of folded towels and sheets filling the basket.

"What in the world? Has Constance started folding the dirty sheets and towels she takes out of the rooms?"

LuAnn shook her head. "These didn't come from the rooms. They came straight from the armoire."

Tess put the potato peeler down and wiped her hands on a paper towel. "Then why are you taking them to the laundry room? Everything in the armoire should be clean."

"Should be," LuAnn said in her best teacher voice. She grimaced. "There was a small carton of milk in the armoire— probably from this very kitchen, given to someone at break- fast time. How it got in with our sheets, I don't know, but it had spoiled and..." She held the basket toward Tess. "Give a whiff."

Tess put both hands in the air. "No, thanks. I can imagine."

Winnie clucked her tongue on her teeth. "Gracious sakes, why'd somebody go and stick a carton of milk inside there? You've got little waste cans all over the place. Who'd be thought- less enough to put trash in an antique wardrobe?"

LuAnn headed for the stairs. "Probably the same person who split the water line in the men's room, tore two sheets to smithereens, stole off with personal items from our office, and broke the mirror in Maple and Mum."

Winnie turned her attention to the steaks she was chopping into stew meat. "It has been quite a week, hasn't it?"

LuAnn chose to treat the question as rhetorical. She carried the basket down the stairs, and Tess followed her. They began tossing towels and sheets into the washing machines. Not until all three machines were humming did Tess speak.

"You might be right about Marcus."

LuAnn placed the empty basket on the folding table and gave Tess her full attention. "Why do you say that?"

"Winnie told me a little bit ago that she gave him copies of the keys to the inn and forgot to tell us."

LuAnn's ire stirred. Winnie did a great job, but she was getting too comfortable if she made decisions like handing out keys without consulting the owners. "Why?"

"To make it easier for him to deliver groceries." Tess glanced toward the loading area door. "She said now he doesn't have to find somebody to open it for him every time."

"Which means he has the freedom to come and go whenever he wants to." LuAnn chewed her lip. So he had the freedom. But was he using it?

The rest of the week went by, thankfully, with no further mysteries or intrigues added to those already plaguing the three friends. Thelma and Irene arrived Saturday for lunch. LuAnn stopped by the sisters' table to tell them about her progress on the timeline. "I've written down everything you've told me thus far. I'm looking online for pictures and more material about Alfred Dawes."

Thelma beamed at LuAnn. "I'm so glad you're writing all of this for future generations. It's good to know about those who've gone before. Kind of makes us accountable to either honor their memories or resolve to do better, don't you think?"

LuAnn couldn't argue with her reasoning. She squeezed the woman's bony shoulder and returned to her duties. The Jenkins family checked out, and LuAnn gratefully accepted their thanks, compliments, and promise to return in the summer for the cousins reunion they'd planned while together for the birthday celebration. She smiled as she told them goodbye, but underneath, sadness hovered. She'd never take part in a cousins reunion, nor would she gather family for a huge birthday celebration. The feeling of aloneness that plagued her at odd times returned, and she was glad when the lunch hour was over and she could escape to her room to shed a few quiet tears.

Early 1857

Elswyth and Reggie continued to live at the Riverfront House, but Prudence wondered how long Mr. Dawes would allow it. Fewer guests frequented the inn during the winter months, and she'd heard talk that come spring a new caretaker would be hired.

On a rainy day in mid-March, Prudence entered the inn through the kitchen door and found Elswyth at the trestle table, weeping. She rushed across the floor and slid her arm around Elswyth's heaving shoulders.

"My friend, has something happened? Why is thee distraught?"

Elswyth lifted her pale, tear-stained face. "A man is coming very soon. A representative for a gentleman named Bickerton. Mr. Bickerton wants to buy the Riverfront House."

Prudence was stunned. "Buy the Riverfront?" Then a wave of happiness washed through her. "But isn't that good news? Maybe the new owner will hire thee to cook or manage his books, and thee and Reggie can stay here."

Elswyth shook her head. "No, Mr. Dawes came to me this morning and told me he wants us out of the house immediately. He said he didn't want to risk Mr. Bickerton thinking that taking care of 'useless widows and their brats' came with owning the Riverfront."

"But where will thee go? What will thee do?"

"We have no one here in Marietta to take us in. And I have very little money to establish myself anywhere else." She folded her arms on the table and rested her forehead on them. "Oh, how I long for Frederick's presence and a return to the happy life I knew before the midnight marauders shattered my world. If only I had the doubloons."

Prudence bit her lip. She'd searched for the coins dozens of times, as had Elswyth. She'd reached the sad conclusion that the doubloons had been carried away by the bandits. Even if they hadn't been, and if they were on the property somewhere, the new owner would take possession of every-thing…including the doubloons.

Elswyth sat up and wiped her tears with her fingers. "They're gone, just as Frederick is gone. I know I must stop thinking about regaining things that cannot be, but—" She drew in a shuddering breath. She caught Prudence's hand. "Will you pray they are found? Reggie and I…we need those coins."

Prudence was already praying for their return. "Of course I will."

Elswyth embraced her. "You're such a precious friend to me, Prudence. If I'm forced to leave Marietta, I will never, ever forget you and your kindness to me."

Prudence embraced Elswyth and asked her heavenly Father the question she kept secret from Elswyth. *Will the new owner support abolition, or the establishment?*

CHAPTER TEN

Sunday morning LuAnn awakened headachy and out of sorts. Even though it was Tess's turn to stay at the inn, she told Tess to go to church.

"Are you sure, Lu?" Tess hesitated in LuAnn's doorway. "Remember, Janice is having lunch with Pastor Ben and Paige, and I made plans to help Jeff Jr. wrap gifts and decorate his tree, so you'll be stuck here all day by yourself."

"I know, and I don't mind." LuAnn shooed her off, and Tess left with Janice, reluctant but resigned.

LuAnn dressed in one of her favorite jogging suits and pulled on fuzzy slipper socks in lieu of shoes. Comfortable, she scuffed down the first two flights of stairs. She paused outside of the Honeymoon Suite, listening for telltale noises that would let her know if Alice was in her room. Silence. Which meant the woman had probably taken possession of the library.

Heaving a sigh, LuAnn descended the final flight and sent a peek in the direction of the library. To her surprise, the long-term guest wasn't in there. She returned to the Honeymoon Suite and knocked lightly on the door while racking her brain for a reason to do so in case Alice answered the door. But there was no answer.

Anxiety struck. If the nosy woman wasn't in her room or in the library, then where was she? Someplace she shouldn't be again? Her pulse thundering, LuAnn darted down the stairs and through the lobby to the check-in desk. The basement door was set firmly in its frame. Even so, LuAnn unlocked the door and peered down the stairway, her ears alert for any unusual sounds. One came. A persistent *skritch-skritch*, as if someone was digging in the dirt.

On tiptoe, she crept downstairs, her pulse pounding so hard it nearly drowned out the scratching noise. She stopped at the bottom of the stairs and searched right and then left. Not a soul around. She started for the hallway leading to the rooms where escaped slaves had taken refuge, but the closer she got to that end of the basement, the fainter the scratching sound became. She reversed direction and crossed toward the elevator. The *skritch-skritch* increased in volume, and a sad whine accompanied it.

Puzzled, as well as concerned, LuAnn darted to the loading area doorway and pressed her ear to the door. Sure enough, the noise came from outside. What on earth . . . ? She hadn't brought her keys, so she couldn't unlock the deadbolt. She trotted back up the stairs to the kitchen, exited the back door, and rounded the corner of the inn. As she did, something dashed at her, and she released a squeal of surprise. Then she quickly squelched it, embarrassed and more than a little sorry, because she'd frightened a small, scruffy dog into cowering at her feet.

She crouched in front of it and held out her hand. "I'm sure sorry, pup." The poor thing could barely see with strands of matted fur hanging over its eyes. His tail rose in a weak wag, and he inched forward to snuffle her fingers.

Stifling a chuckle, LuAnn resisted touching the animal. From the looks of him, he had been on his own for quite a while. She didn't want to frighten him away, but he might have some kind of canine disease. She kept her voice soft and sing-song. "Poor little thing. Were you scratching at the door? Are you hungry? I'd be glad to get you a snack."

The dog sat up and placed one paw in her outstretched hand. Tears stung LuAnn's eyes. Cold, hungry, lost, and he still managed to trust her. She slipped her hand from beneath his paw and slowly rose. "Come with me, boy, and I'll see what I can find for you."

She patted her leg and eased backward, hoping the dog would follow. He trailed her, but when she reached the kitchen's back door and tried to coax him inside, he backed away, lowered his head as if bowing, and barked.

LuAnn patted her leg again. "It's all right. Come on in. I won't hurt you."

The dog backed up a few feet and barked again, jumping up and down on his front feet. Television programs featuring dogs delivering messages flitted through LuAnn's mind. Was he trying to tell her something? Although she felt a little silly and she wished she'd grabbed her jacket before coming out-side, she took a step toward the quivering dog.

"All right. What is it?"

The dog whirled and took off. LuAnn shot after it. Her socks offered little protection against the gravel in the alley and her sweat suit didn't quite block the cold, but she couldn't lose sight of it now. The dog darted behind a trio of garbage cans, then stuck his head out, barked, and ducked in again.

LuAnn crossed to the cans and bent down, resting her hands on her knees. "What're you doing in there?"

The dog emerged and, to her shock, a black-and-white kitten hung by the scruff of its neck from his teeth. He deposited the kitten at LuAnn's feet and looked up at her, tongue lolling and tail wagging. LuAnn crouched and touched the kitten under its chin. The creature arched its back and hissed—so comical considering its small size. It shrunk backward until it huddled between the dog's front feet. Obviously the unlikely companions were traveling together. But from where?

She hugged herself. She needed to get inside, and she wanted these two little vagabonds to come with her. Hoping they'd follow, she took a step in the direction of the inn. "Come on, boy. Bring your friend and follow me."

As if the dog understood, it took a gentle hold on the scruff of the kitten's neck and trailed LuAnn to the back door. She stepped inside, and after a moment's hesitation the dog followed. She closed the door behind her. The dog whined but didn't try to bolt. It dropped the kitten, and the little feline coiled itself around the dog's front legs.

LuAnn gazed down at the pair of bedraggled animals. The health department would give them a citation if they knew she'd let animals invade the kitchen, but LuAnn couldn't bear to put the pair out again. Not until they'd been fed. She scrounged a leftover hamburger patty, mashed potatoes, and gravy from last night's supper and smashed it all together on a plate. She'd intended to heat it at least a bit, but the dog's eager whines chased that idea out the window.

She placed the plate on the floor, then stepped aside. Both animals dug in, the dog's backside wriggling in delight and the kitten holding its ridiculously small tail straight up like a flagpole. Their obvious hunger inspired sympathy. Poor little things... While they devoured the food, she contemplated what to do with them next. She couldn't bear sending them out in the cold on their own again, but what else could she do?

Why not do the practical? She waited until they'd licked up every bit of the gravy and then patted her leg. "Come with me." She moved slowly through the kitchen, and the dog followed. The little kitten scampered after him, as if an invisible thread connected them. The elevator would probably scare them to pieces, but the kitten would never make it up three flights of stairs. She'd have to carry it. If the dog allowed her to.

At the base of the stairs, LuAnn crouched again and stretched out her hand. "Here, kitty, kitty, kitty..."

The dog nosed the kitten toward LuAnn, giving her the feeling it knew exactly what she wanted. She was able to scoop the kitten into her arms. The little thing dug its claws into her sweat suit, but she pulled it off and cradled it in her hands and whispered soothing words as she carried it up the stairs. The dog clicked-clicked beside her, occasionally whining, his brown-eyed gaze locked on his feline friend.

She closed the pair in the bathroom in her apartment and prayed nobody would have an accident until she got them bathed. At least, with it being so cold outside, she didn't have to worry about fleas. But both animals were covered with dirt and tiny bits of dried grass and leaves. The dog gave her no trouble at all, but the kitten yowled as if its fur was on fire when she put it into the warm bath. The entire bathroom was spattered with water and she smelled like a wet dog by the time she finished, but by the end of bath time she knew the kitten was also male.

Using some of her oldest towels, she rubbed first the kitten and then the dog as dry as possible. She kept up a steady stream of quiet talk, partly to calm the animals and partly because it helped to think out loud. "I sure wish you two could tell me where your home is. You're such a friendly pup, you have to belong somewhere. This little friend of yours, though...did you pick him up because he needed protection? If so, you're a great pal."

The dog washed the kitten's head and ears, and the little cat purred. Her heart caught. "If I take you to the shelter, the first thing they'll do is separate you. I have the feeling neither of you would fare well with that. But I'm not altogether sure you can stay here. Especially since I don't have—"

Her cell phone rang. She dug it out of her pocket, and a smile broke on her face without effort. She touched Accept. "Hi, Brad."

"LuAnn...Tess said you weren't feeling well. Would you like me to bring over some chicken soup? They have some at the salad bar in the grocery store."

What perfect timing. "I'm glad you called. I don't need soup, but there are some other things I need..."

LuAnn put her hands on her hips and smiled down at the pair of animals curled together in the dog bed Brad had brought over. In the corner of her room, a litter box stood ready for the next time the kitten needed to relieve itself, and two potty pads for the dog lay on the floor near the litter box. Bags of kitten and dog food were stored under her bathroom sink, and filled pet dishes waited next to the bathtub. The dog had seemed to understand which bowl was his and which was the kitten's, but the little cat had all but crawled into the dog's dish, trying to share. Brad had laughingly declared the cat didn't know it was a cat. The way the kitten cuddled up to the dog, the thought had crossed LuAnn's mind too.

Now that the animals had their tummies full, they'd probably sleep for a while, so LuAnn gestured Brad from her private rooms. She headed to the sitting area she shared with Tess and Janice, and they sank into the matching overstuffed chairs. She shot him a grateful smile.

"Thanks so much for coming to my rescue. What do I owe you for everything you bought?"

He waved his hand. "Not a thing."

She sat up. "Oh, but—"

"No, really. I've been trying to think of a Christmas gift for you. Consider all this pet stuff your gift."

She sighed. "That's really nice of you, but I doubt I'll be able to keep them forever. They have to belong somewhere." She slumped against the chair's cushioned backrest, regret tangling her insides into knots. "I should probably print some fliers and put them up around town. You know, 'Found: dog and kitten,' with a picture and my phone number."

His face creased with sympathy. "You want to keep them, don't you?"

She'd had such pleasure seeing to the animals' needs. Almost like having a four-footed family… "I do, but I know how I'd feel if someone absconded with my pets. I can't be selfish."

"You're a very nice person, LuAnn."

His words warmed her, and heat bloomed in her face. "So are you, for buying all that stuff." He'd even brought a chew toy and a package of felt mice.

"No problem. If you'd like, I'll snap a pic with my cell phone and print up some fliers for you. It'd be no trouble, since I make house-sale fliers nearly every day."

She shouldn't say yes, he'd already done so much, but she nodded. "Thanks."

"Except…" He tapped his chin. "As overgrown as the dog's fur has gotten, he looks more like a rag mop than a dog. He might not be recognizable. How about taking him to the groomer, get him a trim, and then I'll take the picture. It'll be easier to tell what he is if you get rid of some of that hair."

She'd discovered several mats in his fur during the bath. Brad's idea was sound. It might let her have a couple of days with them too. Selfish? Yes. But she decided not to fret over it. "Can you recommend someone?"

"Yep. Sally at Sal's Bathe & Groom, a block from my office. If you'd like, I'll set up the appointment and take the dog over for you." He scrunched his forehead, as if thinking deeply. "It's possible Sally will know where he belongs. A dog like that probably needs frequent haircuts."

LuAnn couldn't argue. "Obviously it's been awhile since he saw a groomer. I guess it's good he got loose from wherever he belongs, though, because I'm betting he's kept that little tomcat alive."

Brad burst out laughing.

"What's so funny?"

"The little tomcat." Humor glittered in his eyes. "You ought to call the cat Tom, and the dog Huckleberry—you know, in honor of them running away together."

She couldn't help but grin. "And in remembrance of Mark Twain. That might make Tess and Janice more amenable to—"

The apartment door opened, and Tess and Janice stepped in. Tess aimed a curious look at Brad, then settled her gaze on LuAnn. "More amenable to what?"

At that moment, the shaggy dog who would forever be Huckleberry in LuAnn's mind trotted up the hallway and plopped onto its bottom next to LuAnn's feet.

Tess held up both hands. "Oh, no. No dogs. Not around me."

CHAPTER ELEVEN

Tess didn't like dogs? But she had to like dogs—she and her husband had a dog for years. Unless she'd only tolerated the dog for her husband's sake. LuAnn stood and scooped Huck into the crook of her arm. "Why not?"

"One, they stink." Tess ticked off the reasons on her fingers. "Two, they make messes in the house. Three, they bark. Four, they chew things. Five—"

"Okay, okay, I get it." LuAnn scratched Huckleberry under his chin. His tail began swishing.

Janice eased around Tess and approached LuAnn, a soft smile on her face. "He's sure a scruffy little thing, isn't he? Where'd he come from?"

LuAnn shrugged. "He was scratching at the basement door this morning. Hungry, lonely, dirty...I couldn't leave him out there." She flicked a hopeful look at Tess. "How unkind would that be, especially at Christmas, to leave a miserable creature out in the cold?"

Tess folded her arms over her chest. "You could take it to the shelter."

Janice *tsk-tsk*ed. "The shelter isn't open on Sunday, Tess."

"Then take it tomorrow morning."

LuAnn sighed. "I can't."

"Why not?"

"Because he isn't traveling alone."

Tess's eyebrows shot high. "You mean there are more of them?"

Brad stood and inched toward the door. "I'll leave you ladies to fight this out. LuAnn, I'll call you tomorrow after I've made a grooming appointment for Huck." He departed, leaving her to face the firing squad alone. Some pal.

Tess dumped her purse and Bible on an end table. "Lu, I love ya, but I will not share my home with a pack of hounds."

LuAnn laughed. "For heaven's sake, Tess, I didn't bring a pack of hounds in here. Come with me." She turned and headed for her bedroom, trusting Janice and Tess to follow. In her room, she pointed to the dog bed, where the kitten lay curled in a fist-sized ball with its white-tipped black paw over its nose. She whispered, "This is Huck's buddy. Meet Tom."

Janice crouched and ran her finger along the kitten's spine. "As in *Tom Sawyer*? I love it." Tom twitched and half rolled onto his back. She grinned up at Tess. "Isn't he adorable?"

Tess's frown remained intact. "Yeah. Real cute. The shelter takes cats too."

Janice rose and shook her head. "Tess, where is your compassion?" Tess turned her face aside. Sighing, Janice turned to LuAnn. "The dog and kitten were really traveling together?"

"Yep. This smart mutt"—LuAnn glanced at Tess, hoping she was listening—"actually led me to the place where the kitten was hiding and brought it to me. He proved that dogs really are loyal."

"That's so sweet…" Janice ruffled Huckleberry's ear and laughed when the dog swiped at her with his tongue. "What was Brad saying about a grooming appointment?"

LuAnn explained Brad's plan to have the dog groomed so it looked more like a dog and less like a mop and then take a photo of the two animals and post it around town. "Such a nice little dog has to belong to someone." Sadness pinched her chest. "Until we find the owner, though, I want to keep both animals here. If we take them to the shelter, they'll be separated. It wouldn't be kind to take them away from each other."

The dog wriggled, and LuAnn placed him on the floor. He climbed into the bed and curled himself around the kitten's sleeping form. His lively dark eyes moved from LuAnn to Janice to Tess, as if asking whether or not they would allow them to stay.

Janice looked at Tess.

LuAnn looked at Tess.

Tess blew out a noisy breath. "All right. They can stay. As long as it's temporary and you keep that furry beast as far away from me as possible." She turned and left the room.

Huckleberry whined and snuggled into the bed, his brown eyes seemingly pinned on Tess's retreating frame.

True to his promise, Brad made a grooming appointment for Huckleberry, and LuAnn allowed him to take the dog in on Monday afternoon. When Brad returned with the neatly trimmed dog prancing at the end of its leash, she hardly recognized Huck.

She knelt and cupped Huck's chin in her hands, grinning when he swiped at her fingers with his soft, warm tongue. "Look at you, handsome boy. I knew you were a cutie but had no idea how much difference a haircut could make."

Brad laughed. "He really did get a haircut too, not just a groom."

LuAnn sent a puzzled look at him. "What do you mean?"

"Actually, Sally gave me some interesting information about Huck." Tess and Janice approached from the café, and Brad tossed a smile over his shoulder at them. "Ah, here's the rest of the Inn Crowd. Now I can fill you all in at once."

Tess pointed at the wriggling dog. "I see he's back. Are you going to put him in your room?"

LuAnn rose and sighed. She took the leash from Brad. "Yes, because Tom is lonely without him." She turned for the stairs. "Why don't you all go sit in the parlor? I'll be right back."

She left Huck and Tom in her bedroom, chuckling at the mutual wash session that began the moment Huck entered the room, then joined Brad, Tess, and Janice in the main floor sitting area. She flopped onto the chair next to Tess. "Okay, what's the scoop on our little canine visitor?"

Brad draped his arm on the back of the sofa, as if settling in for a lengthy chat. "First, Sally's never seen the dog before, so she couldn't pinpoint an owner."

LuAnn would never admit it out loud, but she wasn't disappointed by the news. Maybe she'd get to enjoy several days of the animals' company before handing them over to their rightful owners. Already she'd become attached to Tom and Huck.

"She did recognize the breed though. She says he's a Shih Tzu–terrier mix, and he has a Shih Tzu's hair rather than a terrier's fur. This is a bonus since Shih Tzus shed very little and they're less likely to cause allergic reactions."

Janice beamed at Tess. "See? You don't have to worry about guests sneezing their heads off, after all. He won't bother them."

"He bothers me." Tess fidgeted, bumping LuAnn with her elbow. "Whether he sheds or not, he'll still chew and leave messes and—"

LuAnn put up her hand. "Tess, I love ya, but we've heard it all. Let Brad finish, okay?"

Brad cleared his throat. "There are rescue groups in place who re-house Shih Tzus—apparently it's a highly sought-after breed—so she said if no one steps up as the dog's owner, she could give you the names of a couple of groups that would be happy to foster Huckleberry until a new home is found."

LuAnn sat forward. "But what about little Tom? He's so attached to Huckleberry. And Huck clearly looks at Tom as his kitten. I mean, when I left them, Huck was washing Tom's ears."

Janice laughed. "I've seen him give Tom a bath. The kitten purrs up a storm. It's adorable."

"*Blech.*" Tess rolled her eyes. "Dog slobber."

Janice nudged Tess's knee. "Oh, stop. He didn't lick you. What's your problem with dogs, anyway? Did you get attacked by one when you were little or something?"

"No, I did not." Tess stood. "If that's all, I'm going to go help Winnie with tomorrow's pies." She headed for the kitchen.

LuAnn sighed, watching after her friend. She needed to get to the bottom of Tess's resistance to Huck. She turned to Brad. "I guess it's time to take a picture, now that Huck is all cleaned up. That is, if you're still willing to make the fliers."

"I am." He patted his bulging jacket pocket. "I brought my good digital camera, so let's get to the photo shoot."

LuAnn and Brad went up the stairs and encountered Constance on the second-floor landing. She wore a puzzled expression. LuAnn paused. "Is something wrong?"

"Well..." Constance glanced up the stairs. "You'll probably think I'm imagining things, but when I was putting clean sheets on the bed in Apples and Cinnamon, I could have sworn I heard a dog's whine. It seemed to come from above my head."

LuAnn laughed. "You aren't imagining things. A little dog and cat are staying temporarily in my apartment."

Constance's eyes widened. "A dog and cat? Can I go up and see them?"

LuAnn shrugged. "Sure. Brad's going to take a picture of them so he can make some fliers to post. You might as well meet them."

The three of them climbed to the fourth floor, Constance more smiling and eager than LuAnn had seen her before. LuAnn led Brad and Constance to her rooms and opened the door. Huck greeted them with frantic yips and much dancing.

Constance sucked in a breath. "Oh, I know what the jitter-bugging means. He needs out."

LuAnn started to pick him up, but Constance reached in and snagged him. She turned pleading eyes on LuAnn. "Do you mind?"

"Um, no. Be my guest."

"Thank you!" Constance took off with Huck in her arms.

Brad laughed. "You might have to fight her for custody if that dog ends up free for adoption."

LuAnn shrugged. "As much as I'd love to keep him, Tess has done nothing but avoid him and mutter under her breath since he arrived. It wouldn't be fair to keep him when she's full of animosity."

Brad's lips quirked. "Ani-mosity? Did you intend to make a pun?"

She blinked twice and released a self-conscious laugh. "Okay, let's change that to hostility."

"Hmm, being hostile in a hostel."

LuAnn held up both palms, surrender style. "Enough with the puns."

Brad smirked but fell silent.

Tom crept his way across the floor, then pounced on LuAnn's shoelaces. She smiled at the kitten's antics. She'd seen Tom bat at Huck's ears or tail with the same enthusiasm. Huck was always very patient with the kitten. She jerked her attention to Brad. "Do you think Tom and Huck came from the same home, or is it possible Huck found the kitten and decided to take care of him?"

Brad rubbed his jaw. "Hmm, good question. They seem very attached to each other, but as young as Tom seems, I think the latter is more likely. If there'd been a mother cat in the picture, Huck wouldn't have been able to take Tom away from her. Not without a fight. Mama cats are pretty protective."

"That's what I thought. Which means if Huck is claimed by his family, they probably won't want to take the kitten too."

He grazed her arm with his fingers. "And you're kind of hoping that's what happens, aren't you? So you can keep him?"

She offered a weak smile in reply.

"Maybe you can. Tess doesn't have any opposition to the kitten's presence, does she?"

"Not that she's said. She's been too busy complaining about Huck." LuAnn sat on the end of the bed and lifted the kitten into her lap. She stroked his little tummy, and he attempted to kick her fingers away. "I think, if someone comes to claim Huck, though, I'll probably ask if they'd consider taking Tom too. They've become...family. It would be cruel to separate them now."

"You don't think they'd adjust?"

Her heart panged. "Maybe. Maybe not, though. I mean, when you lose someone you love, the hurt never completely goes away, does it?"

Before Brad could answer, Constance returned with Huck. She put the dog on the floor, and he pranced to the bed and put his front feet on LuAnn's knees. He nosed the kitten, as if ascertaining all was well. Tom's purr revved into overdrive. The two loved each other. If Huck went, Tom would have to go too. LuAnn would sure miss them. She patted the mattress, and Huck leaped up. She set Tom beside him, then moved out of the way of the camera.

Brad took several pictures and returned his phone to his pocket. "I'll email the flier to you for your approval before I make copies." He turned, then stopped. Constance was still standing in the doorway.

"Constance, did you need something?"

Constance held up a gallon-size plastic bag. "What should I do with these dog biscuits?"

LuAnn's heart rolled over. "How kind. Did you get those for Huck?"

Constance shook her head, her forehead puckering into lines of confusion. "No, Miss Sherrill. I found the bag next to the back stoop when I took Huck outside. But I think maybe Marcus brought them."

"Marcus?" LuAnn tipped her head. "Why?"

"Because when Huck saw him in the kitchen with Winnie, he nearly jumped out of my arms to get to him. When I brought him back in after he did his business, Marcus was gone, but Huck went straight to the chair where Marcus was sitting and whined, like he wanted him." She shrugged. "I got the feeling Marcus and Huck were already friends."

CHAPTER TWELVE

On Tuesday morning during breakfast, Brad delivered a stack of forty fliers with a full-color photo of Huck and Tom prominently displayed beneath the banner FOUND. Under the photo, he'd placed LuAnn's cell phone number with instructions to call with queries.

"Thanks—this looks great." She set the fliers on the check-in desk. "Would you accept a cinnamon roll and coffee as payment?"

"Now that's an offer I can't refuse." He grinned and strode toward the café.

When the breakfast rush ended, LuAnn braved the cold and spent a couple of hours attaching the mini-posters to lampposts, trees, bulletin boards, and shop windows, all the while hoping no one would notice them.

Thursday morning, when Constance arrived at work, she took LuAnn aside. "Miss Sherrill, would it be all right if Huck spent the day with me instead of staying closed up in your apartment?"

LuAnn hesitated. "Well… I completely trust you to keep track of him, but what about Tom? Won't he be lonely up there all day by himself?"

"Cats are independent," Constance said, her tone reflecting certainty, "but dogs are pack animals. They need socialization. He'll be a lot happier and healthier if he's allowed to roam and be around people."

LuAnn shrugged. "I suppose we can give it a try."

Tess wandered by, coffeepot in hand. "Give what a try?"

LuAnn repeated Constance's request. Tess grimaced. "Are you sure you want to let him roam? He'll probably bother everybody in the café, beg for bacon, or bark at them."

LuAnn turned a firm look on Constance. "If he doesn't behave, you'll have to take him to the apartment. Deal?"

Constance beamed. "Deal!"

LuAnn kept careful watch, but Huck didn't cross the café threshold even once. He didn't enter any of the guest rooms either. Instead, he lay in the hallway outside the door with his chin on his paws and watched Constance work.

At the end of the day, when Constance delivered Huck into LuAnn's keeping, LuAnn asked a question she hoped Constance wouldn't find amusing. "Do you think Huck understands what we say to him?"

Constance didn't even smirk. "I think he recognizes some words, and he senses what we expect from him. Dogs are very intelligent and intuitive. He understood little Tom needed looking after and took care of him. He knew which door to scratch to find a kind soul."

LuAnn touched Constance's arm. "Thank you. That was a nice thing to say."

The young woman shrugged, her cheeks turning pink. "It's true. A lot of people wouldn't welcome a strange dog and cat into their home." She glanced right and left, as if making sure no one was listening, then added, "If Tess had been here, I wonder if Huck would've bothered scratching."

LuAnn laughed. "Maybe not."

Constance offered a rare smile. "When I was a child, we had a little dog named Duchess. She liked everybody except this one neighbor. She would growl every time he walked by the house, but we never knew why. Until he was arrested for burglarizing several homes. My mom thought maybe he'd tried to break into our house and Duchess remembered it, so she didn't trust him after that." She leaned down and ruffled Huck's ears. "If you want a judge of character, watch a dog. He'll tell you who's trustworthy and who's not."

Constance left, but LuAnn couldn't stop thinking about what she'd said. If a dog could judge character, Huck had deemed Constance trustworthy. He also, according to Constance, liked Marcus, although LuAnn hadn't witnessed it for herself. As for Alice Busby...

LuAnn started up the stairs, and Huck climbed up next to her, his toenails clicking on the steps. Alice had skirted around Huck with more apprehension than even Tess showed. And Huck skirted around her too. He never barked or growled at the woman, but his skittishness made LuAnn wonder if he knew something the rest of them didn't.

She put Huck in with Tom, who was so happy to see his doggy companion he nearly climbed on Huck's back. Then she returned to the main floor. Three couples, longtime friends, were due to arrive midevening for a three-day retreat away from their kids—their Christmas gift to each other—and she'd agreed to do the checking-in since Tess wanted to finish Christmas shopping with her son, and Janice had plans with Paige.

She reached the ground floor. At the same time Alice trotted from the direction of the library. The two of them nearly collided. Alice drew back and laughed. A nervous laugh, LuAnn thought.

"Please excuse me. I didn't see you."

LuAnn glanced at the ever-present notebook in the woman's pudgy hands. "You were probably focused on your novel. How is it coming? Well, I hope."

"Oh, my, yes." Alice nodded so hard her frizzy bun bounced and a bobby pin fell to the floor. "I've reached my midpoint— the big twist."

LuAnn hid a chuckle with a cough. "You've reached . . . what?"

"The midpoint. The place where the story takes an unexpected turn that leads the heroine in a new direction." The author tapped her notebook with her pen. "Before I started writing I studied the three-act structure for novel-writing. Act one is where you set up the heroine for the conflict, act two forces the heroine to confront the challenge, and then in act three you bring her to a satisfying resolution." She beamed. "Smack in the middle of act two comes the big twist. Such an exciting place to be."

Suddenly her eyes widened and she searched in every direction, as if being pursued by a bee. "Where is that little dog?"

"In my apartment."

"Oh." The woman seemed to wilt. "What a relief."

LuAnn's scalp prickled. "Why is that?"

She pursed her lips. "I'm dreadfully allergic to dogs. If one so much as brushes against me, I break out in a rash. Consequently I have to keep my distance."

Could it be Huck avoided Alice not because he didn't trust her, but because he sensed she was afraid of him? LuAnn shook her head. "You don't have to worry about Huckleberry. He doesn't have fur."

The woman's face puckered into a confused scowl. "Did you shave him?"

LuAnn couldn't hold back a soft laugh. "No. But the groomer said he's a Shih Tzu mix, and that particular breed of dog has hair instead of fur, which makes them hypoallergenic. So chances are good he won't give you a rash."

Alice stared, openmouthed, for several seconds. Then she blinked. "Well. I've never heard of such a thing. But maybe the next time I see him, I'll give him a little touch. See what happens. If you're willing to buy anti-itch cream for me if I break out."

LuAnn was interested in how Huck would react to Alice's approach. "I'll buy the biggest tube available."

"Well, then, tomorrow we'll experiment. As for now..." She giggled the most girlish giggle imaginable. "I have a dinner date, so I must ready myself." She scurried up the stairs before LuAnn had a chance to question her about her "date."

Tess and Janice had already left, and Winnie was putting on her coat when LuAnn entered the kitchen. Winnie pointed to the refrigerator. "I just finished rolling out the cinnamon rolls. Would you come down at six tomorrow morning and take them out of the fridge and put them on the counter so they can rise? If you put the first couple of pans in the oven at about seven thirty, they'll be ready to go when the first customer arrives. I've been so busy, I forgot to tell you, but I won't be in until ten or so."

LuAnn leaned against the counter. "Everything okay?"

Winnie shrugged. "Oh, sure. A checkup first thing in the morning, making sure my blood pressure medicine is doing its job."

"I didn't realize you took blood pressure medicine."

"Because it isn't such a big deal I need to tell folks about it." A wry grin dimpled her cheeks. "Marcus is just sure I'm gonna fall over dead from a heart attack because of all the cooking I do here, but I keep telling him there's no need to be such a worrywart. I love working here." She squeezed LuAnn's arm. "Thanks for letting me be part of your inn family." She headed out the door.

Family . . . The word seemed to echo in LuAnn's head. Then another part of Winnie's comment pushed the single word aside. "*Marcus is just sure I'm gonna fall over dead from a heart attack.*" Her years of teaching had taught her that teenagers weren't exactly known for their logic. Could fear for his grandmother's health inspire the young man to create expensive clean-ups at Wayfarers, thinking it would force the Inn Crowd to release employees to save money? She rushed to her notebook and recorded the thought before the reverberating *family* erased it from her mind.

By the end of the breakfast rush Friday morning, the Inn Crowd had decided Winnie's presence was an absolute necessity. Adding cooking, baking, and plate-filling to the duties of order-taking, serving, and clearing tables proved how much the woman did around the kitchen. They all welcomed her with enthusiasm when she arrived a few minutes past ten, in time to start preparations for lunch.

Winnie received their hugs and laughed. "You all act like I've been gone a month instead of a few hours."

LuAnn took Winnie's coat and hung it on a peg. "This morning felt like a month. I think we need to raise your pay now that we know how invaluable you are."

Winnie grinned and shook her finger. "Careful there, Miss LuAnn, or I might hold you to that." She slipped on her Wayfarers Inn apron, her smile bright. "Now all of you, scat out of my way so I can get these soups going. Gotta earn my keep, you know."

Tess and Janice remained in the kitchen to help Winnie, and LuAnn went after a broom to sweep up crumbs from the dining room floor. The whirr of the vacuum cleaner carried from the library area, and LuAnn stepped over its cord on her way to the utility closet under the stairs. Then she stopped and whirled around, staring at the cord. It ran under the closed office door. She followed the cord to the library.

Constance was pushing the vacuum over the area rug, her back to LuAnn. Huckleberry sat at the edge of the rug, seemingly supervising. When LuAnn approached, the little dog trotted to her, and Constance glanced over her shoulder. She pressed the Off switch with her foot, and silence fell. She turned to face LuAnn. "Yes, ma'am?"

LuAnn crouched and petted the dog. She pointed to the cord. "Is this plugged into an office outlet?"

Pink filled Constance's face. "Yes. Do you mind? I can't reach the outlet outside the office with the Christmas tree there, and it's the best place to plug in since it's centrally located to the whole parlor area."

Which meant she'd utilized the outlet before. "How did you get into the office? We generally keep that door locked." LuAnn tempered her tone. She didn't want to accuse, but she was curious.

The pink deepened to crimson. "Well, um, one of the keys on my ring"—she patted the bulging pocket of the hospital-type scrub she wore over her street clothes—"opens it. I only use the outlet and always lock the door behind me. If you don't want me using the outlet anymore, I won't. It's just so convenient."

LuAnn hadn't realized they'd put an office key on the housekeeper's ring. She would talk to Tess and Janice about whether or not to remove it. She straightened and patted Constance's arm. "Go ahead and use it for now. But that might have to change. Not because you've done anything wrong."

Had Constance taken the diary from the office? Despite endless searching, the printed pages had not been found. "But guests trust us to keep their valuables safe in there. We wouldn't want something to come up missing and for you to be accused."

Constance nodded, her expression solemn. "I understand." She wiggled the handle on the vacuum cleaner. "Do you mind if I finish in here? I need to vacuum in Mrs. Busby's room next. She dragged sand in from somewhere. The little particles could scratch the wood floors. It was in here too, but I think I've about got it all."

"Go ahead." LuAnn took a step back, and Constance tapped the foot button. The vacuum roared to life. Huck bounced back to the spot he'd vacated and sat, the tip of his pink tongue sticking out in his doggy way of smiling. LuAnn stood for a moment, watching Constance glide the vacuum over the rug. She had work to do too, but she wanted to make a couple of new entries in her notebook.

Constance has access to the office.

Alice dragged in sand, probably from the riverbank.

Why the sand entry was significant, LuAnn couldn't determine. But somehow she knew she needed to record it for later contemplation.

CHAPTER THIRTEEN

LuAnn's conversation with Winnie about blood pressure had given her the perfect idea for the cook's Christmas gift. On Saturday morning between breakfast and lunch, she put Huckleberry on his leash and walked to a local salon. The day was cold but calm, no wind blowing at all, and the sun beat down brightly. By the time she reached the salon, she'd even worked up a bit of a sweat.

She hooked the leash's hand loop under one leg of the iron bench outside the place of business, then took Huck's chin in her hand. "I'll be right back. You stay put, you hear?" He flopped onto his stomach and rested his head on his front paws. Convinced he'd be fine, LuAnn entered the salon and purchased a gift certificate for a massage, pedicure, and manicure. She knew from personal experience how relaxing each treatment was, and she hoped Winnie would have the same experience. Someone with high blood pressure needed to relax.

The cashier rolled the certificate into a tube and tied it with a bold red ribbon. She even tucked a tiny plastic sprig of mistletoe into the bow. LuAnn smiled. How festive! She wouldn't need to wrap this gift. Tube in hand, she exited the salon and lifted the leg on the bench to free Huck's leash. "All right, Huckleberry, let's—"

Huck lunged, and the leash snapped away from LuAnn's reaching hand. Barking, the dog shot up the sidewalk.

"Huck! Huck!" LuAnn pounded after the escaping dog. The weight of her boots and her bulky down coat slowed her progress. Huck had no such encumbrances. He darted between other shoppers, his leash dancing behind him like a kite's tail, an occasional shrill bark carrying to LuAnn's ears.

Just when she thought her lungs would explode from sucking in the cold air, a gray-mustached man wearing a battered Stetson stomped on Huck's leash and brought the dog to an abrupt halt. He scooped up the wriggling ball of fuzz and met LuAnn in the middle of the block. LuAnn was panting hard, but she managed to choke out a thank-you.

The man grinned, his sun-leathered skin crinkling at the corners of his eyes. "No problem." He glanced at the nearby lamppost, where one of the Brad-made fliers seemed to stare at them. "Is this the dog from the poster?"

"Yes. I haven't had any luck finding the owner." LuAnn took a firm grip on Huck's leash and waited until the rescuer put Huck on the ground. Huck strained against the leash, whining and looking up the block. "I don't know what got into him. He's been on several walks, and this is the first time he's tried to run away."

The man rubbed his chin. He looked in the direction Huck seemed to be trying to drag LuAnn. "It kind of looked like he was chasing the boy who works part time at the grocery—you know, the one who delivers orders to customers. Have you met him?"

"Yes, I'm pretty sure I have." Constance had mentioned she suspected Marcus of leaving dog biscuits for Huck. So had Huck spotted Marcus and run after him, hoping for a treat? "But I think he would have stopped and let Huck catch him."

"Well then, maybe he saw his owner and wanted to get to him."

She wouldn't tell the kind stranger, but that explanation made less sense to her than Huck chasing after Marcus. If the owner was here on the street, surely he would have seen or heard Huck. Or at least have noticed the fliers. Wouldn't he have tried to catch Huck? Unless he'd decided he didn't want the dog anymore.

She sighed, her breath forming a cloud in front of her face. "Since he can't talk, I guess I'll never know. Thanks for catching him for me though. I was scared he would run out into traffic." Huck flopped onto his belly and lay still, brown eyes staring ahead. She shook the now crushed certificate. The sprig of mistletoe had fallen off somewhere too. "That was a bad thing to do, Huckleberry. I won't take you on walks if you're going to try to run away from me."

As silly as it was, she felt rebuffed by the dog's behavior. He might have run away from his first home, but she hadn't expected him to run away from her. She gave the leash a light tug, and Huck got to his feet. "Come on now. Tom is waiting for you."

Usually the mention of the kitten's name made Huck's ears shoot up, but oddly he only whined softly and continued to gaze sadly up the block. The man bent over and ruffled the hair at Huck's neck. "Behave yourself now, fella." He tipped his cowboy-style hat at LuAnn before sauntering off.

Huck walked obediently beside LuAnn all the way back to the inn, but he'd lost the bounce in his step. She took him to the apartment, and he perked up when Tom scampered across the floor and rubbed against his legs. She left the pair closed in her room and went back to the main level. Because the purchased certificate had gotten so smashed during her run, she untied the rumpled ribbon, flattened the certificate as best she could, and put it beneath Brad's coffee table book, along with Irene and Thelma's pie certificates. If it didn't straighten out, at least she'd have a story to go with it.

She started to close the door on the little cupboard, but she gave a start. A stack of pages filled the spot where the diary had been. Then she realized the stack *was* the diary. The pages were all willy-nilly rather than neatly tamped, and several corners were bent or torn, but it was back. She slammed the door closed and hurried to the kitchen where Winnie was rolling biscuits and Tess and Janice were peeling vegetables.

LuAnn pointed over her shoulder with her thumb. "Guess what? The diary is in the cupboard again."

Janice turned from the counter, shame-faced. "Yes. I put it in there this morning."

Both Tess and LuAnn gaped at her. Tess spluttered, "You've had it all this time?"

Janice shook her head. "No, Larry had it."

LuAnn pressed her fingertips to her temples. How had Janice's five-year-old grandson gotten ahold of Prudence's diary? "What?"

Janice sighed and flicked an embarrassed look across the trio of other women. "Stacy came in to buy a half-dozen cinnamon rolls to share at work, and Larry was with her. He asked for drawing paper. We were busy that morning, so I opened the office and told him there was lots of paper and to help himself. It didn't occur to me that he'd taken the diary until Stacy found it in his room and brought it back. Well, she brought back the pages that Larry hadn't colored on or turned into paper airplanes." She cringed. "We'll have to go through and figure out what pages are missing and have another copy made for you."

LuAnn collapsed into a kitchen chair. "So Larry took it." Which meant Constance and Alice Busby were innocent of wrongdoing. At least where the diary was concerned.

Janice nodded. "I'm sorry. The next time he asks for paper, I'll get it myself."

"We have it back. That's what matters." Tess smirked. "You don't suppose Larry stole off with the sheets, do you?"

Janice laughed and returned to whisking the peel from a carrot. "No, he wasn't here when the sheets turned up missing."

LuAnn doubted they could blame Larry for the split water line either. She started to tell the others about Huckleberry's escapade, but Winnie spoke first.

"'Nough of this jabbering now. Folks'll be showing up in less than half an hour, and we need to be ready for them. Everybody, shake a leg."

The women laughingly saluted and got to work. The lunch shift passed quickly, and when they began the cleanup, LuAnn told them about Huck's wild race up the sidewalk. "The man who stopped him wondered if Huck had seen his owner, and that's why he took off."

Janice's brow crinkled. "If my pet came running at me, I'd stop and let him catch me."

"Me too," LuAnn said, "but maybe the owner decided he no longer wants Huck. After all, I haven't had a single phone call since the day I posted the fliers. With all the Christmas shopping going on up and down the street, his owner would have to be blind to not notice at least one of the fliers. The man who stopped him recognized him right away as the dog from the posters."

"How could anyone discard that sweet little dog?" Sadness colored Janice's face and tone.

Tess cleared her throat. "I hope you remember, LuAnn, that if his owner doesn't step forward, that 'sweet little dog' will need to go to the shelter."

Winnie *tsk-tsk*ed. "Miss Tess, you are a hard-hearted one. How can you turn away such a friendly pup? Why, if Miss Lu hadn't found him first, I would've taken him home with me in a heartbeat."

Tess whirled on Winnie. "Then why don't you? He'd be good company for you, Winnie."

Winnie pursed her lips. "I suppose he would, if I spent as much time at home as I do here, but I couldn't take him without taking the cat too. I can't have a cat. Cats make my eyes swell up and make me sneeze."

"Oh." Tess heaved a sigh. "Well, I wish whoever lost that dog would come claim it. The longer it's here, the harder it'll be for—" She snatched a butcher knife from the block and began chopping one of the peeled potatoes into chunks. "For LuAnn to get rid of it."

Constance rounded the corner. "Excuse me, ladies, but I heard Huckleberry whining. I think he needs to go out. Would you like me to take him?"

LuAnn dug in her jeans pocket for her apartment key. "Yes, thank you, Constance. Be sure and put him on his leash, though. The little scamp got away from me this morning."

Constance nodded and scurried to the elevator. Minutes later the elevator returned, and she emerged with Huck prancing at the end of his leash. Apparently he'd gotten over his upset of the morning, because he held his fluffy tail high, and his typical doggy grin was in place. Constance led him through the kitchen, but as she passed Tess, Huck whined and jumped up, putting his front feet on Tess's leg.

"Hey!" Tess shifted aside. "Quit that."

Huck barked and lunged again. Constance scooped him into her arms. "Stop it, Huckleberry. What's wrong with you?" She trotted to the back door and went outside.

Tess slapped at her apron. "Now I've probably got dog hair on—" She rubbed her hand across one of the apron's patch pockets. Curiosity bloomed on her face. She slid her hand into her pocket and pulled out a dog biscuit. She used the biscuit to point at each of the other women by turn. "Okay, whose bright idea was this?"

Janice nudged LuAnn and snickered. "She tries to tell us she doesn't like dogs, but she carries a treat for him in her pocket."

Tess squared her shoulders, her expression indignant. "I did not put that treat in my pocket."

The other three women burst out laughing.

"Stop laughing!" Tess placed her hands on her hips. "One of you had to have done it."

LuAnn cleared her throat and brought her laughter under control. "Why would one of us put a dog treat in your pocket?"

"As a joke. Or as manipulation."

Janice arched one brow. "Manipulation?"

"Yes, to get me to give it to the dog and make friends with him. Well, it won't work. You can't make me be friends with that dog."

LuAnn shook her head. "You are being silly, Tess. None of your friends would've put a dog treat in your pocket, knowing how you feel about Huckleberry. It must've gotten dropped in there by accident."

Tess's lips formed a wry line. "By accident? Really?"

LuAnn imitated Tess's expression. "Yes. Both Janice and I like treating Huck. Somebody probably thought they were putting the biscuit in one of our apron pockets."

Tess silently pointed to her name embroidered on the bibbed section of the apron.

LuAnn put her hands up. "All right then, I don't know. But none of us would set that little dog up for rejection, so you can erase our names from the list of suspects."

Winnie clanked a handful of silverware into the dishwasher tray. "Either way, it doesn't matter. This kitchen won't clean itself. So let's get to it."

CHAPTER FOURTEEN

Sunday morning, LuAnn checked the calendar that hung beside her dresser. December 16. Halfway through the month, only nine days till Christmas, and she still didn't have gifts for Constance or Pastor Ben and Paige. Tess and Janice had taken shopping trips with their children and claimed they'd finished their gift-buying. The wrapped packages under the tree in their shared apartment proved their industriousness. Ordinarily organized and ready well in advance, LuAnn had failed miserably at Christmas prep.

At breakfast, she said, "Janice, it's your morning to stick around, but do you have plans with anyone this afternoon?"

Janice smiled over the top of her coffee mug. "Not today. Why?"

"I need to finish my Christmas shopping, and I was hoping you wouldn't mind if I stepped out for a little while," she explained.

Janice shrugged. "I don't mind staying here so you can shop till you drop."

LuAnn chuckled. "I have no intention of dropping, but I would like to finish my shopping. I can't believe it's almost Christmas already. The past months have really flown." As much as she tried, she couldn't keep melancholy from creeping into her tone.

Tess squeezed her arm. "This'll be a hard one for you. The first holidays without a loved one always are. But we're here for you, Lu."

LuAnn sniffled and blinked, bringing the prick of tears under control. "Oh, I know you are, and I appreciate it. But I don't want either of you worrying over me. You need to focus on your kids and grandkids. They're more important."

Janice didn't try to refute LuAnn's words, but her brow remained set in a series of worry lines. "Well, this afternoon while you are out, I want to go through your diary pages and figure out which ones are missing. Right now that document reminds me of Larry's gap-toothed smile. I want to fill in the blanks."

They all laughed, and a bit of the tension seemed to ease. After church, LuAnn climbed in her car and drove to Front Street. She window-shopped for nearly an hour, then she entered a store with an eclectic mix of trendy women's clothing, artwork, and gift items. On one display, a kit containing a battery-powered set of clock hands and twelve picture frames seemed to leap out at her. She picked up the box and read the directions for creating a one-of-a-kind clock with family photographs in place of numbers. Since Pastor Ben and Paige were expecting their first child, what better gift than a way to showcase the baby's pictures?

She tucked the box under her arm and browsed some more, but nothing that yelled "Constance" made itself known.

She paid for the clock kit, and when she stepped back out on the sidewalk, a gust of wind lifted her scarf and tossed it over her eyes. The temperature was dropping, the wind was increasing, and the thought of more shopping lost its appeal. She slid behind the wheel of her car and aimed for the inn.

Janice was sitting on the parlor love seat, a book in her hands, when LuAnn entered. She set the book aside and hurried across the floor. "Did you find something wonderful?"

LuAnn showed her the box. "Do you think Pastor Ben and Paige will like this?"

Janice clapped her hands and beamed. "It's perfect! They'll love it. It makes me wish I'd seen it first." She laughed, then flicked a worried look over her shoulder. She caught LuAnn's elbow and steered her toward the kitchen. "Let's find a big bow to go with it."

"I have big bows in—"

"I put a box of bows on a shelf in the pantry." Janice spoke over LuAnn's mild protest. Once in the kitchen, she escorted LuAnn to the pantry and closed them inside.

"Janice!" LuAnn gaped at her friend. "Why the cloak-and-dagger routine?"

Janice put her finger against her lips. "Alice is in the library. I don't want her to overhear us."

LuAnn released a disbelieving laugh. "Who cares if she hears us talking about a Christmas gift for our minister and his wife?"

"Not about that. About what I'm going to say now."

LuAnn set aside her amusement. "What is it?"

"I went up to check on Huck and Tom when I got home from church. While I was up there, I couldn't resist playing with Tom for a little bit—he had so much fun batting at a dangled piece of yarn."

LuAnn shook her head. "Janice, playing with the kitten doesn't seem like something that should be kept secret."

"Shh! When I came back down, I found a trail of wet sand leading from the front door to the check-in desk right up to the basement opening." Janice used a low, ominous tone that set LuAnn's teeth on edge. "I looked, and sure enough, bits of sand were on the stairs. By the time I reached the bottom, it was almost all gone, like the person's feet were finally clean, but then I spotted a few particles shining under the light. Then I went back upstairs, and I found—"

"Janice?"

Both Janice and LuAnn jumped. Janice leaped toward the pantry door and swung it open. Alice waited outside the door, her round face wreathed in a smile.

"Oh, you are in there." She held out a Styrofoam take-out container. "Would you put this in your refrigerator? It's my leftover lunch—chicken fingers and sweet potato fries. It was too much to eat all at once, so I'd like to have the rest for my supper, but I don't have a refrigerator in my room, so . . . "

Janice laughed. A nervous laugh. "Did you forget about the little refrigerator in the dining room, next to the microwave? You can put the box in there and then get it whenever you're hungry and reheat it."

The woman made a pouty face. "Oh, my, I did forget about that refrigerator. I'm sorry I bothered you." She leaned side-ways a bit and seemed to examine the pantry. "I'll let you get back to...whatever you were doing." She turned and disap-peared from view.

Janice snapped the door closed and planted her back against it. Her wide eyes fixed on LuAnn, and she whispered, "She's everywhere, like our own personal private detective."

"I agree." LuAnn set the clock box on a shelf and folded her arms over her chest. "I don't believe for a minute she forgot about the guest fridge. She wanted to listen in on our conversation."

Janice nodded. "But why is she so curious about the things we say? You don't suppose she—"

The pantry door opened, and Janice yelped. This time Tess stood looking in, puzzlement on her face. Janice grabbed her arm, yanked her into the pantry, and closed the door. Tess bounced a frown from LuAnn to Janice. "What in the world are you two doing in here?"

"Hiding from Alice," Janice said.

Tess shrugged. "No need for that. She's not even here." She pushed the pantry door open and stepped into the kitchen. "She left as I came in. She had her coat and her notebook with her. I asked where she was off to in the cold, but she only smiled and said she'd see me later." She chuckled. "She's one odd duck."

"And sneaky." Janice gave LuAnn a nervous look as she moved from the pantry. "Do you think she heard us talking about the sand?"

Tess's brows pinched together. "Sand? What sand?"

Janice repeated everything she'd told LuAnn, then added, "What I was going to say when Alice interrupted me, was that the particles of sand also led to the library. Where Alice was. I hate to say this, but I don't trust her."

LuAnn nodded slowly. They'd made fun of her for suspecting Alice of ill-doing, but finally they were coming around. It should have made her gloat. But she was too worried to gloat. Why would Alice be wandering around on the riverbank? Was she trying to access the tunnel? But why? Had she made the rope of sheets Constance found in the trash can? The joy of finding a perfect gift for Pastor Ben and Paige slipped to the far recesses of her mind, crowded out by concern and confusion.

She blurted, "Should we tell Alice we need the Honeymoon Suite and hope she takes the hint to leave?"

Tess's eyebrows rose. "Of course not. We can't send away a paying guest with no guarantee we'll be able to replace the income."

"Besides," Janice said, her face drooping, "she'd probably just move into one of the smaller rooms. She spends most of her time in the library anyway."

LuAnn swallowed an argument, but she wanted to find out if the strange happenings would cease if the whodunit writer departed from Wayfarers.

Monday morning, LuAnn awakened early thanks to Tom pouncing on the bed. Although covered by a sheet, blanket, and light quilt, she still felt the little cat's attack on her feet. She sat up and caught the kitten, drawing him against her chest. He purred up a storm, but he had no interest in cuddling. He wriggled loose and bounced across the mattress, dived on her feet, and bit down on the quilt.

She burst out laughing, which was the perfect way to start a day after a night of worry. She snapped on her bedside lamp and squinted at her cell phone. Her alarm wasn't due to sound for another hour. "You little scamp!"

Huck's mouth stretched in a yawn, a whine emerging at the same time. He stretched, then padded from the dog bed to the edge of LuAnn's bed and looked up with hopeful brown eyes.

She laughed again. "All right, come on up. Maybe Tom will use you as his play toy and give my feet a break."

The dog crouched, his backside twitching, then, like a spring being released, he bounded onto the bed. As LuAnn had hoped, Tom pranced over and wrapped his paws around Huck's neck. The two of them began a wrestling match.

LuAnn got up, tugged on her robe and slippers, and patted her leg. "C'mon, Huck. Let's go out."

The dog leaped to the floor and followed LuAnn out of the apartment and down the stairs. They rounded the corner to the dining room, and Huck suddenly stopped. His ears rose, his eyes bright and alert, and then he yipped and took off so quickly his feet slipped on the wood floor. Barking, he darted through the dining room and into the kitchen. LuAnn followed so closely the tip of his tail swished against her ankle. As they thundered across the floor, the back door slammed.

Huck's barking became frantic. He planted his front feet against the door and alternately barked and whined. LuAnn scooped him up with one arm and twisted the deadbolt with the other. Her heart pounded so hard she could barely draw a breath. She clung to the wriggling dog, whispering soothing words as much for herself as for him. Who would be in the kitchen before the crack of dawn?

She whirled and headed for the stairs. Huck would have to make use of one of the potty pads. She wouldn't be putting him outside this morning. Not by herself. Because whoever had been in the kitchen was probably still in the alley, and she wanted reinforcements before she faced the person who hadn't wanted to be caught inside the inn.

CHAPTER FIFTEEN

Constance's hazel eyes nearly popped out of her head when she arrived for work and LuAnn, Tess, and Janice told her about their early-morning intruder. Powdery snow had fallen during the night, and the temperature dipped low. Apparently people were reluctant to venture out, because only Patricia Huston and Jane Davidson, a pair of retired teachers who visited the inn at least twice a week, arrived for breakfast. They sat in the café, drank coffee, and visited while the Inn Crowd, Constance, and Winnie clustered around the kitchen table.

Tess had insisted on calling 911 as soon as LuAnn awakened her and Janice, and an officer had explored the area behind the inn and the basement. The only out-of-the-ordinary things he found were a few shoe impressions in the snow. Nothing in the inn was damaged or missing. He took a couple of pictures with his cell phone so they'd have a record of the footprints, but beyond that all he could do was assign someone to sporadically patrol the area each night.

The other thing the officer said haunted LuAnn. *"There's no sign of breaking and entering. It looks like somebody either let the intruder in through a door or window, or the intruder used a key."* Neither scenario offered comfort. Someone with a key could come and go as he or she pleased, meaning the inn was never secure. If someone was opening the inn to an unknown person, then they couldn't trust their guests. Or, more specifically, they couldn't trust Alice. She was the only long-term guest. So if someone was opening the door and allowing others in without the Inn Crowd's permission, it had to be Alice.

Constance wrung her hands. "Are you going to change the locks? I mean, if an unauthorized person has a set of keys, that would be the easiest way to keep him out."

LuAnn filed the comment away to record in her notebook later.

Winnie shook her head. "I think you need to let that little dog of yours—"

"That dog is not ours," Tess said.

Winnie acted as though she hadn't heard the interruption. "—sleep here on the ground floor. He'll let you know if somebody comes in uninvited. After all, didn't you say the person ran out the door as soon as Huck started barking?"

"Yes." LuAnn recalled Huck's reaction—raised ears, alert bearing, frantic yips, and wild scramble to reach the door. Only now she wondered if the dog's behavior had reflected fear as much as something else. She'd seen him behave similarly when he was excited to see someone, like Tom or Constance. Or the person he was trying to reach on the street last week.

She pushed up from her chair. "Speaking of Huck, he probably needs to be taken out. I'll get him." She hurried from the kitchen. The patrons were still in the café, so she led Huck from the staircase toward the front door, intending to snap his leash onto his collar before they went out. But before she could grasp his collar, he bolted in the direction of the café.

He raced directly to Tess, who was pouring coffee for their guests. He plopped on his behind next to her feet and sat up, letting his front legs dangle in the cutest pose LuAnn had ever seen. She couldn't hold back a burst of laughter.

"Oh, what a sweetie," Jane said.

Patricia ruffled Huck's ears. "You're quite the charmer, aren't you?" Both women smiled at Huck the way old ladies smile at new babies.

Tess, however, backed away from the begging dog. "What are you doing in here? Scat, scat."

Huck remained in his pose and whined, his brown eyes locked on Tess's apron.

A funny feeling gripped LuAnn. She studied Tess's patch pockets. Sure enough, a dog biscuit-sized bulge showed in the left one. She pointed. "Um, Tess, I think I know what he's after."

Tess glanced at LuAnn, then looked down at her apron. With a groan, she reached into her pocket and pulled out the dog treat. "Another one?" She turned a begging look that closely matched Huck's on LuAnn. "Why? Why me?"

"I really don't want to be crabby." Tess held the wrapping paper in place while LuAnn secured a piece of tape. The women had turned the kitchen table into a temporary wrapping station. They'd need to have it cleaned up by morning or risk the wrath of Winnie. "This isn't the time of year to be crabby. So I'm fighting it, but between the supposed break-in, those dog biscuits turning up in my pocket, and the broken back porch light, crabbiness just might win."

LuAnn fastened the paper with one more piece of tape and then reached for the roll of wide red ribbon. "Do you think the person who came in early this morning broke the light? I didn't notice it when the police officer and I were out there, but I didn't specifically look at the light, either."

Tess shrugged. She fingered the roll of green ribbon. "It's hard to say. But it looks to me like the screws holding the fixture to the siding gave way, and when it fell, it disconnected the wiring. I called Thorn earlier, and he said he'd send the electrician to look at it tomorrow." She sighed. "As if we need another unexpected expense. I'm grateful for Alice's long-term reservation, even if she is a little, er, unpredictable."

LuAnn fluffed the bow. The bright red ribbon against the various greens of the holly-printed paper made the package so cheerful. She set it aside and reached for the coffee table book she'd purchased for Brad. Even though she still lacked one gift—Constance's—the urge to wrap packages had overtaken her. She and her mom had always wrapped gifts together, and it helped to have Tess's presence.

LuAnn flicked a look at Tess as she unrolled a festive snowflake-embossed paper. "Has she given an indication when she plans to leave?"

"None, other than to say she wants to finish her book here." Tess grinned. "She keeps calling Wayfarers and its owners her 'inspiration.' Who knows? We might get a mention in the acknowledgments. Or she might even dedicate the book to us."

LuAnn chuckled. "I'd want to read it before we agreed to any of that." She held the blue and green spools against the paper and decided on blue. As she pulled the ribbon from its spool, something occurred to her. She lowered her voice to a whisper. "Is she in the library?"

Tess shook her head. "No, we're safe to talk. She left about an hour ago. Another dinner date, she called it."

LuAnn raised her eyebrows. "Don't you wonder who her date is? Maybe we should follow her some evening and find out."

Tess took the length of blue ribbon LuAnn had snipped free and wrapped it around the book. "No, thanks. I haven't been too keen on her following us around."

"Turnabout is fair play," LuAnn said.

"Do unto others," Tess returned.

"But aren't you curious?"

"Sure I am." Tess sighed. "It's about driven me nuts, finding her sneaking around and listening to our conversations or observing our every move. But I won't subject her to the same treatment."

LuAnn put her finger on the knot and held it while Tess tied a bow. "That might just be what she needs to understand how she's made us feel."

"Maybe, but to be honest, I don't think she'd make the connection. She's pretty..."

"Self-absorbed?" LuAnn pulled her finger free, and Tess tightened the bow.

"I was going to say absentminded, which sounds a little less harsh, but I suppose self-absorbed fits too." Tess handed LuAnn the wrapped book.

LuAnn set the book next to the small scarf boxes and the certificates, which she'd slipped into Christmas-themed envelopes in lieu of wrapping. She tapped her lips, staring at the little pile of gifts. "She could still be here at Christmas. Do you suppose that means she doesn't have a family?"

"Hmm." Tess scrunched her brow. "I hadn't really thought about that. But yes, it could very well be."

Sympathy twined through LuAnn's middle. She wouldn't wish the loneliness she was feeling this Christmas on anyone. Not even Alice. "Well, in case she does end up spending Christmas at Wayfarers, maybe we should have a little something for her. So she has a touch of Christmas."

Janice came around the corner carrying Huck. The dog set his brown eyes on Tess and wriggled. Janice double-stepped toward the back door. "No, Hucky, she doesn't want you. You'll only get your feelings hurt." She sent an accusing look over her shoulder before heading outside.

Tess's lips formed a grim line. "You don't think Janice is sticking those dog biscuits in my pocket, do you? She's been the most vocal about me not wanting that dog around."

LuAnn gathered up the wrapping paper and ribbon spools. "I don't know. If she has, she's been sneaky about it. I've never caught her messing with your apron."

Tess grabbed the scissors and tape and followed LuAnn to the pantry. They put the items away. "If Winnie hadn't put our names on those aprons, the perpetrator wouldn't be able to figure out whose apron was whose. Whoever's doing it probably thinks if I find it in my pocket I'll give it to that dog and eventually make friends." A stubborn expression crossed her face. "But they're wasting their time. I won't make friends with it even if somebody fills my apron pockets with dog biscuits every day for the next year."

The back door slammed. Janice called, "Somebody bring me some paper towels so I can clean Huck's feet before I put him down."

LuAnn hurried and grabbed a handful of paper towels. While Janice held the squirming dog, LuAnn wiped the snow and moist dirt from Huck's feet. Then Janice put the dog on the floor. He trotted straight to Tess and did his sit-up-and-beg routine.

Janice laughed. "Tess, how can you resist that?"

"Like this." Tess hurried out of the kitchen.

CHAPTER SIXTEEN

The electrician arrived shortly after ten Tuesday morning as the last of the breakfast crowd was leaving. Perfect timing, as far as LuAnn was concerned. She took him out back and showed him the drooping fixture, then stood shivering on the stoop while he performed an examination that reminded her of a doctor giving a patient a thorough perusal. Finally he sighed and turned to her.

"I hate to be the bearer of bad tidings, but whoever put this fixture up didn't seal around the screw holes. Moisture's gotten in over the years, and this board is going to have to be replaced before I can put up a new light."

LuAnn hugged herself. The cold was seeping through her coat. "We'll need a new light too?"

He nodded. "I'm afraid so. When it fell, all the wiring pulled loose. I checked to see if I could rewire it, but the moisture's shorted it out. The thing is toast."

She blew out a breath, a little cloud forming in front of her face. "Okay. So...how long will it take to get this fixed? This is the only light back here, and we have a little dog that needs to be let out. I'm not keen on standing out here with him in the dark." Especially considering that a stranger was coming and going.

"Can't say as I blame you." He dropped his tools into the box at his feet. "I'll be glad to rewire a new light out here, but somebody else will need to replace this board first. In the meantime, though, I'll put a solar-powered motion-detector light above the door. I have a couple of them in my truck, and I can take care of that before I leave today. The solar-powered ones won't light up the whole area, but it'll give you enough light to let the dog out. Sound okay?"

LuAnn didn't see much choice, so she nodded.

"Gimme a call when you've got that board replaced and a new fixture purchased, and I'll come back and get you fixed up. Have a good day now, Ms. Sherrill." He disappeared around the corner, and LuAnn entered the inn. She shrugged out of her coat and then joined the women in the kitchen.

Tess shot her a worried frown. "I can tell by the look on your face it isn't good news. What did he tell you?"

"Before he can replace the light, we need someone with construction experience to replace the board where the light was. You were right that the screws gave way. The siding is rotten."

Tess sighed. "This is one time I wish I wasn't right." She waved her hand toward the office. "Go call Thorn."

Thorn agreed to come by later in the day and give them an estimate. As LuAnn left the office, she encountered Alice coming from the library. The smile she'd been wearing faded when she met LuAnn's gaze.

"Oh, my, you seem distressed. Is something wrong?"

LuAnn tried to laugh, but the sound fell flat. "Just a little electrical problem, Alice. Nothing to worry about."

"But you're worried. I can tell." She put her hand on LuAnn's forearm and nodded wisely. "Writers have a sixth sense about such things."

This time LuAnn's laugh was genuine. Alice hadn't meant to be funny, and LuAnn probably shouldn't have laughed, but she couldn't help it. Sometimes the woman's eccentricities were just too amusing to ignore. She squeezed Alice's hand.

"It's kind of you to be concerned, but the light fixture will be replaced soon and all will be well." Except for the bill that would accompany the replacement.

Alice tipped her head, a frizzy strand of gray hair falling toward her shoulder. "What light fixture?"

LuAnn began inching toward the dining room. "The back porch light."

Alice's eyes flew wide. "Oh no. There's no light back there now?"

Such an odd reaction. LuAnn froze in place and examined the woman's horrified expression. "There will be a light. An electrician is hanging a motion-detector light right now."

Alice heaved a mighty sigh and placed her hand on her chest. "Oh, such a relief."

"Why?" The question came out curt, more so than LuAnn had intended, but her curiosity had to be satisfied.

"Oh, well, it's just that..." Alice licked her lips. Her gaze flitted to the right then met LuAnn's again. "You take that dear little dog out in the back, and didn't you say he ran away from you once? If he ran away in the dark, and you didn't have a light back there, you might not be able to find him, and that would be devastating."

She sounded sincere, but LuAnn wasn't convinced the woman was being completely truthful. Even so, she smiled and nodded. "It's kind of you to be concerned about Huck."

Alice beamed. "He is a sweet little dog, isn't he? So cute and friendly. And he doesn't give me a rash, so I like him very much. I wouldn't want any harm to come to him." Clutching her notebook to her bosom, she turned and scurried up the stairs in her sensible lace-up shoes.

LuAnn stared at the woman's retreating feet. Something about the shape and tread of her shoes tickled a memory at the back of her mind. Then like a lightning bolt, recognition struck. She raced into the office, retrieved her notebook, and scribbled a note. This evening, when all was quiet, she would share her discovery with Tess and Janice.

Thorn arrived midafternoon and began removing the damaged board. He'd told the women he would be as careful as possible to avoid damaging any of the connecting siding, but he wouldn't guarantee it. "Old buildings...you never know what you'll find," he'd said.

While Janice and Tess performed the lunch clean-up duties, Winnie and LuAnn baked pies for the next day's patrons. Around three thirty the front doorbell rang, announcing the arrival of their expected check-ins, an elderly couple named Burl and Eleanor Dockum. LuAnn quickly wiped her hands on a towel and hurried to the parlor.

"Hello, and welcome." She shook first Burl's and then Eleanor's hand. "I'm so glad you didn't let the snow keep you away."

Burl released a deep, throaty chuckle. "Oh, a little snow can't scare us off. We've been looking forward to this getaway for weeks, haven't we, pumpkin?"

His wife beamed up at him, and LuAnn instantly fell in love with both of them. What a sweet, affable pair. She gave them the room key for Moonlight and Snowflakes, went over the inn's guidelines, and then led them to the elevator. "Would you like me to ride up with you and help you get settled?"

Burl shook his salt-and-pepper head. "No, miss, we'll be fine on our own. I've been taking care of this lovely lady"—he turned a tender gaze on his petite, snow-white-haired wife—"for sixty years tomorrow, and I intend to keep doing so for as long as she'll put up with me."

"Sixty years?" LuAnn smiled at them. "Congratulations. Do you have any special plans for your anniversary?"

Burl shrugged. "Coming here is our celebration. We intend to enjoy our room, maybe play a game or two of checkers, and—"

"And reminisce." Eleanor's eyes winked with unshed tears. "We've had a wonderful life together." She tittered and glanced at LuAnn's flour-dusted apron. "But we're keeping you from your duties. It looks to me like we interrupted a baking event."

LuAnn jammed her hands into her apron pockets and grinned. "Pie-making."

Burl raised his head and sniffed, reminding LuAnn of Huck catching the scent of a dog treat. "Apple?"

"Apple streusel, as well as blueberry, peach, and buttermilk."

Their faces broke into identical expressions of delight. "Buttermilk!" Eleanor said. "I haven't had a piece of buttermilk pie in ages."

"Then I'll be sure to set a couple of pieces aside for the two of you first thing tomorrow morning so it will be there for your lunch."

They thanked her and entered the elevator. The doors closed, sealing away their happy faces, but LuAnn carried the image in her mind's eye as she rejoined the others in the kitchen. She shared what the man had said about taking care of his wife for sixty years come tomorrow.

Tears shimmered in Janice's eyes. "Can you imagine? I had planned to celebrate at least sixty anniversaries, but I guess God had a different plan."

Tess slung her arm across Janice's shoulders, leaving a smear of suds on her T-shirt sleeve. "For both of us. If we had made it sixty years, our families would have planned a big party for us. I wonder why no one's hosting one for Burl and Eleanor?"

Sadness descended on LuAnn. "They must not have someone to put together a celebration for them."

Winnie spun around, sending a puff of flour into the air. "Why don't you have a party for them? They came here for their sixtieth anniversary. That means you're responsible for making their day a memorable one."

Janice pressed her palms together and beamed at Winnie. "What a spectacular idea! Who should we invite?"

"Your other guest, Alice," Winnie said, "and all of us will be there."

Janice sighed. "That makes for an awfully small party."

"Why not include whoever comes in for lunch tomorrow?" Tess closed the dishwasher and flipped the switch. The hum of the machine filled the room, and she raised her voice. "We could ask Pastor Ben and Paige to come, maybe Brad and Thorn, but other than that, let the regular lunch crowd be part of the celebration."

"That makes the most sense to me." Winnie picked up the rolling pin and applied it to the crust laid out on the work surface. She clucked her tongue on her teeth. "Hard for me to fathom. They've been married two years longer than I've been alive." She jolted. "One of you, call the grocery. Leave a message for Marcus that I want to make an Italian cream cake. He's familiar enough with my recipes to know what to pick up. Ask him to run the ingredients over as soon as he can." A grin climbed her cheeks. "If you're gonna have a party, you have to have a cake. A three-layer Italian cream cake with cream cheese frosting ought to be just right."

Putting together the details for the Dockums' party filled a significant portion of the afternoon and evening, but by bedtime their plans were set. Constance would bring streamers and balloons in the morning. The Italian cream cake, which smelled as good as it looked, was in the refrigerator alongside a buttermilk pie reserved for the anniversary couple. Pastor

Ben, Paige, Brad, Thorn, Tess's and Janice's children, and Irene and Thelma promised to stop by and offer happy anniversary wishes.

LuAnn crawled under her covers, weary but happy. It felt good to do something special for someone else. Tom climbed the quilt and stalked up LuAnn's frame from toes to chest, then curled in a ball and began to purr. From the dog bed, Huck watched with sad brown eyes. LuAnn patted the mattress, and the dog leaped up. He settled next to LuAnn's hip. With one hand on the dog's ruff and the other on the kitten's warm back, she closed her eyes and spent some time in prayer. At the silent *amen*, she started to drift off.

But a sudden thought brought her to wakefulness. She'd neglected to share the note she'd made with Tess and Janice about Alice's shoes. The shape and tread had been eerily similar to the footprints in the alley's snow yesterday morning. Why would Alice have been in the alley in the early-morning hours? Curiosity twined through her, a variety of explanations vying for prominence. She yawned. Tess and Janice were as tired as she was. She shouldn't get them up. And truthfully, she didn't want to leave her cozy nest. The question would have to wait until tomorrow.

CHAPTER SEVENTEEN

Thorn called early Wednesday morning, just as the women were opening up for breakfast. Tess took the call, and the expression on her face when she entered the kitchen let the others know something was awry. LuAnn pulled in a fortifying breath before asking what he'd needed.

"He's not going to make it over here today like he planned. His daughter called, and her roof is leaking, so she takes precedence."

"As well she should," Janice said.

LuAnn agreed, but they couldn't leave their back wall exposed to the weather, either. Thorn had removed three boards yesterday. New siding needed to go up. "So when does he intend to come finish the job here?"

"He doesn't."

Both Janice and LuAnn drew back.

A grin grew on Tess's face. "He's sending Isaiah over instead. He'll finish it up."

A conniving look flickered through Janice's eyes. A look they'd come to recognize whenever Isaiah Wimber, the young man who worked with Thorn on construction jobs, was mentioned. "Oh, good. I hope he's still here when Stacy stops by to wish the Dockums a happy anniversary."

Winnie picked up the coffeepot and held it out to Janice. "You can do your matchmaking later. Right now, folks are waiting for this hot brew, so scoot."

Janice laughed as she exited the kitchen. Tess and LuAnn took orders, then returned to share them with Winnie. While they waited for Winnie to fry eggs to go with the sausage and toast ready in the warming oven, LuAnn drew Tess aside and told her about the tread on Alice's shoes.

"Do you suppose she could have been the one darting out the back door Monday morning?"

Tess frowned. "To be honest, I'd prefer that idea over having a stranger in the inn, but I don't think those were her footprints out there."

"Why not?"

"They were too big. At least a man's size 10. Have you looked at her feet? She can't wear anything larger than a five, six at the most."

LuAnn's shoulders slumped. "You're right. I wasn't thinking about size. Those were man-sized prints." She shivered. "I wish we knew who—"

"These plates are ready to go. Stop whispering over there and deliver them."

Winnie's fractious demand propelled them to duty. While they took orders and served, they mentioned the anniversary celebration that would take place from noon until one thirty—"If you have a chance, come by for a piece of cake or pie, on the house." They'd decided to make it a true party and not charge for the desserts even though it meant losing a chunk of change. Baking supplies weren't cheap. But the goodwill, Tess reasoned, could drum up more business in the end, and LuAnn and Janice agreed.

When breakfast ended, Winnie and Constance cleaned the kitchen while Tess, Janice, and LuAnn decorated the dining room. Constance had chosen purple, white, and orange streamers and balloons so it wouldn't look like a Christmas party. When everything was hung and balloons tied on thin dowel rods were tucked in vases in lieu of flowers, it looked cheerful and festive. LuAnn hoped the Dockums would think so too.

A few patrons arrived by eleven thirty, and LuAnn directed them to the smaller tables, leaving the large farmhouse table in the middle for Burl and Eleanor. While taking care of diners, she glanced frequently at the elevator doors, willing them to open. She didn't know why this celebration for two people she hadn't even met until yesterday afternoon was so important to her, but she couldn't deny a quivering excitement.

Finally, at five minutes until twelve, the elevator doors opened, and the older couple stepped into the dining room. LuAnn was so glad she wasn't in the kitchen when they arrived, because she would carry the expressions of surprise and joy on their faces in her memory for the rest of her life.

Tess and Janice burst from the kitchen, and they and LuAnn chorused, "Happy anniversary!"

Eleanor clapped her hands to her wrinkled cheeks. "For us?" Tears sprang into her eyes.

Burl's gaze bounced across the streamers and balloons. "How did you know?"

Given his advanced age, he'd probably forgotten mentioning their anniversary when they checked in. LuAnn stepped near and touched his elbow. "Remember? You told me yesterday."

He shook his head. "Not about the anniversary. The colors. Orange and purple." Now tears shone in his eyes. "I coached the Clemson University Tigers back in the '60s. Eleanor and I still follow them even though we moved to Ohio decades ago. The colors bring back wonderful memories." He slipped his arm around his wife's shoulders. "We never had children of our own, but many of the young men from the team have stayed in touch with us over the years. They've become our surrogate children. One of them paid for our room here at the inn as a gift to us."

Janice whispered in LuAnn's ear, "Happy coincidence, or God's leading? I think it's the latter."

LuAnn nodded. She escorted the couple to the table of honor. Brad and Pastor Ben and Paige came in at the same time and joined the Dockums. Each of the Inn Crowd took a few minutes at their table too, and Winnie joined the party and received many compliments on the buttermilk pie and Italian cream cake.

In the middle of the celebration, Isaiah appeared in the doorway between the kitchen and dining room. He seemed perplexed. LuAnn hurried over to him. "Is something wrong?"

"No, but I found something inside the wall where Tory took down the boards. I thought maybe you'd want it." He placed a tarnished rectangle a little bigger than a deck of cards into LuAnn's hands.

She turned the strange item this way and that. Although completely crusted with dirt, she thought the top bore some etchings. One side showed evidence of hinges, which meant it was a box rather than a simple block.

Isaiah rubbed his finger on the box. "I think it's silver, but it's hard to tell under all that grime."

Burl stretched his hand toward them. "What've you got there, young man?"

"I'm not completely sure, sir." Isaiah trailed LuAnn to the table. "Do you have any idea what it is?"

Burl took the box and turned it over in his hands, his brow furrowing. "It looks like a snuffbox."

Pastor Ben chuckled. "A what?"

"A snuffbox. To hold chewing tobacco." Burl shook it, and something clinked inside. "My granddaddy had one similar in size to this. But he kept matches in it for camping trips. Snuffboxes were fairly common in the 1800s." He grinned. "As if putting something like that in a fancy box made it more appealing." He plucked a handkerchief from his pocket and rubbed the top of the box. "Look here—it's got a mama horse and colt embossed on the cover. This is likely an old one."

A shiver of excitement wiggled down LuAnn's spine. "How old?"

Burl shrugged and gave LuAnn the box. "Hard to say, but could be as far back as 1850. An antiques expert could answer that better than I can." He started to return his handkerchief to his pocket, but Eleanor put her hand on his arm.

"That thing's filthy. Set it aside, and I'll wash it in the sink later."

Tess picked up the handkerchief. "I'll wash it with our laundry today and get it back to you before you check out tomorrow."

The older man smiled his thanks and then pointed at the box. "I'm pretty sure that's pewter, which means it's not as valuable as a silver one, but it's still a nice find."

Isaiah gazed at Burl in wonder. "How do you know so much about this?"

Burl laughed. "Son, when you have as many years on you as I do, you pick up a little bit of knowledge about a whole lot of things."

Eleanor leaned forward and beamed at Isaiah. "What he isn't telling you is he's a museum curator, so he encounters all kinds of items. I call him Professor. He's as smart as any college professor."

"Now, now, don't exaggerate." Despite the mild denial, pride glowed in Burl's lined face. "Where did you say you found the box?"

"Between the siding and the interior wall." Isaiah frowned. "A really strange place, considering there's no window or anything there where a person might've accidentally dropped it behind the wall. I'd sure like to know how it got in there."

"Maybe there was a window on the wall at one time," Eleanor said. "Often old buildings undergo transformations."

Isaiah turned to LuAnn. "Aren't there some vintage photos of the inn at the Marietta museum? It would be interesting to see if there was a window in that wall way back when."

Curiosity rolled through LuAnn's chest. "I'll have to explore."

Isaiah returned to work, and LuAnn turned the box in her hand, earning a *clink* with every turn. How long had it been in the wall? Who'd held it before her? It gave her a strange sense of déjà vu even though she knew she'd never seen anything like it before. "This will make a nice addition to the display I want to create to commemorate the inn's complete history."

"It needs a good cleaning first." Brad rose. "Would you like me to drop it by Harry's? He could clean it up and maybe give you an estimate on its value."

LuAnn didn't care a bit about its monetary value, and didn't want to bother the antique dealer with it. "Thank you, but I'll clean it up myself and put it with the other things I've been collecting for my display."

Brad shrugged and smiled. "Suit yourself." He shook hands with Burl and Eleanor and excused himself. LuAnn watched him go, hoping she hadn't offended him by refusing his offer. He hadn't acted offended, but sometimes it was hard to tell what people—especially men, in her opinion—were thinking.

"May I see it again?" Burl held out his hand, and LuAnn placed the box on his weathered palm. He examined the box from all angles and fiddled with the lid. Finally he sighed and returned it to her. "I hoped it might open, but it's tightly sealed with all that dirt. I hope you'll be able to open it. There could be a piece of history inside worth recovering."

Another shiver rattled LuAnn's frame, and she hugged the box to her chest. *A piece of history . . .* How perfect would that be?

CHAPTER EIGHTEEN

The Dockums checked out the next morning, and the women of the Inn Crowd abandoned their duties in the kitchen and café to bid the couple farewell. LuAnn hugged first Eleanor and then Burl, battling a wave of emotion she didn't fully understand. The pair were close in age to her mother, which was no doubt part of her reluctance to see them leave, but she was surprised that she was feeling their departure so keenly.

When the door closed behind the Dockums, LuAnn turned and discovered Alice in the parlor area, watching them over the top of her spectacles. As usual, she had her notebook open, pencil in hand. Unease struck LuAnn with force. What did Alice find so interesting about seeing guests to the door? There wasn't time to explore the answer, because the bell above the door jangled as the door opened.

A deliveryman stepped in, package in hand, and snapped the door closed on the cold wind. "Would someone sign, please?"

LuAnn was closest, so she scribbled her signature on the touchpad of his device, then took the box. It was surprisingly weighty.

"Thank you, ma'am. Have a good day." He bustled out again.

Janice peered at the box, curiosity lighting her face. "I bet it's a Christmas present. Who's it for?"

LuAnn examined the printed address label. "It's addressed to Wayfarers Inn, no specific individual."

"Who's it from?"

"Hmm. It only says Bridgeport Linens from Massachusetts." LuAnn glanced from Janice to Tess. "Did one of you order more linens?"

Tess snorted. "If one of us did it, you'd know. We all have to okay purchases."

"Let's open it." Janice's eyes shone as bright as a child's on Christmas morning. "Maybe there's a note inside."

LuAnn carried it to the kitchen, and Tess and Janice trailed her. Winnie shot them a frown of disapproval when Tess retrieved a pair of scissors from the junk drawer.

"What're you doing now? Taking a break?" Winnie shook a pie spatula at them, grinning. "I don't stay chained to this stove just so you can sit around."

"We'll only be a minute," LuAnn said. "We want to see what came for us." She'd satisfy her curiosity before returning to work.

Tess slit the tape and peeled open the flaps. An invoice marked PAID lay on top. When she lifted it, a snowy-white sheet in plastic packaging came into view. The label indicated a 100 percent Egyptian 500-count cotton top sheet. A second one, identical to the first, rested underneath.

Janice opened the zipper on one package and slid her hand inside. She sighed. "This is soft as butter. Who sent them?"

They searched the box and examined the invoice's front and back, but there was no note to hint at the sender. Tess plopped both packages into the box and set it aside. "I guess we'll have to call the company and ask who paid for them. Isn't it strange that whoever sent them knew exactly what we needed to replace?"

Tess closed herself in the office as soon as the last breakfast customers left and called the linen company in Massachusetts. When she returned to the kitchen, LuAnn scurried over to her. "Well? What did you find out?"

"That trying to get information from the purchasing department at Bridgeport Linens is as hard as extracting information from a mob boss." Tess folded her arms over her chest. "They wouldn't tell me nothin'," she said in a gangster voice. Then she shrugged. "I guess whoever sent them wants it to be a secret. We might never know. But we'll definitely use them. They're nicer than the ones we bought." Her eyebrows rose. "As well they should be. The rep did tell me what they cost—as much as we paid for six of the other sheets."

Winnie whistled. "Somebody must really like you ladies."

LuAnn arched her eyebrows. "Or somebody's feeling really guilty about destroying our sheets."

Tess nodded slowly. "You're right. Who else would know we needed exactly two white sheets?"

Janice chewed her lower lip. "Well, we did talk to some people about the sheets. Pastor Ben, Brad, even Thorn."

"Can you imagine any one of them going to the trouble of buying replacements sheets?" Tess crossed to the sink and pulled on a pair of gloves, then began running hot water in the sink. "Frankly, I doubt either Thorn or Pastor Ben could afford them, and if Brad did it, he wouldn't send them anonymously. He'd barge in with them and hand them over, proud as punch."

LuAnn agreed with Tess's reasoning. She carried a stack of plates to the sink and lowered them into the steaming water. "Well, we owe a big thank-you to whoever did it. The lucky guests who end up sleeping under those sheets will want to come back a second time just to sleep under their buttery softness."

As Tess was sliding the last tray of dishes into the dishwasher, the back door opened and Isaiah called, "Ladies?"

"Come on in," Janice said, a smile in her voice, "and have a cinnamon roll or two. We have several left over."

Isaiah poked his head around the corner but didn't enter the room. "Thanks, Mrs. Eastman, that's real nice. I would if my feet weren't so dirty, but Winnie might chase me off with a broom if I muddied up her clean floors."

Winnie gave a terse nod. "You got that right."

Isaiah laughed. "The new light fixture's up. Thorn chose a reproduction bracket-style lantern attached to a bronzed embossed plate. It looks real nice—probably closer to what hung on the wall originally than even the one that came loose." He scratched his jaw, his expression sheepish. "I was curious, so I visited Ms. Rector at the museum yesterday afternoon. She said according to her records there wasn't a window on this part of the wall, but when the inn was built, there was a porch out here with windows looking out over both ends of it."

LuAnn paused in putting three cinnamon rolls on a paper plate, trying to envision a large porch stretching across the back side of the building. "I wonder why they tore down the porch."

Isaiah shrugged. "My guess is it rotted over time. Being so close to the river, wood takes a beating. Once this building became a warehouse, a porch probably wasn't needed."

"You're probably right." She covered the plate with aluminum foil and carried it to him. "Here's a small reward for your labor."

He grinned. "Thanks, Ms. Sherrill. I'll enjoy these. There's something else I noticed on the planks Thorn took down—kind of interesting. The previous light was mounted to an iron plate about the size of one of Winnie's cinnamon rolls. That plate covered a big knothole in the wood. I bet the first lantern that hung out there—it would've been an oil lantern instead of an electric one, of course—was bracketed to that same iron plate. If I'm right, the iron plate's been on the wall of the inn for more than a century."

LuAnn experienced another delightful chill. "Another piece of history... Did you keep the plate?"

"I sure did." Isaiah waved his hand. "It got modified when the light was changed to an electric one, though. There's a hole drilled in the middle of it for wiring. But still, it's a nice piece. Ought to go real good with that little box I found, huh?"

LuAnn nodded. "That's what I'm thinking."

"I'll get it for you—it's in my toolbox." He ducked around the corner, and the back door slammed behind him.

LuAnn turned and aimed her smile at Tess and Janice. "What do you think about making a shadow box of significant objects found in the inn? The snuffbox, the iron plate, the original deed..."

Janice grinned. "Do you want to see if we can get one of the bones from the skeleton I found in the basement?"

LuAnn laughed. "No. But pages from Prudence's diary would make a nice backdrop for the items, don't you think?"

Winnie opened the oven door and slid a tray of biscuits inside. "I think you've got one of the most creative minds I've ever known." She closed the door and put her hands on her hips. "If you wanna include part of the current owners' history, you need to preserve one of my biscuits and add it to the shadow box."

Tess and Janice laughed, but LuAnn didn't. Her creative mind had leaped to another idea. "Not a biscuit, but a photograph. Pictures of the people who claimed ownership of the inn from the very beginning up until now." Her pulse revved into overdrive. "Thelma and Irene will be glad to share photographs of their family. There have to be pictures somewhere chronicling the building's time as a warehouse, and—"

Tess waved her hands. "Whoa, slow down. If you gather all that, you're going to need a shadow box as big as the grand piano."

LuAnn shook her head. "The photos will go in frames. I'll make a timeline with them, with the dates underneath indicating how long each had possession of the inn." Excitement made her voice quiver. "And of course, the pictures will also go in the history book with lengthier descriptions of the people, their lives, how they used the inn, how the building changed over the years."

Winnie cleared her throat. "When're you gonna find time to put this all together, Miss Lu? Seems to me you stay plenty busy keeping up with what's needed around here to make the guests happy."

LuAnn's spirits sank. If only she could get started now. This very minute. "I...I'm not sure."

Janice crossed the floor and put her arm around LuAnn's shoulders. "Preserving the inn's history is important to you. Winnie could run this kitchen singlehandedly. Constance is fully capable of the housekeeping chores, and Tess and I can handle the remaining responsibilities except when we have a full house. We'll give you as many hours as you need to put your plan into action."

Tears threatened to spill over LuAnn's lower lashes. She blinked rapidly. "Thanks, but I don't want to pass all the work on to you. I need to do my fair share."

"And you will," Janice said, giving LuAnn's shoulder a pat. "But we don't have many reservations from now until the end of the year. So after the café closes for the day, you could use the afternoons and evenings to work on your book, shadow box, and whatever else you want to put together."

LuAnn sent an uncertain look to Tess. "Are you okay with this?" The last thing she wanted was to create resentment by pushing her responsibilities onto Tess's and Janice's backs.

Tess applied a potato peeler to a red potato—Winnie's top choice for the loaded potato soup because they weren't as starchy and wouldn't affect the thickness of the broth. "I'm fine with it. No arguments from me. I think guests will enjoy the information you collect."

LuAnn's excitement returned in a heartbeat, and she released a happy sigh. "Then, if it's all right with you, I'll go to the museum after lunch today. If anyone has photos of this building from its beginning to now, it'll be Maybelline."

CHAPTER NINETEEN

There's sure been a lot of interest in that old building of late." Maybelline put another stack of manila folders on the table in front of LuAnn. "You. That nice young man, Isaiah. A couple who were house-hunting…I don't recall their names."

LuAnn opened the first folder. "Dean and Kay Pankratz?"

Maybelline snapped her fingers. "Yes, that's them. And of course Alice Busby. She's been in at least three times scouring records and making notes."

LuAnn's scalp prickled. She lifted her attention to Maybelline. "Alice has been researching the inn? Did she say why?"

Maybelline shrugged, her expression unconcerned. "She said she's a writer. I assumed she needed information for whatever she's working on. She seemed particularly interested in the tunnel from the river, but I assured her that was no longer accessible." She backed away from the table. "I'm fairly certain there are some newspaper articles from the 1960s about renovation on the building. You might find something of interest in those. I'll be right back." She scurried off, her heels click-clicking on the hardwood floor.

LuAnn frowned. If Alice was asking questions about the tunnel, then she probably had also done some exploring along the riverbank. That would explain the sand they'd found in the inn. She could also conclude that the woman had been in the basement more than once, probably trying to access the tunnel from the inside. But why? To use in her mystery story? She could merely be a snoopy woman, but LuAnn couldn't shake the notion there was something more to Alice's interest than mere nosiness.

The mention of the Pankratzes reminded LuAnn that she hadn't checked with Kay Pankratz about the watercolor painting she'd commissioned. She pulled out her cell phone, located the couple's number in her contacts, and pushed the call button. The woman's perky voice answered after the first ring.

"Good afternoon, Kay, this is LuAnn Sherrill from Wayfarers Inn in Marietta."

A tinkling laugh trickled through the phone. "Yes, LuAnn, how good to hear from you. I imagine you're wondering about your painting."

LuAnn couldn't help grinning. The woman's friendliness was evident even through a telephone conversation. "You're absolutely right. How is it coming along?"

"It's finished as of this morning. Dean and I were talking at lunch about the best time to make the drive over. I realize we're creeping up on Christmas, and we don't want to interfere with your holiday plans, but would Saturday work for you? Maybe, if you have a room available, we could spend the night and then visit one of the churches on Sunday morning. We'll want to find a new church home soon, since by the end of January we'll be living in Marietta full-time."

The meaning of the woman's last sentence hit LuAnn and she gasped. "Oh! You found a house then."

"Yes, ma'am. Brad was so helpful, and he guided us to the perfect house not far from the business district. So Dean and I will be able to walk over and have your delicious soups, biscuits, and pies as often as we like." Kay giggled. "Which will be nearly every day if I have my way. I don't mind cooking, but I'd much rather work on paintings for the little gallery I hope to open."

So not only would Marietta gain new residents but possibly a new business as well. "That sounds wonderful on all counts. I believe the same room you stayed in last time is open this coming weekend. Do you want to reserve it, or would you rather stay in a different room?"

"Surprise us." She laughed again, and LuAnn couldn't help smiling again. The woman's joy was contagious. "I hope you'll like the painting. I have to say, I'm very pleased with how it came out. But if for any reason you aren't satisfied, you are under no obligation to purchase it. It will just go into my gallery and eventually find another owner."

"I'm sure we'll be more than satisfied. Thank you so much."

"You're very welcome. Dean and I will see you sometime early Saturday afternoon. Bye now, LuAnn." The call disconnected.

Too late LuAnn realized she hadn't asked about making prints of the painting for other uses, but she'd ask when the Pankratzes arrived. She called the inn and told Tess to reserve a room for the couple for Saturday night. To her delight, Tess told her they'd had two other calls for weekend reservations too.

"Wouldn't it be great if we had a full house the weekend before Christmas?" Tess's tone held a hint of desperation. They'd anticipated winter being slower than spring and summer, the traditional vacation seasons, but the less they had to dip into savings to cover expenses, the better.

"It sure would." A full house would benefit them financially, but it would also keep LuAnn too busy to miss her mom so much. "I'm going to get back to my research. I'll probably stay here until Maybelline shoos me out the door."

"Which will be at five thirty on the dot." Maybelline bustled into the room, another manila folder in her manicured hands. "I'm going to dinner at the Galley at six, and I'll need a few minutes to freshen up." She plopped the folder with the others, flipped her dyed hair over her shoulder, and spun on a spiked heel.

LuAnn retrieved the mail from their post office box on her way back to the inn. A letter from a previous guest, part of the group who'd come for its matriarch's ninety-fifth birthday celebration, was mixed in with the expected bills and advertising postcards.

Tess and Janice were in the kitchen eating leftover soup and biscuits. Janice grimaced. "We weren't sure when you'd get back, and we were hungry."

LuAnn dropped the mail on the table. "It's all right. You didn't need to wait for me."

Tess pointed to the kettle on the stove. "I turned off the burner but it should still be hot. Ham and beans. There are a few biscuits in the oven too."

"Thanks." LuAnn went to the stove. She scooped beans and chunks of ham and carrots into a bowl. The savory aroma tickled her nose, and her stomach twinged in response. She grabbed a spoon from a cup on the counter and joined the others at the table.

Tess pushed her bowl aside and picked up the stack of mail. She flicked the envelopes into two stacks—bills and junk—but kept hold of the letter. "Jenkins..."

LuAnn offered a quick prayer of thanks and dipped her spoon into the soup. "Open that. It could be a request to reserve the second floor again."

Tess slit the envelope with her butter knife and pulled out a single typewritten page. She flattened it on the table, and Janice leaned in. LuAnn couldn't read it from her angle. But she could read her friends' expressions. Janice's eyes widened in shock, and Tess burst into laughter.

LuAnn swallowed the bite of beans. "What is it?" She reached for the letter.

Tess held it away from her. "Listen to this. 'Dear ladies, I recently learned about something that happened when our family stayed with you earlier this month. Apparently our youngest son, Brandon, sneaked a carton of milk to our room. When his older sister told him he'd get in trouble, he hid it in the large wardrobe next to the elevator. We only became aware of this escapade when Brandon tattled on Kaitlyn for breaking a dish, and she in turn tattled on him.'"

Janice nodded, grinning. "Sounds like typical brother and sister to me."

Tess went on. "'I can only imagine your confusion when you found a carton of milk in a place where it didn't belong. Please accept my humble apologies, and I assure you we will keep a very close watch on Brandon when we return the first week of June for our reunion. That is, if you're still willing to host us.'" Tess rolled her eyes and dropped the letter. "Of course we'll host them."

Janice fingered the letter, scanning the typed text. "Does it say anything about taking some sheets and turning them into a long rope?"

"Not a word." Tess's grin turned impish. "Maybe one of the boys will find another reason to tell on their sister and she'll rat them out about the sheets. After all, if the little one opened the wardrobe to hide the milk carton, he had to have seen sheets."

LuAnn doubted the boys had anything to do with the destroyed sheets and said so.

Janice's face pursed with puzzlement. "Why not?"

"Because whoever ruined the sheets replaced them." LuAnn stirred the soup. "If Mrs. Jenkins ordered sheets and had them sent to us, I think she'd mention it."

"That's probably true," Tess said. "She fessed up about the milk carton, so she'd probably fess up about the sheets if her kids were guilty."

"You're right." Janice rose and picked up her and Tess's dishes. "Well, someone is certainly guilty, and I'd sure like to know who."

"Wouldn't we all." Tess leaned back and released a heavy sigh. "Here we sit having leftover bean soup and biscuits while at the Galley the members of the Chamber of Commerce are probably dining on filet mignon and roasted asparagus."

LuAnn blew on a spoonful of soup, sending up aromatic steam. "Chamber of Commerce?"

"Yes. Brad popped in here while you were gone and dropped off some Chamber brochures for us to put out on the check-in desk. He mentioned the Christmas dinner and suggested—again—that we join the Chamber. We probably should. We've settled in enough now, and the membership fee is a tax write-off."

LuAnn took the bite, chewed, and swallowed. "It's fine with me if we join the Chamber."

Tess flicked a look at Janice. "What do you think?"

Janice grinned. "Let's do it. It'll get us invited to next year's filet mignon dinner."

Tess laughed, but LuAnn couldn't muster a chuckle. Janice sent a worried look at her. "What's the matter?"

Tess nodded, understanding blooming on her face. "Christmas blues. Am I right?"

LuAnn sighed and set her bowl aside. "You're right. I'm trying so hard to keep the Christmas spirit. I know the true meaning is to celebrate Christ's birth. But I can't help but feel..."

"Lonely?" Tess asked.

LuAnn nodded. "Yes."

Janice slipped into the chair next to LuAnn and put her arm around her shoulders. "I know you miss your mom, and I know the two of us can't replace her, but we'll be here for you this Christmas, LuAnn."

"And all the Christmases to come." Tess put her hand over LuAnn's and squeezed. "For as long as you'll put up with us."

LuAnn's lips quivered with her smile. "You two are the best."

A sniffle carried from the café. All three women glanced at the doorway, and LuAnn left the table. She peeked around the corner in time to see Alice Busby's form zip into the library.

CHAPTER TWENTY

Their single guest had left for the evening, so LuAnn allowed Huck and Tom free rein after supper. Huck was accustomed to following Constance around the inn and knew where he was allowed and where he wasn't, but Tom bounded everywhere. Guest room doors were always kept closed, so he couldn't enter the rooms, but he pawed at every door in typical cat fashion. LuAnn chuckled at the kitten's antics and Huck's parental, worried whines as she followed the animals from floor to floor.

Tom went down the stairs one tread at a time in a little sideways hop too adorable for words. Huck stayed right next to Tom even though he was perfectly capable of bounding up and down the stairs quickly. How loyal the dog was to the cat. And how dependent the cat was on the dog. Every few minutes Tom would rub his head against Huck's chin. Once again, LuAnn made a vow not to separate the animals. When—or if—Huck's owner finally came to claim him, she would insist that Tom go too.

Then she'd head straight to the shelter and adopt a dog or cat. Assuming she found another Shih Tzu mix. She'd need something hypoallergenic for the sake of the inn's visitors. Her research for hypoallergenic cats had turned up a hairless creature, but she couldn't imagine having a cat she couldn't pet. So if she got a cat, she'd need to keep it in the apartment. So far Tom hadn't minded being up there, so maybe another cat wouldn't mind either.

She and the animals reached the bottom of the stairs, and Tom pranced to the Christmas tree and began batting at bows. LuAnn laughed. "Oh, no, you don't." She reached for him, but he darted under the tree, clambered over the neatly arranged wrapped empty boxes, and disappeared from view. She heard him rustling around, but she couldn't get to him. Maybe allowing him to explore wasn't such a good idea after all. "Tom, you stinker, come out of there!"

Huck paced beside the tree, whining. LuAnn got down on her hands and knees and slid packages one at a time from under the tree, muttering to herself. She'd spent at least thirty minutes putting them in place for the best display. Would she be able to put them back the way they'd been?

"Tom, come here, kitty." She spoke sweetly as she shifted boxes. She pulled the final box from beneath the tree and, to her surprise, Tom wasn't there. She lifted the edge of the crazy-quilt tree skirt. No kitten underneath either. She sat up and searched the area. "Tom?" Huck whined, and she scratched his neck. The kitten couldn't have wandered off, or Huck wouldn't still be waiting beside the tree. "Where'd he go, Huck, huh? Can you find him?"

Huck whined again and bounced on his front legs. One of the shatterproof ornaments fell from the tree and landed on the floor in front of them. LuAnn gasped. Tom was climbing the tree! "Janice! Tess! Come quick!"

Tess came running from the office, Janice from the library. They slid to a halt next to LuAnn. She pointed. "Tom's in the tree. I've got to get him out of there without tipping the whole thing over. One of you, steady the tree."

"Oh, for Pete's sake..." Tess worked her hands between the branches and gripped the trunk. "Okay, now what?"

"Janice, can you go up a few stairs? If he makes it to the top, you'll be able to grab him from there."

Janice scurried up three steps and leaned toward the tree. "I'm ready. What are you going to do?"

LuAnn gritted her teeth. "Something ridiculous. Pray that it works." She scooped the dog into her arms and held him toward the tree. "Huck, tell Tom to get down."

Huck barked twice, bucking in her arms. She held tight. He barked again. Tom's head poked out from between branches. Janice leaned over the railing and caught him by the scruff of his neck. He yowled, and Huck went crazy in LuAnn's arms. She put the dog down and grabbed Tom from Janice.

She held the kitten beneath her chin while Huck jumped against her legs, whining. "It's okay, Huck. Your kitten isn't hurt." Huck hunkered down but he kept his brown-eyed gaze locked on the kitten.

Tess ran her hand through her hair, leaving it tousled. "Are you going to take him back to the apartment now?"

LuAnn sighed. "Tom, you blew it, buddy. If you can't behave, you can't stay down here with us." Huck accompanied her to the fourth floor, but she only shut Tom inside the apartment. Huck would need to go out, so he might as well stay with her. Back on the main floor, she knelt and straightened the tree skirt, then began returning the packages to their places beneath the tree. She picked up a small, rectangular box and paused. Was this one weighted? But it couldn't be—she'd wrapped empty boxes.

She gave the box a little shake. Sure enough, something bumped around inside. She turned it over and noticed fresh strips of tape holding the obviously torn edges of wrapping paper in place. Who would have opened an empty box, put something in it, and then rewrapped it?

She stood, holding the box away from her body the way one might hold a snake, and called for Tess and Janice. They both returned, Tess looking a little cranky. "What is it now?" Huck whined at her, and she skirted around him to the other side of Janice.

"Did one of you open this and put something inside? Janice?"

Janice drew back. "What? No."

"Tess?"

"Of course not."

"I didn't either, but there is definitely something in here." LuAnn held the box out to the other women. "Shake it."

Tess took it and shook it back and forth. Soft thumps proved something slid around in the box. She gave it back to LuAnn. "There's one way to find out what's in there. Open it."

LuAnn placed the box upside-down on the check-in counter. "Can you get me some scissors, please?" Janice retrieved a pair from the office, and LuAnn carefully cut the tape loose, hoping to preserve the paper for one more wrapping, and peeled back the layers. She hadn't bothered taping the lid shut when she'd first wrapped the box, but it was taped now, mute evidence that someone had tampered with it.

"Be careful." Janice wrung her hands. "Something might jump out at you."

"If you're worried, step back." LuAnn popped the tape and lifted the lid. Nothing happened. She peeked in, then she gave a start. "What in the—" As Tess and Janice pressed close, LuAnn lifted out a small digital tape recorder. She gaped at the other two and whispered, "It's recording."

LuAnn sat up in bed cuddling Tom. She'd intended to read her Bible and pray, hoping to hand the worrisome thoughts plaguing her over to the One who was capable of carrying them, but her mind wandered too much to focus.

Had they done the right thing by putting the recorder back the way they'd found it? Maybe they should have turned it over to the police instead. Wasn't recording someone without their consent a privacy violation? But why would anyone want to record the happenings in the lobby of a bed-and-breakfast? Janice hadn't even wanted to sleep in the inn after the discovery. LuAnn heard her friend's nervous voice in her memory.

"What if there are recording devices all over the place, making a tape of everything we say?"

Tess had disdained the idea, but then she'd shaken every other box under the tree, checked the potted plants, and peeked behind books in the library, which proved she was concerned too. The idea of someone listening to them when they were unaware made LuAnn's skin crawl.

At a quarter after ten the buzzer connected to their apartment from the front door blared. LuAnn started to get up, but she heard Tess call, "Alice probably forgot her key. I'll take care of it." She gladly let her. Alice hadn't stayed out past ten since she arrived at Wayfarers the first day of December. She must be getting friendlier with whomever she was meeting. LuAnn tried to conjure up amusement, envisioning the eccentric woman with frizzy gray hair caught in a messy bun and glasses perched on the end of her nose on a date, but it didn't work.

She heard Tess enter the apartment and come up the hallway. She called her friend's name.

The door creaked open and Tess peeked in, the hall light shining on her copper hair. "What did you need?" She eyed Huck, who sat up in his dog bed but didn't climb out.

"Is Alice safely in her room?"

"Yes."

"What about Janice? Is she okay?"

Tess sighed. "She's more nervous than Huck was when Tom climbed the tree."

LuAnn shuddered. She rubbed Tom's chin and relished the kitten's purr. Such a relaxing sound. "I've been thinking… That thing was probably put there by Alice. After all, she's been observing our every move and trying to eavesdrop. But planting a listening device goes beyond snoopy. It gives me the creeps."

Tess came in and sat on the edge of LuAnn's bed. "To be honest, I'm a little rattled too. If there's one, there could be two. Or more. I think I'll have Thorn come over tomorrow and do a sweep of the building, find out if there are other recording devices anywhere."

"Can he do that?"

"If he doesn't know how, he'll know someone who does."

"That's a good idea. I don't think any of us will rest well until we know for sure we aren't being listened to in every part of the inn."

Tess patted LuAnn's leg. "Sleep, okay? At least if we're sleeping we aren't giving somebody something to record." She laughed wryly and left the room.

LuAnn wriggled downward until her head met her pillow. She snapped off her bedside lamp, closed her eyes, and tried again to pray. Words refused to form. So she resorted to something her mother had taught her—reciting scripture. She borrowed phrases from Psalm 139, a passage she memorized when she was in fifth grade.

"Thou compassest my path and my lying down, and art acquainted with all my ways... Thou hast beset me behind and before, and laid thine hand upon me... How precious also are thy thoughts unto me, O God!... Search me, O God, and know my heart..."

A tentative peace settled on her. God knew her heart and everything else about her. He understood her worry about the recording device. He also knew who had put the recorder in the Christmas box. Her eyes popped open. God knew. Her mother would tell her it was enough for God to know and that faith meant trusting Him to do what was best with the information.

How precious also are thy thoughts unto me…

She closed her eyes and allowed sleep to carry her away.

Chapter Twenty-One

Before they went down for work in the morning, the women agreed not to mention the recording device to anyone other than Thorn. Although they strongly suspected Alice, Tess suggested they shouldn't rule out Constance. If Constance had planted it, they didn't want her to know they'd found it. They also didn't want to worry Winnie. Stressing over whether or not her conversations were being recorded by some unknown person wouldn't help her blood pressure.

Thorn arrived with the very first patrons, ate a hearty breakfast of oat and walnut pancakes topped with fried apples, and then proclaimed—loudly—that he intended to check the plumbing in each of the rooms. "Just to satisfy myself that no other lines are leaking. Water leaks can cause a lot of damage."

Tess exchanged a wobbly smile with LuAnn. "Would you mind if one of us shadows you? It would be good for us to have some basic knowledge of plumbing, just in case we have an emergency."

Thorn shrugged. "I don't mind. So who's coming?"

"I'll go." LuAnn tugged her apron over her head and handed it to Tess. She lowered her voice to a husky whisper. "Is Constance helping in the kitchen?"

Tess gave a quick nod. "Yes. I'll keep her busy there until you're back."

LuAnn glanced over her shoulder as she followed Thorn to the parlor. Apparently their behavior, which felt out of the ordinary and clandestine, didn't strike anyone as odd, because no one seemed to pay a bit of attention to them.

Thorn had placed his toolbox near the check-in desk when he came in, and he opened it and took out a small transistor radio. LuAnn stared at the outdated piece of technology. "What are you going to do with that?"

"Shhh..." His brows dipped with a warning frown. He flicked the On switch and adjusted the dial until only a soft crackle came through the marshmallow-sized speaker. He beckoned her close with a twitch of his finger. She leaned in. "According to my buddy in the police department, the radio will give feedback if it picks up transmissions from any kind of bug. The closer we are to the device, the louder the radio will squeal. We'll be able to play that childhood game 'hot and cold' and find anything that might be recording."

LuAnn recalled playing the game and seeking out hidden items, but back then she'd giggled with excitement. Only apprehension stirred within her now. She licked her lips and nodded. "All right, then. Let's see if we can find 'hot.'"

Thorn stepped close to the tree. The radio released a discordant squawk. Their gazes met, and they nodded in unison. He hurried away from the tree, and the radio went silent again. He whispered, "Now we know this thing works." He glanced back at the cafe. "We'll need to wait until everyone clears out before we can check the dining room and kitchen. Let's hold off on the office too, until the place is quiet. No sense in this"— he bounced the radio in his hand—"alarming any of the customers."

"Good thinking."

LuAnn followed him as he inched his way around the parlor, holding the radio to everything large enough to hide a recorder—furniture, piano, bookshelves, television, and even the pictures hanging on the walls. The radio didn't make a single sound.

He grinned at her. "Nothing here."

She released a nervous laugh. "What a relief."

"We've got a lot of other places to explore, though."

Thorn entered each of the public bathrooms while LuAnn waited outside, then he led her up the stairs. They explored the second-floor guest rooms, with the exception of the Honeymoon Suite, since Alice was inside. The radio gave no evidence of devices, so they went to the third floor and entered every room. Thorn even checked the linen armoire. Nothing.

One last floor and then the café, office, and kitchen to go. LuAnn stopped outside the door to the Inn Crowd's rooms and told Thorn to go in without her.

He paused. "Are you sure? I mean, this is your, er, personal space."

Which is exactly why she didn't want to go in. If the radio started squawking in her room, she'd never be able to be at ease in there again. It was better for her not to know where Thorn found a listening device. Assuming he found one.

She nodded. "I'm sure. Go ahead. But please don't let Huck or Tom out."

He saluted and entered the apartment.

She paced back and forth on the small landing, her ears tuned for any kind of squeal or screech. She heard Huck's welcoming bark, letting her know Thorn had reached her rooms, and she stopped and stared at the closed door until Thorn emerged.

A satisfied grin creased his face. "Nothing. It's all secure."

She nearly collapsed with relief. "Thank goodness."

He patted her shoulder. "I'm sure sorry. This has gotta have you ladies on edge. For the life of me, I can't figure out why someone would want to bug this place. What do they think they'll uncover—some kind of plot to exchange raisins for cherries in the pies?"

LuAnn hugged herself. "I don't know, but..." Should she share the other strange happenings? Of course he knew about the back porch light, which probably hadn't been anything more than an act of time and erosion, and the plumbing line. But she, Tess, and Janice hadn't discussed how much to divulge to the handyman, so she probably should keep quiet. "You're right. It has us on edge."

He headed for the stairs. "Well, I'll leave for now and come back around ten thirty, when the café ought to be empty. Make sure Winnie and Constance are someplace else, so I can check the office and kitchen."

She'd need to make sure Alice was someplace else too. "That sounds fine. But what should we do about the device in the box? Leave it, or take it out?"

He stopped and turned to face her. His eyes lit. "Leave it. I have an idea that might let you find out who put it there."

"What?"

He chuckled. "Never mind that yet. I need to make sure it can be done before I promise anything. But I'll tell you when I come back, all right?"

She might burst from curiosity by then, but she had little choice but to agree. She escorted him to the door, thanked him again, then hurried to the café. More customers had come in, which made her happy. A good morning of business helped their bank account, and being busy kept her mind off her worries.

The hum of the vacuum cleaner, Constance at work on the third floor, provided musical background for Thorn's adjustment under the Christmas tree. Janice was in the kitchen with Winnie, and Tess played lookout for Alice, who'd indicated she wanted to do some shopping and would return by lunchtime. If Alice came up the walk, Tess would let Thorn know, and he would dive into the office and out of sight. LuAnn knelt beside him, ready to hand him whatever tool he pointed to.

She'd questioned the plan he'd concocted. Couldn't they use a hidden camera instead? But Thorn said they'd be able to catch the perpetrator in the act rather than discovering him or her after the fact. He'd added, "And you might not get a good look at their face, which means you'd still have a mystery on your hands." Then Tess had impishly stated that whoever planted the device deserved a bit of a scare, and they'd taken a vote. It passed.

Thorn didn't say a word while he worked, his movements slow and methodical. He'd purchased a simple battery-operated alarm system meant for doors or cabinets that would blare if the door was opened. He secured the alarm base to the floor with duct tape, then placed the box on top of it. If someone lifted the box, it would act like a door opening, and the alarm would sound. He reasoned, correctly to LuAnn's thinking, that the only person who would pick it up was the one who'd hidden the device in the first place, and when he or she did— gotcha! They'd capture their bug-planter.

He backed up from under the tree and gave LuAnn a thumbs-up. She smiled in reply and reached to straighten the tree skirt. He grabbed her wrist and shook his head, a firm silent warning. He rose and tugged her to her feet and led her to the office. Closing the door, he frowned at her.

"You can't touch anything underneath that tree now. If you do, you run the risk of tripping the alarm."

But the skirt was askew. Every time she walked past the tree, the imbalance would taunt her. If she couldn't have everything perfect, she at least wanted the decorations in the inn to be perfect in appearance. "Not even a tiny adjustment on the tree skirt? It looks... off-center."

"I'm sorry about that. I had to shift it to get to bare floor. But seriously, you're gonna have to leave it alone." He finally grinned. "With any luck, whoever put that thing under the tree will come to get it in the next day or so, and you'll be able to put everything right again before Christmas."

She hoped he was right. "Okay."

They exited the office at the same time Tess announced, "Well, here's Alice, back from her shopping." She opened the door and the woman bustled in, her arms filled with shopping bags.

Alice shot a startled look at Thorn. "Oh, dear. Has there been another plumbing problem?"

He picked up his toolbox, as casual and unconcerned as if he were taking a walk on a beach. "No, ma'am, everything's under control. Tess, LuAnn, call me if you need me, but I doubt there'll be a need." He touched his fingers to his forehead and strode out the door.

Alice turned to Tess. "Would you assist me with these bags, please? My arms are about to fall off."

Tess laughed and took a few of the bags. "It looks as if you bought out the whole town. You must have a very large family to need all these presents."

Alice smiled and shrugged.

Tess flicked a look at LuAnn and then smiled again at Alice. "Will you be with them for Christmas?"

Alice set off for the staircase. "I can't say. I've made a promise to myself to finish my story before I leave here, and I still have much to write. So...we shall see!"

CHAPTER TWENTY-TWO

LuAnn felt as if she were walking on eggshells all day. She guarded her words, afraid the device was capturing everything she said. When she couldn't see the tree, she constantly listened for the alarm. After lunch clean-up, when Winnie had left, LuAnn admitted to Tess and Janice, "I wish the alarm would go off now. This waiting is making me stir-crazy."

Janice put her arm around LuAnn and squeezed, a comforting gesture. "Why don't you use the desk in the library and work on your timeline? Constance will see to Huck. There's very little wash to do, and we have tomorrow's rolls and pies ready to go."

LuAnn looked from Janice to Tess. "You won't think I'm lazy?"

Tess chuckled. "We know better than that. I plan to start gathering our tax information, so I'll be in the office. I can answer the phone or the door, if necessary."

Janice released her hold and popped her apron over her head. "I'm meeting with Paige as soon as I change clothes." She grinned impishly. "I'll probably stay and have supper with her and Pastor Ben, so I'm the truly lazy one." She hung up her apron, then seemed to freeze.

LuAnn waited for her to turn around, but she didn't. "Janice, what's the matter?"

Janice shifted her head and peeked at Tess. She bit her lower lip.

Tess put her hand on her hip. "What is it?"

Janice slipped her hand into Tess's apron pocket and withdrew yet another dog biscuit. "Our treat-elf struck again."

"And of course, in my pocket." Tess huffed and threw her arms wide. "When did that happen? I wore that thing up until half an hour ago, and it did not have a dog biscuit in the pocket then. Who's been in here?"

Janice tapped her chin. "You, LuAnn, Winnie, Constance, Marcus, and me. Well, Marcus was only here for a minute, long enough to meet Winnie at the door, so maybe we shouldn't include him."

"Yes, we should. We have to include everyone. Well, except the three of us." Tess strode across the kitchen and snatched her apron from its hook. "I'm considering sewing the pockets closed."

Janice's lips twitched as if holding back a snicker. "Or you could rig them. You know, put a mousetrap in there. I bet that would end someone poking around in your pockets."

"I'd probably end up snapping my own fingers. But you know what? I'm not going to put this out where it's easily accessible. It's going in the pantry from now on." Tess folded it with the pockets tucked inside the neat square and carried it to the pantry. She grinned, raising her eyebrows. "Just see if someone can get a dog treat in there now." She waved and left the kitchen.

Janice trailed out after her, and LuAnn followed. She'd left her notebook and research materials in the drawer of one the library bookcases, so she went straight to the reading area of the parlor. Alice was seated at the small desk in one of the bookcase units. She quickly closed her notebook when LuAnn neared.

LuAnn bit back a grin. If the woman was going to be an author, she'd have to get used to other people seeing her writings. "Do you mind if I join you?" She opened the drawer and removed the information she'd copied at the museum yesterday.

Alice leaned sideways, peering into the drawer. "No, I don't mind. As long as you're quiet. I can't concentrate well when there's a lot of noise around me."

LuAnn considered suggesting she write in the privacy of her suite, but she didn't want to sound ungracious. "I'll be quiet. I also find it easier to concentrate when there are no distracting noises." She bumped the drawer with her hip, intending to close it, but Alice's hand plunged into the drawer and grabbed the pewter snuffbox.

She held it aloft. "Is this the box the young electrician found in the wall?"

LuAnn kept her gaze locked on the box. "Yes."

"It's so nice and clean now." Alice examined it from every angle. "What did you do to it?"

"Scrubbed it with an old toothbrush and then rubbed it with a loofah sponge."

"Ah. Good thinking. Neither the bristles from the toothbrush nor the mesh would damage the surface, but both are effective dirt removers." She shook it near her ear, smiling. "It still rattles."

"Yes."

Alice pushed up on the lid's lip with both thumbs, gritting her teeth and grunting.

"I'm afraid it won't open." As hard as she'd tried, LuAnn hadn't been able to pry up the lid on the box. "All the years of lying in moist dirt has sealed it well."

"Such a shame. Aren't you curious about what's inside?" She turned it upside down and pulled with her fingers.

"Of course, but I don't want to damage it by getting too rough with it."

Alice abruptly ceased her efforts and handed the box to LuAnn. "There must be someone who can open it."

LuAnn slipped the box into the pocket of her jeans. "After Christmas, when the shopping season is over, I'll take it to a jeweler and see if he can open it. Until then, it will have to remain a mystery." She closed the drawer and picked up her stack of pages. She settled in one of the wingback chairs, pulled up her feet, and placed the pages on her upraised knee. She began to read, dimly aware of the *skritch-skritch* of Alice's pencil adding lines to her story.

While she read, she organized the material in her mind, envisioning pages in a photo-and-text book similar to a coffee table book. She planned to divide the book into decades, beginning with the year the inn was built, and ending with the current ownership. It would be easy to give the most recent decade substantially more pages than the others, since they'd taken so many pictures of their renovations. But she'd need to choose only a few to put in the book. Too many color pages would add up. If she decided to make extra copies of the inn's history to sell to guests, the cost needed to be reasonable.

LuAnn read the printed pages, jotting an occasional note in the margins. The sound of a clearing throat pulled her from her focus. She turned in the chair and found Tess waiting, her face crinkled as if she'd tasted a lemon.

LuAnn laughed. "What's that all about?"

"Your dog is whining. Can't you hear him?"

For once Tess hadn't referred to Huck as "that dog." Improvement. LuAnn bounced up. "Constance usually takes care of him during the day, so I wasn't thinking about him."

"Constance clocked out at five thirty, like always. So he's all yours."

Alice sat straight up, slapping her notebook closed. "Is it that late already? Oh my, I completely lost track of time."

LuAnn offered the woman a smile. "I guess we both did. All right, Tess, I'll get Huck as soon as I put these things away." Tess departed, and LuAnn took the pages to the office, placed them in the cabinet with her copy of Prudence's diary, and put the snuffbox on top of the entire stack. She stepped out of the office and almost tripped on Alice, who waited outside the door.

"LuAnn, I just love these bubble lights." Alice fingered one of the lights. "When you have time, could you write down where you found them? I'd love to put some on my own tree next year."

LuAnn eased past the woman. "Let me take care of Huckleberry, then I'll find the mail-order catalog for you."

LuAnn waited on the back stoop, shivering. She shifted from foot to foot and huddled in her jacket. When would Huck finish his business? Full dark had fallen, but the newly installed lantern lit the entire area well. The motion detector light attached several inches above the door went off and on again as Huck paraded back and forth, nose to the ground, searching for the perfect location.

"Huck, come on, boy, it's bedtime. Hurry up, huh?"

The dog paused and looked at her. His tail swished twice, and then he went back to snuffling. If she didn't know better, she'd think he was trying to track somebody. That thought made her shiver harder.

"Huck, finish up." She flicked a nervous look left and right. "Let's go in."

To LuAnn's relief, the dog finally squatted. She reached for the door handle, expecting him to leap up on the stoop, but instead he lifted his head and sniffed the air. Then he zipped past her, as fast as if running from a raging bull, and disappeared behind the garbage cans. LuAnn stepped from the stoop and trotted over the hard ground to the row of trash cans, certain the dog would emerge with a kitten the way he had last time.

"Huck! Huck, come out of there!"

He popped out with something in his mouth, but it wasn't a kitten. He held a rumpled bag. A potato chip bag?

"Oh, ick, Huckleberry. Drop it!"

With a whine, he released the bag. She picked it up and started to toss it in the trash can, and Huck sat up on his haunches and let his front paws droop in his begging pose. The only time he assumed that pose was for—

She uncrumpled the bag. Sure enough, it was for dog biscuits. The picture on the front perfectly matched the treats Constance had found on the stoop and the ones that had been showing up in Tess's apron pocket.

LuAnn turned for the house, patting her leg. "C'mon. Let's go in."

Huck scampered ahead of her and leaped up on the stoop. She lifted him into the crook of her arm and entered the back door. He wriggled, trying to get the bag, but she held it well away from him. She wanted to show it to Tess and Janice, and he'd probably rip it to shreds trying to get to the remaining crumbs inside.

She cleaned his feet with paper towels and put him down. With the wadded bag in her hand, she headed for the office. Huck trotted along beside her, tail up and head held high. She couldn't resist grinning at him. He really was a cute dog. Surely someone, somewhere, was missing him.

The office door stood open, and Tess was at the desk, making use of the calculator on her cell phone. Huck nosed her leg. Her eyebrows dipped. "You, what do you want? Shoo." Huck whined and backed up, then sat and gazed at Tess.

LuAnn stepped in front of him and showed Tess the bag. "Huck found this on the ground by the trash cans. He acted like a bloodhound out there, sniffing all over the place, and he followed whatever scent he'd discovered to the trash. Someone is obviously bringing these things specifically for him."

Tess swiveled the office chair to face LuAnn. "Okay, I understand some people are dog people. I completely get that. You could even say I've been one in the past. But what I cannot figure out is why the 'dog person' who brings these things here wants me to be the carrier. Why not just give them to the dog themselves? Why make me the go-between?"

"I have no idea." LuAnn balled the bag as tightly as possible and dropped it into the waste can. Huck rose and whined, looking at the can longingly, but LuAnn scooped him into her arms. "No you don't. You aren't going to chew on that and tear it to smithereens. You might swallow some of it and choke."

Huck licked the underside of her chin, and she laughed. She caught Tess observing them, and she believed she witnessed something akin to jealousy in her friend's gaze. But the look disappeared so quickly, she couldn't be sure.

"You're going to catch a disease, letting him lick you like that."

LuAnn shrugged. "According to some experts, dogs' mouths are cleaner than humans'."

"That's not saying much."

LuAnn sighed. "Tess, do you really hate Huck?"

Tess stared at the dog for several seconds, her expression unreadable. Finally she shook her head. "No. I don't hate him.

But I won't let myself love him." She shifted abruptly and picked up her phone.

LuAnn debated about questioning Tess further, but Huck wriggled, stealing her attention. "I'll leave you to your figuring. Are you coming up soon?"

"As soon as I balance the checkbook." She flicked a frown at the dog. "I hope he'll be asleep by the time I get there."

LuAnn chuckled as she climbed the stairs, carrying Huck. "You know, Hucky, methinks that damsel protests too much. Underneath all her bluster and fussing, she probably really does like you. You keep up your cute little begging act, and you just might win her over after all."

When they reached the second-floor landing, Alice's door opened and she stepped out. Her gaze collided with LuAnn's, and she gasped. So did LuAnn.

"Alice? Wh-what have you done to yourself?"

CHAPTER TWENTY-THREE

Huckleberry bucked in LuAnn's arms, and she put the dog on the floor, still gaping at their guest.

Alice touched her fingers to the flesh-toned cap covering her scalp. "Oh...this?" She laughed, the sound shrill. "I...sleep in it. Like a nightcap." Another fake-sounding laugh spilled. "I'm sure it looks a fright."

LuAnn couldn't argue with that statement. "You sleep in that? Isn't it uncomfortable?"

"Not when you get used to it." Alice bent over, gave Huck's neck a quick scratch, then straightened and moved backward over the threshold into her room. "I'm sorry I startled you. I was going to get a bottle of water from the little refrigerator, but I think I've changed my mind. Good night, LuAnn." She closed the door.

LuAnn took Huck on upstairs. The scent of peppermint tea greeted her as she entered the apartment.

Janice looked up from the table, where a teacup sent up a swirl of steam. Her smile quickly faded. "What's the matter? You look like you've seen a ghost."

"Not a ghost, but..." LuAnn glanced down at Huck. "Go to bed, Hucky." The dog trotted up the hallway and entered

LuAnn's room. LuAnn glanced at Janice's cup. "Is there more where that came from?"

"Sure." Janice gestured to the antique dry sink and the electric teapot. "Help yourself."

LuAnn snagged a cup from the shelf and filled it with aromatic tea. She sat across from Janice. "You're not going to believe this, but I'm pretty sure Alice Busby wears a wig."

Tess came in, and she gave LuAnn a confused frown. "Did I hear you say Alice wears a wig?"

LuAnn nodded. While Tess poured herself a cup of tea and joined the others at the table, LuAnn described what she'd seen. "At first, I thought she was bald. It took me a minute to realize her hair was covered up by a wig cap. She said she wore it to sleep in, but I don't believe her. The only reason you'd have something like that on is if you were in the habit of wearing a wig." She took a sip of tea, her thoughts tumbling one after another. "If a person was going to wear a wig, why wear a frizzy gray one pulled into a messy bun?"

"And not a trendy, cute messy bun the young girls wear these days," Tess said, "but one that looks like it was fashioned by a weed eater."

"Exactly!" LuAnn nodded at Tess. "It doesn't make sense."

Janice pushed her cup aside and folded her arms on the table. "Have you stopped to consider she wears a wig that matches her natural hair so no one suspects she's got on a wig?"

Tess scratched her ear. "Huh?"

"There are women who, for various reasons, don't want to wash their hair every day. Maybe on Alice's 'off' days, she wears the wig."

Tess gawked at Janice. "You mean, half the times we've seen her, it's been her hair, and the other half the wig?"

Janice shrugged. "I don't know. But it's a possibility." She ran her fingers through her messy platinum curls. "If I got a wig, it would definitely be something more in vogue than my real hair, but then I'd have to wear it every day or I'd startle people. Or myself, when I got a glimpse of my reflection."

LuAnn laughed. She squeezed Janice's wrist. "I think most people would focus on your gracious smile and not pay a bit of attention to your hair, but could we set aside discussion about why Alice wears a wig? I'd like to talk about the dog treats and who might be buying them. It's got to be someone who uses the back door on a regular basis."

"And you've come to this conclusion because..." Tess held out her hand, as if inviting LuAnn to complete the sentence.

"Because the empty bag was by the trash cans near the back door."

"Someone could come in the front, go out back to throw something away, then go out the front again," Janice said.

LuAnn shrugged. "Okay. That's true." She held up a finger. "But the bag wasn't actually *in* the trash can. It was on the ground *behind* the trash cans. Which tells me whoever discarded it was in a hurry. He or she didn't want to be seen, shall we say, holding the bag. So a quick toss and no cares if they missed or not. So...who of the people who come and go around here, whether by the front or back door, wouldn't care if they missed the trash can?"

Tess looked at Janice, who looked at her. They chorused, "Marcus."

"And it's unanimous."

Tess sat back and crossed her arms over her chest. "Remember how nuts Huck goes whenever Marcus comes around? I think he sneaks the dog treats on the sly."

"For what reason, though?" Janice rose and fetched the teapot. She refilled her cup. "I mean, why not give Huck the treats right in front of us? Why try to hide it? Furthermore, why hide them in your apron pocket, Tess? Assuming he's doing that."

Tess laughed, shaking her head. "Who knows why young people do what they do. Maybe he's embarrassed for us to see his softer side. Maybe he's trying to prank me. Maybe he's trying to entertain himself at our expense. Who knows?" She threw her hands wide. "What's more, there's a whole lot of other things I don't know, such as who broke the mirror, who ruined our sheets and replaced them, who split the water line, who put the recording device under our Christmas tree, who dragged in sand and left a trail to the basement, and who left our basement door unlocked."

Janice placed the teapot on the dry sink, aiming a puzzled frown over her shoulder. "Do you think the same person is responsible for everything?"

"I hope so!"

LuAnn choked on her sip of tea. "You *hope* so?"

Tess nodded as Janice slowly sank onto her chair. "Yes. I don't want to think there's a whole gang of people plotting against us. One adversary at a time is enough."

LuAnn yawned. "Ladies, it's late. I think we should table that question until the person who planted the bug under the Christmas tree retrieves it. When we know who that is, we'll probably get answers for everything else too. Besides, we have guests coming tomorrow, and we should get our rest so we're awake enough to welcome them. I move we adjourn."

"I second that motion." Tess stood and gathered up the teacups. "Morning'll be here before we know it."

Morning arrived at exactly 2:17 a.m., when the alarm Thorn had placed beneath the box blared loudly enough to wake half the town. Or so it seemed with it cutting through the silence of the night.

LuAnn scrambled from under the covers, grabbing for the robe she'd draped over the end of the bed four hours ago. She met Tess and Janice in the hall, and for a few seconds they bumped into and stumbled around each other like they'd been cast in a Three Stooges remake. Finally they gathered their bearings and raced out of the apartment and down the stairs, thundering as loudly as an entire herd of stampeding elephants.

Alice stood in the shadowy doorway of the Honeymoon Suite with her hands over her ears. "Is that a smoke alarm?"

"No, ma'am," Tess hollered as she ran by. "Please stay in your room."

When they reached the bottom of the stairs, Tess pushed Janice toward the office. "Call 911." She caught LuAnn's elbow and pulled her toward the kitchen. "Lu, check the back—see if anyone's behind the inn. I'll check the basement."

Gasping for breath, LuAnn raced for the back door. Its deadbolt was locked, which even in her muddled state let her know no one had exited there. She whirled toward the front door, but as she entered the dining room, Janice intercepted her.

"It wasn't an intruder!"

"What?"

Janice made a horrible face and pushed her fingers into her ears. "How do you make that thing stop?"

LuAnn searched her mind for Thorn's instructions on silencing the alarm. She dropped to her knees, yanked the box aside, and snapped the alarm's jaws closed. Silence fell.

Tess trotted around the corner. "No one's in the basement, and the door's locked tight. Did—"

Janice waved her hands. "Nobody broke in. It wasn't an intruder."

LuAnn's ears were still ringing. She stood and shook her head to dislodge the high-pitched squall. "How do you know?"

Janice pursed her lips and gestured to the tree, Vanna White style. A tiny black-and-white face peered at them with round golden eyes from the middle branches.

Tess groaned. "Tom..."

Janice pulled the kitten from the tree. "How did you get down here?"

LuAnn slapped her hand to her forehead. "I probably let him out. I came down about eleven. I couldn't remember if I'd taken the stew meat from the freezer and put it in the fridge for tomorrow's—or today's, now—beef and barley soup." She rubbed the kitten's head with two fingers. "I probably didn't get the door fully latched."

Tess yawned. "And of course he had to climb the tree. What else would a cat do in the middle of the night?"

Someone knocked on the front door, and a flashlight's beam came through the glass. Janice cringed. "There's the answer to my 911 call. In all the excitement, I forgot to call them back and tell them it was a false alarm."

Tess trudged toward the door. "I'll take care of them. Go on up. Let Alice know we aren't under attack. And please, lock up the cat."

"Winnie, honestly, it isn't funny." LuAnn tried to glare at the cook, whose merriment continued to roll despite Tess's huffs and Janice's pursed lips. Maybe someday their early morning race to catch an intruder that turned out to be their very own kitten would be funny, but her nerves were still too rattled to find humor in it. Worse than the lost sleep, their secret had been exposed.

Alice showed up for breakfast the minute the café opened, two hours earlier than her usual routine, and she told and retold the story about the police coming in the middle of the night to catch a *cat burglar*. The news would be all over town by sundown. The person who put the box under the tree would never try to come for it now.

Winnie grinned while filling a plate with pancakes and scrambled eggs. "Don't get *purrr*snickety with me, Miss Lu. Catching a cat burglar is funny."

LuAnn gritted her teeth and picked up the plate.

"If you weren't all crabby from running up and down the stairs when you should've been sleeping, you'd be *feline fine* like me." Winnie threw back her head and guffawed.

LuAnn carried the plate to Brad, who'd joined several others around the farmhouse table. She plunked the plate in front of him, stifled a yawn, and said, "Can I get you anything else?"

"I'm fine for now, thanks." Sympathy glimmered in his blue eyes. He offered her a sad smile. "You look beat. Will you ladies have time to grab a nap this afternoon?"

"I doubt it. We're expecting several guests."

"That's a good thing, yes?"

Of course it was a good thing. She only hoped they'd be able to greet the arrivals with a modicum of enthusiasm, given their exhaustion. She nodded. Another yawn threatened, and she couldn't squelch this one. She hid it behind her hand. "I'm so sorry."

He shook his head, his eyes twinkling. "LuAnn, you'll fall asleep standing there if you don't start moving."

She lurched away from the table and started for the kitchen, but Patricia Huston waved her over. She stopped at the table and its familiar occupants, forcing a smile. "Would you like some more coffee? Another roll?"

"No, thank you." Patricia rested her elbows on the table and linked her hands beneath her chin. "I wanted to ask a question. Why did you put a burglar alarm under the Christmas tree if the boxes are empty?"

LuAnn frowned. "How did you know they're empty?"

She raised one shoulder. "When I was here last, I commented to Constance how pretty the boxes were decorated, and she said it was kind of a shame to make an empty box so festive." The woman tipped her head, and her brow furrowed. "Isn't it kind of silly to protect empty boxes?"

Jane flicked Patricia with her napkin and laughed. "Here now, don't be catty."

LuAnn bit back a groan.

"I doubt the burglar would know they were empty. The alarm was probably meant to give any intruder a good scare." Jane looked at LuAnn. "Am I right?"

The explanation was as good as LuAnn could have created, given her current state of grogginess. "Yes. That's right."

Jane draped her napkin over her lap. "See? So it wasn't so silly after all. And now that people know the inn has safeguards in place, the owners can rest assured no one else will try to sneak in and steal from them." The two put their heads together and chatted.

LuAnn left their table and welcomed and seated two newcomers. She waited while they read the menu board and then took their orders. Since the orders didn't require the grill, she took care of the plates herself, not at all disappointed about avoiding Winnie for a few more minutes. The woman still wore an ear-to-ear grin.

LuAnn took a tray and filled it with the plates, two mugs, and a carafe of coffee, then delivered the items to the waiting patrons. They smiled their thanks, and she smiled in reply and reminded them to holler if they needed anything else. She tucked the empty tray under her arm and turned toward the kitchen, but a movement at the opening between the café and parlor caught her eye.

Tom Davis waited in the middle of the floor, his hands deep in his jacket pockets. His unsmiling countenance gave LuAnn the impression he hadn't come for breakfast. She passed the tray to Janice and whispered, "I'll see what he wants."

Janice gave her a worried look and nodded.

As LuAnn approached Tom, he pulled one hand free of his pocket and held it out to her. She took it, and he gave it a solemn shake. "I'm sorry to show up without warning like this"—he glanced toward the café—"but I thought it'd be better for me to talk to you ladies face to face, and it needed to be as soon as possible."

LuAnn licked her lips, suddenly afraid to ask the question that had to be asked. "Is something wrong?"

He ducked his head and tapped the toe of his boot against the floor. "Yes, ma'am, I'm afraid so. And it's a pretty big something wrong."

CHAPTER TWENTY-FOUR

Tom suggested they take their conversation to somewhere private, so LuAnn led him to the office. She closed the door behind them and managed a weak smile. "Now...what can I do for you?"

"Well, ma'am, when I ran the new plumbing in this building, I bought a spool of flexible plastic tubing so I could cut whatever length I needed. I had no idea it wasn't a certified PEX line."

She wished she'd asked Tess or Janice to join them. Her sleep-deprived brain and taut emotions made it difficult for her to understand what he was saying. "What's the difference between certified and uncertified, um, pecks line?"

He made a sour face. "A whole lot. I used the last of the spool in the bathroom of a new house addition, and after only two weeks one of the shower lines split and flooded their crawlspace. Cleaning up the mess is my responsibility. If the line had been certified, the company where I bought it would be responsible."

"I see." LuAnn pulled in a deep breath, trying to flood her blood supply with oxygen that might feed her numb brain. "So there's the possibility the lines here could split too?"

"One of 'em already did. The line we put in the men's room."

"How can you know for sure it wasn't deliberate?"

"The line we took from the house looked like somebody'd taken a knife and slit it. Same as the line over here." He shook his head. "But now I know that a knife didn't do it. The line was thin at that point, and the water burst it."

"So if the line wasn't intentionally cut..." LuAnn forced herself to think. "That means we could have faulty water lines elsewhere in the inn."

He puffed his cheeks and blew out a mighty breath. "Yes, ma'am, that's exactly what it means." He held up his hands, palms out. "Now, I'm gonna replace every inch of it and not charge you ladies so much as a penny. It'll take time, but not as much as it did to run it in the first place, since we can use the old line to pull new lines through from the faucets and so forth to the water control board."

The lights on the Christmas tree blinked, painting cheerful little dots on the side of the plumber's face. So incongruous to the deep furrows lining his brow. She grabbed the back of a chair. "How much time?"

"A quarter to a half hour per line, depending on which floor it feeds from."

She silently tried to count the number of plumbing lines in the inn. Her head began to ache.

"I suggest we start with the lines you use the most, like the kitchen and the rooms that're occupied." He went on talking, and she did her best to focus. "Me and my workers'll shut down the water line to each room one at a time, replace the lines, then turn it on again so nobody'll be inconvenienced for long."

"When do you intend to replace the lines?"

"Well…" He pulled off his ball cap, pushed his fingers through his hair, then slapped the cap into place again. "I'd like to get started today. Now. I've got three men waiting outside." He hung his head and shoved his hands in his pockets, looking for all the world like a little boy who'd broken his neighbor's window with a baseball. "I really am sorry, ma'am, and I'll do everything in my power to make the replacement as easy as possible for you and your guests."

She stepped away from the chair and squeezed his elbow. "Please don't apologize. You didn't deliberately run faulty lines. You were misled, and you're making it right. That's what matters." Even as she spoke reassuringly, worrisome thoughts cluttered her mind. By this afternoon, three more rooms would be occupied. Would he and his workers be able to make those rooms safe by the time the guests arrived?

Although she, Tess, and Janice ordinarily made decisions concerning the inn as a team, this was an emergency. They would understand her need to act alone. "Please bring in your workers. I'll give you the locations of the rooms you can start with. When we close for breakfast, you can replace the kitchen lines." She cringed. She hoped none of the lines would split before he got to them. "Does that sound like a workable plan?"

His shoulders slumped, and he heaved a huge sigh. "It does. Thank you for being so understanding."

She smiled. "Getting angry won't fix the lines, will it? Before your men start, though, please come to the dining room for a cinnamon roll and some coffee. We'll call it fuel to get your engines running."

"Thank you, ma'am, but we've got a lot of work to get done." His grin turned impish. "So please make those rolls to go."

A genuine laugh left her throat, and it revived her more than even the three cups of coffee she'd consumed. "That's a deal." She turned toward the café, and a yawn built up in her chest. She lowered her head to hide it, and her gaze landed on the edge of the Christmas tree skirt. It was still askew. She could fix it, since the alarm had been tripped. She leaned down and caught the fabric between her fingers, and then she stared in disbelief. The box with the recorder was gone.

By the end of the day, the Inn Crowd agreed that they would recommend Tom to anyone looking for a plumber. He and his workers paired off, tackling two rooms at a time, and they proved themselves as industrious as bees. By five that evening, they'd changed out all but the plumbing lines to the fourth-floor apartments. He offered to stay until every line was replaced, but Tess shook her head.

"That isn't necessary. There are several unoccupied rooms only one set of stairs down. To be on the safe side, we'll use those bathrooms tonight and tomorrow morning. So go home, get a good rest, and come finish up tomorrow."

His relief was evident, and he thanked them each with firm handshakes and promises to be back first thing in the morning. Janice saw him to the door, and then she plodded back to

Tess and LuAnn, who leaned on the reception desk. She, too, propped herself against the desk and sighed.

"We did it. We made it through this day. If we can serve guests, handle four plumbers running all over the building, and keep our sanity, we can do anything."

"'I can do all things through Christ which strengtheneth me.'" LuAnn quoted the verse from Philippians on a wheezing breath.

Tess raised one fist and cupped her bicep with her other hand, making a fierce face. "Yep. We can do it."

Constance came down the stairs and caught them laughing. She bounced a hesitant smile across each of them. "Is it okay if I ask you something?"

Tess waved her over. "Sure, Constance. What do you need?"

She approached, wringing her hands. Even after three weeks, she still always seemed nervous. "All the bathrooms are clean and ready in case someone shows up without a reservation, but Huck isn't very happy. I don't think he's liked being shut in all day."

LuAnn released a light laugh. "No, I'm sure he hasn't, but we really didn't have much choice today. We couldn't have one of the plumbers tripping over him."

"Oh, I know." Constance's eyes went wide. "I wasn't criticizing. I wondered if… Could I take him for a walk? I think he'd enjoy the exercise, and I'm sure you all are too tired to do it."

Tess released a weary chuckle. "You're right about that. Go ahead. Take him." She lifted her brows. "Take him all the way home."

"Pets aren't allowed in my apartment. But I wish they were." Her tone turned wistful. "I'd love to have a little dog or cat."

"Well, then, you can borrow him as often as you like."

Constance's hopeful face shifted from Tess to Janice and LuAnn. "So it's all right?"

LuAnn answered. "Of course."

"Thank you." Constance hurried up the stairs.

Tess watched after her until the sound of her footsteps receded. Then she whirled on LuAnn and Janice. "All right. It's quiet and no one's around, so we can talk."

Janice fiddled with the neck of her Christmas-themed sweatshirt. "Are you sure? Where is…?" She glanced toward the library.

"I don't know where she is, other than not here." Tess grinned, which erased the tired droop of her eyelids. "She must have found a friend in town, because she's been gone a significant amount of time."

"That's…nice," Janice said, the words separated by a yawn. "Whatever you need to talk about, make it quick. I've got to take a nap before dinner, or I won't last through the evening."

Tess's grin faded. "The missing recorder box. Let's see if we can figure out when it disappeared."

"Well…" Janice's brow pinched. "It was there when the alarm went off."

LuAnn pressed her memory. "And it was there when we came down to get breakfast started. I know, because I checked under the tree to see if Tom had dislodged any ornaments. That was early—a little before six."

"What time did you notice it was gone?"

LuAnn looked at Janice. "What time did the plumber come in? Did you look at the clock?"

Janice shrugged. "I didn't notice the clock, but we were pretty busy, so I'll guess somewhere around eight since that's the start of our busy time."

"So between six and eight..." Tess drummed her fingers, her scowl deep. "That's not a very wide window of opportunity, which means we can limit the pool of suspects to—"

Footsteps—of the human and canine varieties—interrupted her. Tess clamped her lips closed, and they all watched the staircase for Constance's descent. Huck bounced along beside her, his tail and ears high.

Constance offered them a smile. "I won't keep him out long since it's so cold, but I think a walk to Jeremiah's and back will do him a lot of good."

"Bundle up." Janice shook her finger at Constance, the gesture motherly. "We don't want you coming down with something."

Constance dipped her head. "Yes, ma'am."

Huck whined and nudged Tess's leg. She scooted backward a foot, and the dog crowded close to Constance again. Constance leaned over and picked him up. "We'll go out the back door since my coat's back there." She hurried off with Huck's wagging tail seeming to propel her along. After a minute or two, the back door latch clicked.

"—Constance, Winnie, Alice, and us."

It took a moment for LuAnn to realize Tess was finishing the sentence Constance had interrupted. She drew in a breath, centering her thoughts. "You're forgetting all the people who came in for breakfast. Any one of them could have helped themselves to the package."

"And Marcus." Janice pinched her chin, seemingly deep in thought. "Remember? He dropped off Winnie's blood pressure medicine on his way to school."

Tess tipped her head. "Did he come out here though? He usually comes and goes through the back."

Try as she might, LuAnn could not recall seeing Marcus come or go. "If he went out the front, it would've been really easy for him to grab that box and take it with him."

Tess's gaze seemed to drift from the tree skirt to the front door. "I don't know why he'd want to record what goes on here, but a young person like him would know how to use any kind of technological gadget." She aimed a grim look at LuAnn. "Get your notebook and write this down, Lu. After we've had a good night's rest, we'll give it some more thought."

CHAPTER TWENTY-FIVE

LuAnn dragged herself out of bed at five thirty Saturday morning. Huck raised his head and released a little whine when she padded across the floor, but then he wriggled back into the bed and closed his eyes.

She yawned as she descended the stairs, the bag of necessities she'd put together before going to bed in her hand. A dull ache plagued her lower spine, and her knees popped twice. Sixty-three wasn't old, but neither was it young, and time and age were making themselves known in her joints. And her stamina. A full night of sleep hadn't completely eradicated the fuzziness holding her brain captive.

The hot shower eased the pain in her back and washed away much of her weariness. She passed Tess on the stairs on the way to her apartment, and she offered a good morning that sounded authentic. Tess grunted in reply. LuAnn swallowed a laugh. A shower would hopefully stir Tess's good humor back to life.

After dressing, she bent down and ruffled the soft hair on Huck's head. "Okay, fella, time to go out. Let's go."

She tiptoed down the flights of stairs, holding Huck. No sense in waking their guests before the sun peeked over the horizon. In the kitchen, she put him on the floor, and the two of them walked side by side to the back door. As she reached for the handle to let Huck out, the motion-activated light above the door came on. Startled, she lurched backward. A key clicked in the lock, the door opened, and Winnie stepped inside.

LuAnn nearly slid down the wall into a puddle of relief. "Winnie..." She glanced at the clock. "You're a half hour early."

Winnie gaped at LuAnn. "So are you. I didn't expect anybody to be down here yet. What're you doing up?" Huck whimpered, and she nodded knowingly. "Ah. You're taking him out. Here you go, Huck." She moved aside and held the door open. Huck shot out. She grinned at LuAnn. "I hope I didn't scare you too bad. You don't have high blood pressure, do you?"

LuAnn managed a short laugh. She peered out the window, watching for Huck's return. "I never did before, but I might now after that fright. You didn't come over to let Huck out, so why the early arrival?"

Winnie hung her coat on the hall tree and snagged her apron from its hook. "Oh, I had a little... personal errand... to do."

Huck scratched at the door, and LuAnn let him in. She grabbed him before he could race across the floor with his dirty feet and turned for the paper towel holder. She caught Winnie glaring at the remaining aprons on the hooks. "Is something wrong?"

Winnie tapped the empty hook where Tess's apron usually hung. "What happened to Miss Tess's apron? It wasn't here yesterday either, but she had it on when we were working, so I know she didn't lose it."

Awareness crept through LuAnn's mind. Her mouth dropped open. "Winnie... You..."

Winnie's eyebrows rose, and she touched her bodice with her fingertips. "I...what?"

"You've been putting the dog biscuits in Tess's pocket."

Winnie smacked her finger to her lips. "Shh." She looked up, as if Tess could hear them through the ceiling. "Don't be saying that out loud."

LuAnn wiped Huck's feet and put him down. He pranced over to Winnie and whined. She bent over and scratched his chin. LuAnn put her hands on her hips. "Why did you do it? You have to know it was driving her crazy."

"Oh, I know." The unconcerned comment accompanied a grin. Winnie straightened, and Huck sat up on his haunches. She rewarded him with a biscuit from her pocket. "But it was for her own good."

LuAnn leaned against the counter and folded her arms. "How so?"

"She acts all fidgety and nervous around Huck, but I'm not buying it for one minute. She's holding that little dog at arm's length, probably trying not to get attached, so when his owner shows up, she doesn't end up missing him too much. But it's not fair to Huck to be treated like that. So I figure, give Huck here a reason to take to Tess, and eventually Tess will take to him. Makes sense, doesn't it?"

LuAnn could imagine one of her former students coming up with an excuse like that. She would've set him straight too.

"It might make sense to you, but it made no sense at all to Tess and only made her more nervous about Huck."

For a moment, Winnie's face drooped into a pout. Then she brightened. "We haven't given it enough time yet. It'll work. You'll see." She sauntered to the refrigerator and pulled out a carton of eggs. "Long as you're up, why don't you fetch me Miss Tess's apron. I bet you know where it is. I've got one more biscuit in my pocket from the last bag Marcus bought, and I'll transfer it to hers."

"Oh, no." LuAnn backed up. "Leave me out of this."

Winnie sent LuAnn a hopeful look. "You aren't gonna tell on me, are you, Miss Lu?"

Should she? Tess would be greatly relieved to know who their "dog treat elf" was. But the pleading look on Winnie's face was as hard to resist as Huck's begging. She sighed. "No, I won't tell Tess. But neither will I tell you where to find her apron." She scooped up Huck. "C'mon, Hucky, you can stay in the office until the plumber is done in the apartment."

Several times during the morning LuAnn came close to telling Tess who'd been sneaking dog biscuits into her pockets. But then she'd remember Winnie's hopeful face and change her mind. She kept an eye on Winnie, though. If somehow the woman managed to drop a biscuit in Tess's apron pocket, LuAnn would find a way to sneak it out before Tess was aware. It was the least she could do to protect her friend's sanity.

Saturday morning passed in a blur. The last shopping Saturday before Christmas must have brought half the town out early, and everyone wanted one of Winnie's cinnamon rolls or a stack of oat and nut pancakes. They ran out of rolls and pancake batter before nine, and Janice made a quick change on the menu board—apple-walnut, blueberry, or cinnamon-streusel muffins. All three varieties waited in the basement freezer. When Winnie tucked away a few muffins from every batch as an "emergency stash," LuAnn had questioned her reasoning, but this morning she praised the cook for her foresight.

They also ran out of orange juice, but at least they had plenty of coffee, and LuAnn nearly wore herself out weaving from table to table and keeping the mugs filled. She plopped into a chair after the last breakfast customer left and put her head in her hands. "If lunch is this busy, I'm leaving on vacation immediately afterward."

Tess tapped her on the shoulder. "You can't. Tomorrow's your turn to stay here in the morning, remember?"

She remembered now. She sighed. Even though the spoiled milk, split water line, and missing diary had been explained away, there were still a few events that needed answers. If only they knew who'd planted—and taken—the bug, had torn the sheets to pieces, broken the mirror, and traipsed sand where it didn't belong. Somehow the incidents must be connected, but neither she nor her partners, despite frequent conversations and pondering, had been able to solve the puzzle.

Tess bumped her again. "The plumbers left about a half hour ago, so you can take the dog back to our apartment now."

LuAnn gaped at her. "They were here?" She hadn't even seen them, she'd been so busy. She'd wanted to give them the thank-you note she'd written. They'd put in long hours without a word of complaint, and they deserved the free breakfast coupons she'd included in the card.

Tess shrugged. "Probably had other jobs to get to." She flicked her fingers at LuAnn. "Go get that dog out of the office, wouldja?"

LuAnn forced her stiff joints to unfold and trudged toward the office. When she was halfway across the floor, the front bell jangled and Brad stepped in. Even though it was Saturday, he wore a suit and crisp white shirt, but he'd skipped the tie. The top button of the shirt was undone and his collar lay open, giving him a casual, approachable appearance. All at once she felt frumpy in her work apron and blue jeans.

She crossed to meet him, wishing she had time to brush her hair from its simple ponytail or freshen her makeup. "Morning, Brad." Embarrassment made her pulse race, and her voice emerged on a breathless rasp.

He flashed his familiar smile. "Morning."

"I hope you aren't here for a cinnamon roll. They sold out. It was pretty much a zoo here this morning."

He laughed. "Yeah, well, Christmas shoppers. The parking spaces are filled up and down the street, and people are milling on the sidewalks like ants on a sugar mound."

That was how it had been in the café. "We might have a frozen muffin or two, though."

He shook his head. Not that she could blame him. He probably wouldn't want to risk chipping a tooth on a frozen muffin. "I don't need a muffin, but there is something I need from you, Tess, and Janice."

She tipped her head, curious. "What's that?"

"A photograph." He looked around and then pointed. "There, on the stairs next to the tree."

LuAnn wiggled her finger in her ear. Surely she hadn't heard him right. "Why do you need a photograph of us?"

"For the Chamber of Commerce website. Tess mentioned you all were ready to join the Chamber. That means we'll feature your place of business on the website. We always put a photo of the business front and another of the owner. Our web designer plans to update the site right after the first of the year, so he asked me to take some photos, since I know you ladies well."

"I guess we can do that, but..." She glanced down at herself, then fixed him with a wary look. "You don't need it *now*, do you?"

He laughed again. "No, no, you're busy now, and I didn't bring my digital camera with me. Tell me what time works best for you, and I'll put it in my calendar. I'd like to get it taken as quickly as possible, though, so Rick will have everything he needs when he sits down to make the updates."

LuAnn raised her finger. "One minute." She dashed to the kitchen, explained what Brad wanted to Tess and Janice, and then hurried back. "Will today around five work for you? That seems to be the quietest time here for us."

He pulled out his phone, poked it a few times with a stylus, then slid both items back into his pocket. "Perfect. I'll be back at five." He started toward the door, then paused and faced her again. "LuAnn? I hope you don't think I'm forward for saying this, but I think the business owners picture of the three of you will be the cutest on the entire website. You remind me of triplets separated at birth—somehow you all just seem to belong together." He grinned, waved, and stepped out the door.

CHAPTER TWENTY-SIX

After the lunch crowd cleared and they finished the kitchen clean-up, the Inn Crowd made a mad dash to their apartment to get changed for what Janice called their photo shoot. LuAnn didn't want to put such a formal title on it, but she couldn't deny a desire to make the photograph a good one. The image would be on a website for potential guests to see—it needed to create a good impression—and, even if it seemed a little vain, she really did want her, Tess, and Janice to be the cutest business owners on the website.

Cleaned up, hair freshly styled, makeup refreshed, and dressed in business casual attire, the three made their way down the stairs together. Alice met them at the landing and looked them up and down. She touched her frizzy hair with one hand and planted her notebook against the bodice of her faded gray dress with the other. "Well, don't you all look nice? Are you going out tonight?"

"No," Janice said. "We're having our picture taken."

"To put in Christmas cards?"

Why hadn't LuAnn thought of that? She smiled at the woman. "It's probably too late for that, but it'll be used on a website."

Alice nodded and went upstairs. The women stood in a little cluster near the check-in desk, Janice tugging the hem of her blouse and LuAnn smoothing a few stray wisps of hair. Tess glanced at her wristwatch. "We're ahead of schedule."

Janice giggled. "Maybe we were eager."

Tess shrugged. "Maybe. What should we—"

The front door opened, and Dean and Kay Pankratz entered. Dean pulled a small rolling suitcase, and Kay held a large portfolio under her arm. LuAnn scuttled around the desk and pointed at it. "Is that our..."

Kay grinned, showing a pair of dimples. "It is. Do you want to see it?"

"Of course I do!"

Kay placed the portfolio on the floor and leaned it against her legs. She opened the flap and slid a sizable framed painting from the protective cover. Grinning, she held it in front of her. "What do you think?"

"Oh..." LuAnn gazed in amazement. How had the woman so perfectly captured the charm and warmth of the building? The muted colors melting together yet also somehow distinct from one another formed a nearly breathtaking image. "It reminds me of a reflection on a pond. Stunning."

While the owners of Wayfarers Inn oohed and aahed over the painting, Constance came down the stairs. She crossed to the group and peeked over Janice's shoulder. LuAnn gestured her forward.

"Look, Constance. Isn't it pretty? It's Wayfarers before it was Wayfarers."

The young woman's hazel-eyed gaze swept from corner to corner of the painting. Her lips began to quiver. "It's...it's lovely."

LuAnn hadn't expected such an emotional response to the painting. Sympathy rolled through her. The teacher in her emerged, and she put her arm around Constance's waist. "We're going to hang it where it will be easily seen by everyone who enters the inn. It allows our visitors to have a snapshot of the past. It's important to preserve the history, don't you agree?"

"Yes. Yes, I..." Constance swallowed. Tears filled her eyes. Then, without warning, she burst into tears. She jerked free of LuAnn's light grip. "I have to go home." She darted out the front door.

Janice gaped after Constance. "She didn't even take her coat. Should we go after her?"

Tess put her hand on Janice's shoulder. "Constance strikes me as a private person. I think we would embarrass her. Let her have some time to compose herself. She'll come back for her coat, and we can talk to her then."

Kay slipped the painting back into the portfolio. "I hope I didn't do something to upset her. The painting really seemed to bother her."

LuAnn took the artist's hand. "The painting is perfect. Whatever is bothering Constance isn't your fault. Please don't feel bad." She patted Kay's hand. "Shall we get you two checked in? And then perhaps we can talk Dean into helping us hang this marvelous piece of artwork."

Brad arrived promptly at five, only a few minutes after Dean placed the painting on its hanger. He spent a moment admiring it and complimenting the artist. Kay mentioned her desire to open a small gallery at some point in the near future, and he immediately offered to help her locate office space. LuAnn swallowed a chuckle. Sometimes he acted like a used car salesman.

Dean and Kay left for dinner, and Brad turned to the Inn Crowd and held up his camera. "Are you ladies ready?"

Janice touched her curls. "As ready as we can be."

He guided them to the staircase. He instructed Tess to stand on the second step, LuAnn on the first, and Janice on the floor next to the newel post. "Tess, one hand on the railing, the other on LuAnn's shoulder. LuAnn, place your hand over Tess's—that's right—and then your free hand on Janice's shoulder."

A delightful feeling wiggled through LuAnn's frame. The only group photos she'd ever been a part of were faculty shots for high school yearbooks. This photo was much more personal. How she hoped it looked as good as it felt.

Janice held out her hands. "What do I do?"

Brad released a light chuckle. "It will seem odd, but stick out your left thumb. Now make a fist around it with your right hand, and lay your fingers over your knuckles."

Laughing, Janice followed his instructions. "Like this?"

"Exactly like that. Let your hands drop but slightly angle them toward your left hip."

Janice giggled again. "You were right, this does seem odd."

"But it looks great. Trust me." He backed up a few steps, tipped his head, and frowned. He moved a few inches to the left and tipped his head the opposite direction. LuAnn battled the urge to snicker. She'd seen a pigeon beg for bread crumbs exactly the same way. He stood straight and beamed at them. "Perfect. Okay, ladies, on the count of three..."

He snapped at least a dozen pictures—some at the staircase, some by the grand piano, and more standing on either side of Kay Pankratz's watercolor painting. His serious expression tickled LuAnn, and she hoped amusement didn't shimmer in her eyes. Finally he lowered the camera and winked at them. "All done."

LuAnn skirted Janice and approached him, gathering courage as she went. "I know this is for the commerce website, but would you email them to me so I can make some prints? I might want one for myself."

"Me too," Janice said, hurrying to join them.

"And me," Tess called from the stairs.

Brad smiled. "I tell you what, I'll print three copies of each pose for you." They all started to protest, and he put up his hand, shaking his head. "No, it's no trouble, and you can consider it my Christmas gift to you all."

LuAnn shook her head. "You already gave me one—the dog and cat supplies, remember?" The photographs were a much better gift.

His blue eyes met hers. "I guess you get double."

Tess snickered, and LuAnn shot a disapproving glare over her shoulder. She pinned Brad with the firm look that always ended a student's nonsense. "It's too much, Brad. I appreciate your offer to print the pictures, but I either need to pay for them or the pet supplies."

Brad shrugged. "I tell you what, let me come in every morning in January for a cinnamon roll, and we'll call it even."

She stuck out her hand. "Deal."

He took her hand and smiled at her with such warmth, she wondered if she'd made a mistake. She gently withdrew her hand and turned to Tess and Janice. "All our guests are in and we're dressed for public viewing. How about driving to the River Town Grill for dinner?"

Brad cleared his throat. "River Town might be booked, considering it's the last Saturday night before Christmas."

A crestfallen expression crossed Janice's face. "Oh, that's right."

"I planned to grab a pizza at Over the Moon." Brad slipped one hand into his trouser pocket. "You all are welcome to join me."

"All of us?" Janice gestured to the group. "Maybe someone should stay here."

Tess sauntered across the floor. "I think it'd be okay for us to go. Our guests are all checked in, they have keys to let themselves in and out, and we can put a sign on the door with a phone number if someone shows up unexpectedly. I think we could all use an evening out."

"Sounds good to me." LuAnn headed for the stairs. "But I need to let Huck out before we go."

"Another reason not to have a dog," Tess muttered.

LuAnn chose to ignore her.

LuAnn enjoyed their time at Over the Moon. The casual atmosphere put her at ease, and she found herself relaxing more and more as the evening progressed. She was disappointed when Tess mentioned they'd been away from the inn for almost two hours and they should get back.

Brad drove them to Wayfarers and pulled up in front of the inn. LuAnn started to thank him for the enjoyable dinner, but Janice gasped, "Constance!" LuAnn looked out the window and spotted Constance next to the front door, her arms wrapped around herself and her head low.

LuAnn leaped from the car and ran across the sidewalk. "Constance, my goodness, you look half frozen." She dug for her key, but Tess found hers first and unlocked the door. Janice and LuAnn ushered the young woman inside. LuAnn took hold of Constance by her shoulders. "What in the world were you doing, standing out there without a coat? Are you trying to catch pneumonia?"

Constance shuddered. "No, ma'am. I forgot my coat and came back to get it. But no one was here, and I seem to have misplaced my key. So I decided to wait outside."

Janice trotted toward the kitchen. "I'll get you some hot cocoa."

Tess turned for the parlor. "I'll get an afghan."

Constance's gaze bounced back and forth from one lady to another. "No, it's all right. I'll get my coat and—"

LuAnn steered Constance after Tess. "You'll get warm first. Come on. No arguing."

Constance seemed to lose her ability to fight. She scuffed alongside LuAnn and settled in the middle of the sofa. LuAnn sat next to her, battling the urge to gather the young woman close. How she seemed to need mothering.

Tess draped the afghan across Constance's knees, and she grabbed it and pulled it up to her chin. "Oh, that feels good."

Janice came in and handed Constance a steaming mug. The rich aroma of chocolate met LuAnn's nostrils, and even though she'd just had a good dinner, her appetite stuttered to life. She caught Janice's eye. "Is there more?"

Janice grinned. "I'll be right back." She scurried off.

Tess sank down at the other end of the sofa and put her hand on Constance's knee. "I'm glad you came back. We were all worried about you."

Constance grimaced. "That's nice of you. I don't know what came over me. It was that painting. It... I..." She sent an uncertain glance left, then right. "There's something I need to tell you all. A... confession I need to make."

CHAPTER TWENTY-SEVEN

Each with a cup of cocoa warming her hands, the women settled into the cushioned seats, and LuAnn offered Constance an encouraging smile. "Go ahead. We'll listen."

Constance took a deep breath, closed her eyes for a moment, then began. "My mom's in a nursing home in Canton. She had her first stroke ten years ago, when she was fifty-two."

Janice clicked her tongue on her teeth. "So young..."

"Yeah. I know. She had a second stroke three years after the first one, then a mild heart attack the year after that. She got stents put in, but she never fully recovered. She needed somebody. I'd just finished coursework to become a CNA—you know, Certified Nursing Assistant—so I stayed home and took care of her."

LuAnn's heart rolled over in sympathy. "Wasn't there anyone else in the family to help?"

Constance shrugged, her head low. "My dad died when I was eleven. I have an older brother, but he was already married with a couple of little kids when Mom had her first stroke. I didn't have any other obligations, so..."

LuAnn swallowed. "You gave up a lot for her, Constance."

"I guess." The young woman looked at LuAnn, her eyes seeming to plead. "But she's my mom. What would you do?"

Exactly the same thing. LuAnn nodded. "But she's in a nursing home now, which gives you the opportunity to pursue your own interests. Why take a job here instead of at a hospital or even at the nursing home where your mother is staying?"

Constance leaned forward and set her mug on the coffee table. She pulled the afghan high again, as if trying to hide herself. "This is probably going to sound stupid, but when I was a little girl, my granddad would drive past this place and tell me about his great-grandfather, who was the caretaker at the Riverfront House."

Janice sucked in a sharp breath. "The caretaker...he was murdered... From the diary, remember?"

LuAnn and Tess nodded.

Constance continued as if Janice hadn't spoken. "Granddad tried to buy the hotel before they turned it into a warehouse, but the bank wouldn't give him the money. He never stopped talking about it, though, how different his life would've been if his great-grandfather hadn't been killed. I got the feeling his father was bitter about it, and he passed that bitterness to Granddad. My mom said Dad had a little bit of that in him too, but I don't really remember him being bitter. Mostly curious."

LuAnn tipped her head. "Curious about what?"

"The supposed treasure."

Tess sat forward. "There's a treasure here?"

Constance shifted the afghan a bit. "It's only a rumor. Nobody in the family could ever prove it. But Granddad said Frederick Stanfill was killed because he wouldn't hand over a treasure to riverboat pirates. He was trying to hide it somewhere, but he died before he could tell his wife what he'd done with it. She never found it, and then of course she lost her job, so she couldn't keep looking for it." She sighed. "It's probably just a story, a tall tale passed down through generations."

Tess touched Constance's shoulder. "Did you apply to work here so you could look for the treasure?"

"No. If there was a treasure, it's probably long gone considering how many people have passed through this building. I wanted to work here so I could..." She sent a self-conscious glance across each of them. "...feel connected to my ancestors. Granddad and Dad are both gone. But the inn's still here. I kind of feel like I'm honoring my dad and grandfather by making the inn shine." She hung her head. "I guess that sounds pretty stupid."

"Not stupid at all." LuAnn used her staunchest tone. This young woman needed bolstering. "I'm sure they'd be very proud of you. Not only for the good care you've given the inn, but for the good care you've given your mother."

"Not anymore, though. I hated leaving her in that home, but she insisted. She said she was holding me back from living my own life."

How many times had LuAnn's mother said the same thing to LuAnn? She squeezed Constance's knee. "Your mother loves you very much."

Finally, Constance lifted her head. "I love her too. After Christmas, I'm thinking about moving to Canton so I can find a job close to the home. That way I can visit her more often than I can now."

Janice clapped her hands together. "That's a wonderful idea. Say, would you like to have the pages in Prudence's diary that mention your ancestors?"

Constance's forehead pinched. "I don't know what diary you mean."

LuAnn explained about finding the century-plus-old diary written by a woman who helped slaves escape via the Underground Railroad. "Since she mentions your history, it only seems right that you should have the pages."

A smile quivered on Constance's lips. "Do you have it here? I'd like to see it."

Janice jumped up and retrieved the diary from the office. It took a little while to find the entries about the caretaker—Frederick Stanfill—and Constance fidgeted, clearly eager. At last Janice pulled the correct entry free and read it out loud. "I'll make a copy of it, and you can take it with you."

"Thank you." Constance beamed.

Something clicked in LuAnn's brain that hadn't the first time she'd heard the passage read aloud. "The light..." She took the page and stared at it. "Prudence presumed his reference to the light meant the light of heaven. But what if..."

Tess reached across Constance and tapped LuAnn's leg. "What if what?"

LuAnn stood, her fingertips tingling. "Oh my goodness, what if..." She began pacing. "Isaiah said the light fixture by the back door covered a hole. He thought it was a knothole. Which means the hole was there when that part of the inn was constructed. The drawings at the museum of the original, which show the now missing porch, also show that a lantern was mounted near the back door."

She stopped pacing and whirled around to face the women. "What if 'the light' was code for lantern? What if Frederick dropped it through the knothole? That could explain how the snuffbox ended up between the siding and the interior wall."

Tess jumped up. "There's something rattling around in the snuffbox. Could it be the treasure?"

Janice sat with her mouth hanging open. Constance tossed the afghan aside and stood too. "Wait… Knothole? Snuffbox? You aren't making any sense."

LuAnn laughed and put her arm around Constance. "I'm so sorry. When the electrician wired our new light by the back door, he had to remove a length of wood that had rotted from water damage. He found an antique snuffbox behind the wall. We intended to put it with the other items that are part of the inn's history, but if it was Frederick Stanfill's, it really ought to go to you."

If Constance's eyes widened any further, they'd pop from her head. "Have you opened it?"

"No. Something *is* clinking around inside of it, but the lid is crusted shut from years of dampness and dirt. I planned to take it to a jeweler after Christmas and have him open it, but maybe you should be the one to do that."

Constance sank down slowly and perched on the edge of the sofa. "Something that belonged to my great-great-great-grandfather. I can hardly believe it."

Tess sat beside Constance and bumped shoulders with her. "If it's a treasure box, it's holding an awfully small treasure."

Constance laughed. "I'm sure the treasure talk is family lore. I would like to know what's inside, though. Even if it's only petrified chewing tobacco."

LuAnn gave a decisive nod. "And you will find out. I'll get the box for you right now." She entered the office and opened the cabinet. Where was the snuffbox? Hadn't she put it with the pages of research? She searched every cupboard, but the metal box wasn't there.

Constance's happy laughter filtered from the sitting area. "This is so unbelievable. I never thought I'd actually have something that belonged to my ancestors."

LuAnn's heart sank. How would she tell Constance that Frederick Stanfill's heirloom was gone?

Even though they promised to find the snuffbox, Constance's disappointment was palpable and nearly broke LuAnn's heart. Tess closed the front door behind the housekeeper and turned a disbelieving stare on LuAnn and Tess. "This is getting ridiculous. That thing didn't sprout legs and walk away, so where did it go?"

LuAnn began collecting the empty mugs. "I'm sure I left it in the office cabinet."

"I'm sure you did too. You aren't exactly known for being careless." Tess folded the afghan and dropped it over the back of the couch. "Okay, let's think this through. Who knew the snuffbox was in the office?"

"Both of you. Me." LuAnn remembered something, and her shoulders slumped. "And Alice."

Tess's expression turned grim. "Alice again."

Janice looked from Tess to LuAnn. "But we keep the office locked. How would she get in there?"

"I can speculate." Tess folded her arms across her chest. "She's in the library a lot, so she could notice when we're using the office and when we step away from it. I'm guilty of leaving it unlocked when I leave to grab a cup of coffee or a snack or go to the ladies' room. She could have sneaked in when we weren't looking."

Janice nodded slowly. "So what do we know for sure about Alice Busby? Besides that she tends to be nosy, is always writing, and possibly wears a wig."

Her hands full, LuAnn headed for the kitchen. "Tess, grab my notebook from the office, and let's sit in the kitchen and think this all through." She left the mugs in the sink and joined Tess and Janice at the table. Tess had already opened the notebook, and LuAnn turned it so the writing was facing her. She put her finger at the beginning of the list. "All right, let's look at these. The first weird, thus far unexplained, happening is the mirror 'falling' from the wall. I wrote that Constance was the only person close by, but I honestly don't know where Alice was at that time."

"It's long enough ago, I don't remember either." Tess made a face. "As sneaky as she's proven herself to be, she could have been close by, and you might not have noticed."

LuAnn nodded and returned her attention to the list. "The missing diary and damaged water line have been explained away, but what about the sheets? Could she have taken and then replaced the sheets?"

Janice's mouth formed an *O*. She grabbed Tess's arm. "Didn't you say the replacement sheets were really expensive?"

Tess nodded.

"Well, Alice has done a lot of shopping while she's been here, and she paid for three weeks in advance without batting an eyelash. Doesn't it seem as though she'd have the means to buy two very expensive sheets?"

LuAnn circled the note about sheets and wrote *Alice?* above it. Another notation leaped out at her. "All the sand... We know for sure she dragged in sand at least once, because Constance talked about sweeping it from the floor in Alice's room. That makes me think she was probably the one who left it on the stairs to the basement too. After all, she knew how to get down there. I caught her coming up from the basement."

Janice rested her chin in her hand. "But what would she want down there?"

Tess raised one eyebrow. "I can't help but think she was looking for the tunnel exit. For what reason, I don't know, but finding the tunnel door would involve prowling around the riverbank *and* prowling around the basement."

LuAnn circled another note.

"And you know what else?" Tess's tone turned introspective. "Originally I pegged Marcus for sticking that recorder under the Christmas tree, but I'm shifting the blame to Alice.

All the snooping she's done, all the eavesdropping... Setting up the tape recorder so she could listen in when she isn't here fits. Plus, with her room right at the top of the stairs and the Christmas tree at the bottom, it wouldn't take much effort for her to take or leave the box the recorder was in."

LuAnn gazed at the list of notes and considered Tess's comments. Everything she'd said was reasonable, and LuAnn's logical side couldn't find an argument against any of it. Even so, some questions remained. "Why would she want to find the tunnel? Why would she shred and then replace a pair of sheets?"

Tess shrugged. "I don't know. But I think it's time to ask her those questions." She stood. "And there's no time like the present."

CHAPTER TWENTY-EIGHT

LuAnn, carrying her notebook, followed Janice and Tess up to the second-floor landing. Tess knocked on the door to the Honeymoon Suite, and the click of heels sounded against the wood floor. The door opened and revealed a petite woman with chin-length streaked-blonde hair.

Tess reared back. "Who are you?" Then she leaned forward, squinting. "Alice?"

The woman fluffed the flipped bottom of her bobbed hair and moved out onto the landing. "It's me."

Janice circled her the way a shark might circle its prey. "It *is* you."

LuAnn's mouth hung open, but she couldn't close it. Disbelief froze her frame. Alice stood before them completely transformed. No more messy bun. No wire-rimmed glasses on the end of her nose. No glasses at all. Trendy short boots replaced her sensible shoes, and she wore a crimson red tunic over patterned leggings in lieu of a granny dress.

Alice smiled and gestured to the pile of suitcases and shopping bags inside the door. "I was just getting ready to call for a cab. I'm taking the red-eye to Indianapolis. My project is finished, so it's time for me to go home."

"You…We…" Tess sputtered like a rusty engine. She shook her head. "Before you go, we need to talk."

A wary look flitted across Alice's face. "Oh?"

LuAnn finally found her voice. "Yes. Let's go the parlor."

Alice led the way and seated herself in one of the over-stuffed chairs. LuAnn, Tess, and Janice sat in a row on the sofa. A hysterical laugh built in LuAnn's throat. If Brad took their picture now, he'd probably think he was photographing an inquisition.

Alice crossed her legs and linked her fingers on her knees. "Now, what can I do for you?"

LuAnn looked at the list in her notebook, ready to address each issue, but Tess spoke first.

"Are you really a novelist?"

Alice chuckled. "I might have misled you a bit on that."

"Misled?" Tess raised her brows. "Isn't that another word for lied?"

The woman offered a cavalier shrug. "Perhaps a little white lie. I am a writer, but I write for an exclusive travel magazine. Maybe you've seen my name—Allison Busfield?"

Janice clapped her palms to her cheeks. "Oh, my goodness…the reviewer for *Traversing America*?"

Alice—or Allison—held her hands in a gesture of *you got me*. "Every year, we choose one new, unique destination spot and highlight it in our winter edition. I've been gathering information to feature Wayfarers Inn."

LuAnn exchanged startled glances with Tess and Janice. She aimed her puzzled frown at Allison. "Why didn't you come out and say so? We would have told you anything you wanted to know, and you wouldn't have needed to stay for almost a month."

Allison smiled a sly smile. "Oh, but I didn't want to write only about the structure. The curator at the Marietta Underground Railroad Museum could have told me its complete history. I wanted potential visitors to know who would see to their needs while they were here." She sighed, shaking her head as if suddenly sorrowful. "Some inns are lovely places with extravagant accommodations, but the owners leave the business in the hands of managers who have no real emotional attachment to the property. Other owners are active in the operation but give the impression that their guests are an imposition rather than truly welcomed there."

She sat back and draped her hands over the chair's armrests. "I've spent a good portion of the past weeks observing your interactions with guests of all varieties, and I have to say, you've impressed me. I'm sure there were times you wanted to boot me out the door because I was in places I wasn't supposed to go."

LuAnn tilted her head, pen poised. "Like the basement?"

Allison's eyes twinkled. "Yes, LuAnn. Yet you were always gracious and kind. To my delight, I discovered you were even gracious and kind when no one was looking."

Tess inhaled so sharply LuAnn marveled that she didn't swallow her tonsils. "So you did plant the bug."

Allison's red-painted lips twitched into an impish grin. "I did. I'm sorry, but it was the only way I could determine that your treatment of guests was genuine. Believe me, I've encountered some very good actors and actresses—smiling and kind to your face and then speaking disparagingly when they think you're not around."

Allison Busfield was a good actress too. She'd played the role of an eccentric, snoopy wannabe writer to perfection.

A warm smile ignited the woman's eyes. "Ladies, the kind treatment and attention you offer your guests is exactly what our readers are seeking. They want a true getaway spot where they can relax, be pampered, be treated like…well, like family."

Tess leaned forward and rested her elbows on her knees. "There's something I don't understand, though. What were you doing in the basement?"

"I wanted to confirm a few things for myself." Allison waved her hand the way someone shooed away a fly. "I found a short blurb about the building's involvement with the Underground Railroad, which stirred my intrigue, but there are hundreds of places with subtle connections to various historical happenings—interesting but impersonal. I wanted to stand in the same hidden rooms where runaway slaves took a brief respite. This structure sheltered countless weary travelers longing for a place of peace."

She heaved a regret-laden sigh. "I could never find the tunnel from the river, though. I went out at least three times. The fact that it's well hidden is probably a safeguard for you, but how I would have liked to have seen the underground pathway the slaves traversed." Fervency colored her tone. "This building is not only a stopping point, it's a crucial part of many souls' journey to freedom. It deserves more recognition than a tiny plaque and a brief mention.

"Additionally, you"—she pointed to each of them by turn—"are continuing that tradition. You've opened your doors and your hearts to visitors. You offer them a few days of restoration and renewal. My article will include every bit of what I've uncovered about the inn itself *and* my personal experiences as a guest. Believe me, it is all complimentary, and I truly hope it will encourage others to come experience the inn's history and welcome for themselves."

Janice wheezed out, "Wow."

Tess released a wry laugh. "I don't know whether to thank you or throttle you."

The woman laughed, a merry sound that invited LuAnn to smile even though she'd been completely hoodwinked. "Hold that thought until I've divulged everything."

Janice yelped, "There's more?"

"Yes, indeed. I'm guilty of destroying your sheets. I hope the replacements I ordered were acceptable."

LuAnn made a checkmark in her notebook. "They're *better* than acceptable."

Tess scratched her head. "What compelled you to turn sheets into a rope?"

"It was all part of my research." Allison sat up and spoke animatedly. "When I was reading about the inn's history, I came upon a short article from the early 1900s. A guest who was being sought by law enforcement escaped out the third-floor window and made his way to the river, where he hid on a paddleboat before he was ultimately discovered and turned over to authorities."

She raised one eyebrow. "I'm afraid I sometimes get too involved in my research, and I couldn't resist exploring a means to make it from the window to the ground without breaking one's neck. In case you ever need an escape, two sheets torn into thirds and knotted securely into a rope are just long enough to allow someone to scale the rope and drop safely to the ground." She laughed. "Of course, I didn't try it myself. Even I won't go that far for the sake of research, but the young man who comes to the inn every day offered to climb down it for me."

Tess nudged LuAnn and muttered, "Marcus."

"The sheets aren't the only thing I ruined." Allison looked down at her lap. "Very early in my stay, I tried to borrow a mirror from another room. I wanted a mirror in front and behind in order to see the back of my head." Her eyes widened. "You wouldn't believe how difficult it is to hide a full head of hair under a wig cap." She shrugged. "Unfortunately, it was much heavier than I anticipated, and I dropped it."

LuAnn gazed at her in astonishment. "Brad and I ran upstairs as soon as we heard the crash, and I didn't see you anywhere. Where were you?"

She chuckled. "When you and Mr. Grimes were in the room, I was hiding in the closet. Since then, I've taken taxi rides all over the county, visiting antique stores in search of a comparable replacement. I finally resorted to an online search and located one in Indiana that should look very lovely on the wall. It will be delivered shortly after Christmas."

A grin twitched on Tess's mouth. "You really are sneaky."

"Sneakier than you know." Suddenly her expression turned sheepish. "The snuffbox…"

LuAnn held her breath.

"I took it."

She let the air escape. She made another checkmark. So far, they'd aimed their suspicions in the right direction.

"It's at a local jeweler. I intended to surprise you by mounting both the snuffbox and its contents—whatever they may be—in a shadow box, as you've talked of doing, for your wall. I'm sure operating Wayfarers takes a significant amount of money, and I wanted to not only relieve you of that expense but also have a small part in contributing to the history of the place."

Tess chuckled. "I've decided. I'd rather hug you than throttle you."

Allison burst out laughing. She stood and opened her arms wide. Tess hugged her, then LuAnn and Janice each gave her a hug. The writer slipped her arms around LuAnn's and Janice's waists, and Tess completed the circle.

Allison's eyes glistened with tears. "I hope you'll forgive me. In order to get a true depiction, a lengthy stay was necessary, and I didn't dare divulge my real reason for being here if I wanted to witness your genuine character." She paused and met each woman's gaze by turn, smiling warmly. "I must say, you ladies have impressed me with your kinship and your kindness. You have something very special."

CHAPTER TWENTY-NINE

After waving goodbye to Allison Busfield, the Inn Crowd ladies returned to the parlor. Although it was after ten o'clock, they were too wired to sleep. LuAnn flipped her notebook open and scanned down the list she'd made.

"Well, it looks like we've pretty much wrapped everything up, with the exception of who left the basement door open and who was prowling around in the kitchen in the wee hours of the morning."

"And who keeps leaving dog biscuits in Tess's apron pocket," Janice said. "Don't forget the dog biscuits."

LuAnn grinned. "I won't."

Tess pursed her face into a comical scowl. "Neither will I."

LuAnn hadn't divulged Winnie's secret, but she didn't think she'd need to. Tess's comment about not allowing herself to love Huck let her know Tess held no real animosity toward the little dog. She only wanted to protect herself from getting hurt when Huck finally went to his real home. LuAnn completely understood Tess's concern, but it was too late for her to protect herself. She already loved Huck and "his" kitten.

Janice sighed and flopped back onto the sofa. "Do you think it would upset anyone if we put up a sign tomorrow about closing the café on Christmas Eve day? Of course, we'll need to feed our inn guests breakfast, but LuAnn could easily cover that."

"I think that's a good idea." Tess wriggled into the cushions on the opposite end of the sofa. "If we won't have the café open, will we really need Constance and Winnie to come in? How about we call them tomorrow after church and give them an extra day off?"

LuAnn held up one hand. "All in favor, say 'aye.'"

"Aye," they chorused.

Tess closed her eyes, a smile playing on the corners of her lips. "That was really nice of Allison to take the snuffbox to the jeweler. I hope he's able to open it without damaging it." She opened one eye and peered at LuAnn.

Tess whistled. "Wouldn't it be something if the snuffbox really was hidden by Frederick Stanfill and there was a treasure still inside it? Of course, we'll need to contact the jeweler soon. The snuffbox is Constance's, and she'll need to make the decision about what to do with the treasure, if there really is one."

LuAnn smiled, considering Constance's reaction. "It would be amazing."

"Amazing for Constance," Janice said, her voice sad, "but not so much for her great-great-great-grandmother. I bet she could have used those coins after her husband died."

"That's true." LuAnn sat up. "I wonder what happened to her. Is there anything else in the diary about her?"

Janice bounced up as if she'd just enjoyed a lengthy nap. "It wouldn't hurt to look. Now I'm curious too." She retrieved

LuAnn's copy, and the three of them scanned pages. Suddenly Janice exclaimed, "Ta-da!"

Tess peeked at the page. "What did you find?"

"Listen." Janice held the paper at arm's length. "'April 6, 1857. My heart nearly broke to tell my dear friend and her wee son goodbye. The new owner of the Riverfront House does not have need of her assistance, so she and little Reggie will go to her mother's home in Steubenville until she can find a job to support her son. We hugged long and with many tears at the riverboat dock, and I told her how sorry I was that she had not found the dowry from her father. She was sorry as well, but then she said something that humbled me: 'I do not have my dowry, but I have something of greater value that can never be lost or taken away. My heavenly Father goes with me wherever I go. He will not forsake me, and I will, as the Apostle Paul proclaimed, be content with what I have.' I pray I will always hold tight to faith and contentment the way my dear friend Elswyth did on this sorrowful day.'"

Janice put the page back in the stack. "'My heavenly Father goes with me...'"

"'I pray I will always hold tight to faith and contentment.'" LuAnn swallowed the lump that filled her throat. "What a wonderful prayer for all of us."

Christmas Eve morning, as Janice and Tess served baked french toast stuffed with cream cheese and topped with strawberry sauce to their guests, and LuAnn ran a sink of hot, sudsy water, a key turned the lock in the back door. To LuAnn's surprise, Winnie entered the kitchen, and Marcus slunk in on her heels.

LuAnn dried her hands and gave Winnie a puzzled look. "We gave you the day off, remember?"

"I'm not here to work." Winnie aimed an imperious finger at the kitchen table. "Sit."

Marcus sat. LuAnn almost did.

Winnie yanked off her coat and slapped it on the hall tree. "Are folks still eating?"

LuAnn nodded. "Yes. The first group is already done, but the second group came down about fifteen minutes ago. It could be a while." She glanced at Marcus, who hunkered into his jacket the way a turtle hunkered into its shell. She lowered her voice to a whisper. "Is everything okay?"

"Nope." Winnie didn't bother lowering her voice. She pulled out a chair, sat, and folded her arms over her chest.

Winnie's silent fury made LuAnn's stomach quiver. The woman was never shy about speaking her mind, so something terrible must have happened to clam her up. LuAnn touched her shoulder. "Would you like a cup of coffee or—"

"Don't need a thing. See to your duties, Miss Lu. We'll talk later."

LuAnn rinsed the early group's dishes and then stacked them in the industrial dishwasher's tray. While she worked, she sent surreptitious glances to the pair at the table. Even when Tess or Janice came in, Winnie kept her lips pursed tight. Marcus wouldn't look at anyone. By the time the last group of guests finished eating and exited the dining room, LuAnn's nerves were as taut as the strings on a new violin.

Tess and Janice entered the kitchen the way children might enter the principal's office. They paused beside the table, and Tess cleared her throat. "I want to tell you 'Merry Christmas,' but I'm afraid it might not end up merry."

Winnie sighed, and the stern lines around her mouth relaxed. She patted the chair next to her. "Miss Tess, Janice, LuAnn—sit, please. We've got some talking to do."

Tess took the chair next to Winnie, Janice sat the end of the table, and LuAnn sat across from Marcus.

Winnie poked her grandson on the shoulder. "All right. It's time. Talk."

Marcus's dark, resentful gaze roved around the table.

Winnie poked him again. "Sit up like a decent person and talk."

Marcus straightened. His face angled toward the pantry, he clamped his jaw so tightly the muscles quivered.

"Marcus Everett Washington, speak."

LuAnn cringed. Winnie would make a good drill sergeant.

Marcus swiveled on his chair, but he aimed his gaze somewhere beyond the Inn Crowd rather than meeting their gazes. "Grandma wants me to apologize for using the key she gave me and coming in without you knowing I was here. She says I was trespassing. But all I was doing was looking out for her."

LuAnn rested her folded hands on the table. The years rolled back, and she might have been sitting across the desk from one of her rebellious students. "Why are you worried about her, Marcus?"

He looked at her out of the corners of his eyes. "Lots of reasons. She's got high blood pressure, and she's starting to get arthritis in her spine. But she gets up two hours before the sun and comes over here and cooks and cleans up. You all expect too much from her—I heard her say it herself."

Winnie squawked, "What? When did I say that?"

"A couple weeks ago. You were right there at the stove and I heard you say you felt chained to the kitchen." He scowled at the Inn Crowd. "You're taking advantage of her."

Winnie huffed. "That's nonsense. I wanted to help here. You know how much I like cooking and baking. I've cooked and baked for others for years all by myself. Here I've got plenty of help, and—" She jerked as if something poked her with a tack. Her eyes narrowed to slits. "I don't recall you being here when I made that comment. How'd you hear me?"

Marcus stared at the pantry door again.

Winnie nudged him. "I want an answer."

He mumbled, "I peeked in on you."

"You *peeked in* on me?" Winnie's voice boomed.

"Yes, ma'am." He whirled to face her. "Two or three times a week, early, before I went to school, or on my lunch period, or between school and my job. And, Grandma, every time I peeked in on you, your face was all sweaty, and you were doing most of the work while the others just filled plates and carried them out."

Winnie shot a dumbfounded look at LuAnn, Tess, and Janice. LuAnn had no idea what to say. Apparently neither did

Tess or Janice, because they sat in silence too. Winnie turned to Marcus. "Just how were you able to *peek in* on me?"

"I took your keys and made a copy of the one to the back door so I wouldn't disturb anybody."

"You mean so you wouldn't get caught."

Marcus's jaw jutted. "That too."

Winnie flipped her hands and sent a look around the table that said *What am I supposed to do with this boy?*

LuAnn had an idea. "Marcus, as long as folks are apologizing, we"—she gestured to Tess and Janice—"need to tell you we're sorry."

Winnie's eyebrows rose, but Marcus's pinched low. They said in unison, "Why?"

"For a while, we thought you might be doing bad things around here."

"Like what?" Again, they spoke in tandem.

Tess covered her mouth with her hand, clearly hiding a smile, and Janice ran her finger over the embroidered letters on her apron, as absorbed as if she'd never seen them before. LuAnn didn't dare make eye contact with either of them, or she'd dissolve into laughter. "Well, for cutting a water line under the sink in the men's bathroom."

Janice nodded. "Dragging sand all over the basement."

Tess lowered her hand. "Planting a bug under the Christmas tree."

Identical expressions of shock formed on grandmother's and grandson's faces. Marcus shook his head. "All I did was come in from time to time and check on Grandma. I didn't do any of that other stuff."

"I know." LuAnn reached across the table and placed her hand over the young man's wrist. "We made assumptions about you. Those assumptions were wrong. You've made assumptions about us too. Could you be wrong?"

Marcus puckered his lips and didn't answer.

Winnie turned to face Marcus. "You bag groceries and stock shelves at the grocery store. How would you feel if I came to your work and spied on you?"

Marcus shrugged. "I probably wouldn't like it."

"Then maybe you ought to think about that 'doing unto others' I taught you when you were a little boy. It applies to adults too, you know."

"I know."

"And you can bet we'll be talking about this more when you take me home."

"I know."

Winnie dug in her pocket and pulled out a key, which she slapped onto the table. "That's the extra key I made so Marcus could get in the loading dock door without pestering us." She held out her hand to Marcus, and he pulled a key from his jeans pocket. "And here's the key he made. From now on he'll just have to pester us, because he's lost his coming-and-going privileges."

LuAnn looked from the keys to Marcus. With his head low and his shoulders slumped in defeat, he looked half his age. Sympathy stirred in her chest. She said softly, "Marcus? I asked you why you were looking in on your grandmother, and you gave me some medical reasons. But I think there's a deeper reason why you don't want her to work too hard. Am I right?"

He nodded, the movement stiff.

"What is the reason?"

He glanced at Winnie, glanced at LuAnn, and lowered his gaze again. "She's my grandma. I love her."

Without pause, LuAnn said, "She's our dear friend. We love her too. And, Marcus?" She waited until he raised his head. "I promise we won't take advantage of her, okay?"

"Yeah. Okay."

Tess pointed at him. "And you need to promise to quit with the dog biscuits."

Marcus sat straight up. "But why? Huck really likes those things." Suddenly his expression turned sheepish. "I found him in the alley behind the grocery store, and I used the biscuits to get him here. I hoped Grandma would find him and decide to keep him. Then she'd have to stay home more to take care of him."

Tess shook her head. "I'm sorry your plan failed, and if you want to give him a treat now and then, fine, but he doesn't need to eat them out of my apron pockets."

He gawked at Tess. "Huh?"

Winnie sucked in her lips. LuAnn stood. "Tess, I think Marcus has had enough scolding for one day. Let's let him off the hook now, okay?" She and Winnie locked gazes, and LuAnn winked.

CHAPTER THIRTY

Tess and Janice left after lunch to have some time with their families. LuAnn took a book to her room and propped herself against a stack of pillows. Tom curled on her lap, and Huck lay at her feet. She'd barely opened the book when her cell phone rang. Brad's number showed on the screen. She set the book aside and answered. "Hello, Brad. Merry Christmas."

"Merry Christmas to you. Are you busy?"

"Just sitting here with Tom and Huck, enjoying the quiet."

"Do you mind a little noise?"

"What did you have in mind?"

"Aunt Thelma and Aunt Irene would like to drop by some information they've collected about Howard Bickerton. The real Howard—the one who bought the inn from Constance's ancestors."

LuAnn gently dislodged Tom from her lap and stood up. "I'd love to see it."

"Good. I'll bring the prints I made for you too. We should be there in less than five minutes."

"Sounds fine." They disconnected the call, and LuAnn hurriedly brushed her hair, applied a bit of blush and a slash of peach-colored lipstick, and added another coat of mascara to her eyelashes. Huck accompanied her down the stairs, and they reached the main level as the bell above the door announced her visitors' arrival. Brad ushered his elderly aunts over the threshold, and LuAnn greeted Thelma and Irene with hugs. "It's so good to see you. Merry Christmas!"

The pair wished her a merry Christmas in return, then Irene shoved a large envelope at her. "Here. For your history wall."

Thelma *tsk-tsk*ed. "Goodness, Irene, you could be more genteel about it."

LuAnn laughed. "Let's sit down, and I'll look at it." They sat around the coffee table in the parlor, and LuAnn tipped the envelope. Several printed pages as well as a half-dozen large black-and-white photographs spilled out. "Did you bring me a selection?"

Thelma's bright eyes danced. "Brad's been scouring the museum archives and internet sites for pictures connected to the inn for as far back as the records go. He printed all those."

Brad waved his hand as if shooing away Thelma's comments. "Now, you make it sound like I've gone on a scavenger hunt. It wasn't that much work."

"Mm-hmm." Thelma exchanged a knowing look with her sister. "Anyway, use what you want of those, but if you don't want them, you won't hurt our feelings."

LuAnn fanned them across the table. "I'm sure I'll use all of them. Thank you, all of you."

"You're welcome." Brad reached inside his jacket and removed a smaller envelope. "Here are the pictures I took of you, Janice, and Tess. I'll let you ladies decide which one you like best, and that's the one we'll put on the Chamber website."

She took the envelope. "Thanks. I'll wait to open this till Tess and Janice are here. Then we can look at them together."

"That seems fair." Brad clapped his hands on his knees. "Well, we have other stops to make—I think these two have presents for everyone in town."

LuAnn jumped up. "I have presents for you too. Let me get them." She retrieved the gifts from the office and handed them out.

Thelma and Irene were thrilled with their certificates, and Brad seemed awed by the book. Seeing their delight lifted LuAnn's heart, and the joyous feeling carried her through the remainder of the afternoon.

When Tess and Janice returned, she told them about the pictures Brad had delivered.

Tess held out her hand. "Let's see them."

LuAnn spilled the images on the parlor table alongside the ones Thelma had brought. The three of them examined all of the pictures, and Janice bumped LuAnn lightly with her elbow, a grin rounding her cheeks.

"This is such a good idea, Lu, including each of the families who've invested a part of themselves into this wonderful old building."

LuAnn considered Janice's comment. One phrase echoed in her mind. *Each of the families...* Tears stung her eyes, and she sniffled hard. She picked up one of the photographs that Brad took of her, Tess, and Janice on the stairs beside the towering

Christmas tree, their smiling faces aglow. A traditional family? No. But family all the same. They were her sisters of the heart. Her gift from God to ease her ache of loneliness.

She placed the photo on top of the others and held her arms wide. "Group hug!"

Tess rolled her eyes, Janice laughed, but both surged in and grabbed hold. They hugged, rocking slightly, and LuAnn let the tears roll down her cheeks.

Janice pulled back slightly, alarm on her face. "Are you all right, Lu?"

LuAnn smiled through her tears. "I'm more than all right. I'm...perfectly content." *Thank You, Lord.*

Dear Reader,

Thank you for spending a little more time in Marietta at Wayfarers Inn. It was a pleasure to write a story centered on Christmas, my favorite time of the year. I found particular joy in giving LuAnn the Christmas ornaments that have long graced my family's Christmas tree—bubble lights, reflector globes, and handblown Santas. But I think my favorite part of this story was the introduction of Huck and Tom, the scruffy little dog and "his" kitten.

I could easily imagine the friendship between Huck and Tom, because we had a dog and cat who were best buddies. Our Dachshund Meine Kleine Schnitzel, nicknamed Meinie, "adopted" a timid ball of fluff that grew into the most beautiful cat. Every day Meinie and her kitten, Isabella, dozed together in patches of sunlight, took turns playing fetch with terrycloth ponytail holders, and washed each other's ears. The pair were so close that when Meinie had a stroke and died in January of 2008, Isabella mourned so deeply that she also passed away later that year.

I really think friendship is one of our most precious gifts. Proverbs 17:17 says, "A friend loveth at all times." We saw the reality of the scripture played out with Tess and Janice supporting LuAnn through her first Christmas without her mother and in a variety of other relationships in the story.

Each of us needs a friend who loves us at all times, and we can all find one in Jesus, who is the Friend who never leaves us or forsakes us.

May God bless you as you journey with Him!
Kim Vogel Sawyer

ABOUT THE AUTHOR

In 1966 Kim Vogel Sawyer told her kindergarten teacher that someday people would check out her book in libraries. That little-girl dream came true in 2006 with the release of *Waiting for Summer's Return*. Since then, Kim has watched God expand her dream beyond her childhood imaginings. With almost fifty titles on library shelves and more than 1.5 million copies of her books in print worldwide, she enjoys a full-time writing and speaking ministry. Empty-nesters, Kim and her retired military husband, Don, live in small-town Kansas, the setting for many of Kim's novels. When she isn't writing, Kim stays active serving in her church's women's and music ministries, traveling with "The Hubs," and spoiling her quiverful of granddarlings. You can learn more about Kim's writing at KimVogelSawyer.com.

CHRISTMAS IN MARIETTA

The first Christmas in Marietta featured a two-for-one deal. The settlers celebrated both Thanksgiving and Christmas on December 25, 1788.

In 1788, Marietta was a brand-new settlement, the first in the Northwest Territory of the United States, which was the first territory outside the original thirteen colonies. The town was a fortified community elegantly named Campus Martius (Latin, meaning "Field of Mars"). The New England settlers in Marietta were probably not used to celebrating Christmas. Their Puritan ancestors had actually banned Christmas celebrations in 1659, because they believed that Christmas, in practice, was more drunken revelry than pious observance. Christmas had been reinstated but was still only loosely observed by New Englanders in the late 1700s.

A proclamation dated December 17, 1788, was issued by His Excellency Arthur St. Clair, Esquire, Governor and Commander in Chief, stating that "For as much as it is incumbent on all men to acknowledge with gratitude their infinite obligations to Almighty God for benefits received...do hereby ordain that Thursday the 25th of December be observed as a day of solemn Thanksgiving and Praise..., and I do prohibit all servile labor on that day."

On Christmas/Thanksgiving morning, a three-gun salute from Fort Harmar, answered by a three-shot cannon blast from Campus Martius, gave the day a rousing start. All residents attended a community church service, during which Judge Parsons gave a sermon from the second verse of Psalm 103.

One of Marietta's citizens, Dr. Drown, wrote about the day in a letter to his family in Providence: "It being Christmas, public worship was introduced by reading...in the Church Prayer Book. Gen'l Parsons read a sermon adapted to the occasion. Good singing. I dined at General Goodale's and as this is such a new country, perhaps you will like to know our bill of fare. A boiled dish, Turkey, beef and bacon, cabbage, turnips and potatoes, butter, etc., A roast turkey 17 pounds. A turkey pie, custards, wheat bread, etc." Surely no one left the table hungry!

Today in Marietta, Christmas celebrations begin with a parade the day after Thanksgiving. Shop owners in the historic city district offer special deals to shoppers and give tours of the loft levels of the buildings. Of course Santa Claus and his elves make a visit, and church bells toll to welcome the Christ Child. I'm relatively certain LuAnn, Tess, and Janice participated in the community celebrations for their first Christmas in Wayfarers Inn, and no one left the table hungry.

SOMETHING DELICIOUS FROM OUR WAYFARERS INN FRIENDS

Wayfarers Inn Buttermilk Pie

Ingredients:

½ cup butter, melted

1½ cups sugar

3 eggs, beaten

1–2 teaspoons vanilla

3 tablespoons flour

pinch of salt

1 teaspoon cinnamon or
nutmeg, if desired

1 cup buttermilk

1 deep dish pie shell (your
own recipe or store bought)

Directions:

Preheat oven to 400°F. Beat butter and sugar together until fluffy. Add eggs and beat until well blended. Beat in vanilla. Set aside. In a separate bowl, sift the dry ingredients together and add to batter alternately with the buttermilk. Beat until smooth. Pour into unbaked pie shell and bake at 400°F for 10 minutes; reduce heat to 350°F for 50–60 minutes until filling is a golden brown and a knife inserted in the center comes out clean.

Allow pie to cool to room temperature before cutting. Store in refrigerator.

Read on for a sneak peek of another exciting book
in the Secrets of Wayfarers Inn series!

At Face Value
by Ocieanna Fleiss

Thee, Lord, is a God of justice. I know this, but my eyes see the weak suffering at the hands of the mighty. I see scars on backs and in hearts, families shattered, hope overthrown by hopelessness. Lord, how long? Will Thee ever free the slaves, Thy children? Set the captives free, please, Heavenly Father, and help me to serve Thee faithfully.

—Prudence Willard, Marietta Ohio, January 1, 1863

Marietta, Ohio
January 21, 1863

Pastel rays filtered through gaps in the meager barn's aging slats like the new year breaking through ruins of the old. Prudence Willard, solitary in her morning chores, tossed feed to her goose, Patience. "Be glad thee is suited for the cold, miss!" Even beneath her knitted gloves, Prudence's hands were nearly numb. "'Tis my duty to rise with the sun and feed thee, God's creature, and I do not mind the task." She threw down another handful of corn. "I mind it less when freezing cold does not beset my feet when they touch the floor."

The white-feathered goose tilted her head questioningly, and guilt dusted Prudence's conscience. "Forgive me," she said with a simple bow. Patience recommenced eating, so Prudence believed she was forgiven.

Softly humming her favorite hymn as she worked, her mind wandered. What would this new year hold? Opportunities to help free more lost souls from the shackles of slavery? She hoped so, but her deepest desire echoed that of every abolitionist—an end to the despicable practice altogether. How hard she prayed, how forcefully abolitionists pressed President Lincoln and the Congress. Those efforts, as well as the profound influence of *Uncle Tom's Cabin,* did thankfully contribute to the commencement of this war to free the slaves. When the war began, she thought slavery's end would be forthcoming. It had been almost two years since the battle at Fort Sumter thrust brother against brother. Yet still the weak suffered. Still injustice reigned.

A bald eagle's call floated to her, jarring her from her thoughts. *Come now, enough of this pondering.* The goose nipped at her, seeming to be more eager for breakfast than normal. "Have patience, Patience." She shook out the last bit of corn.

Her goose's antics made her smile, and Prudence peered out the open door at the snow-blanketed fields, glowing a peachy gold as they reflected the Creator's magnificent sun-rise. She let her gaze follow the gentle descent to the river—frozen solid. Maybe she and Jason would take Moses to play on the ice later. Laughter would do them good.

Charity, her horse, whinnied loudly.

"My!" Prudence responded. "Thee is pushy this morn—"

But something stopped her words, and she spotted what was spooking her animals. She gasped.

A woman lay motionless in the hay of Charity's stall. Scenarios hastened to Prudence's mind. Had this stranger heard this was an Underground Railroad stop? Or was she simply seeking shelter from the cold?

"Dear Father, help me!"

Prudence knelt next to her. The woman appeared frozen… gone. Was she?

Curled up in a ball in the corner, her head rested against the wall and her knees faced inward. Her hair had frosted over, her eyebrows too, making them white, like an old woman's.

Prudence laid a gentle hand on the woman's shoulder, covered only with a thin coat. The freezing traveler didn't move, so Prudence traced her arm down to her youthful hand. She was no old woman.

And then another shock.

A wedding ring. Obviously forged from a rough metal, likely pounded into shape with a hammer.

Someone loved this precious one. She pictured her and her sweetheart jumping the broom in the back of their mas-ter's barn, rejoicing in love even in the midst of hate.

Prudence twisted her head to glance outside. "Where is thy husband?"

Not seeing anything, she focused back on the woman, who still hadn't moved.

Then, adjusting her arm, she spied her middle. She gasped again. "Do not let this dear sister and her baby be gone," she pleaded.

As an answer to her prayer, the woman moaned, then slightly opened fearful eyes.

"Child, thee is going to be all right. Thee and thy little one."

The woman managed to nod, and her ebony-eyed gaze searched Prudence's. A silent moment lingered, and Prudence's own past pregnancy invaded her thoughts—the first one. Her sweet Hope, whom she held for but moments before the breath of life slowly stopped and the Shepherd took the little one in His arms. That couldn't happen to this dear soul. In a rush, she stood.

"Stay here. I'll be right back. The Lord is with thee."

But as Prudence raced to the house to fetch Jason for help, an unwelcome thought snagged her. She banished it. Who was she to question God's ways?

Could this afternoon be any more glorious? Tess Wallace basked in the crisp, winter air as her ice skate blade scraped across the frozen river. "Listen up, legs," she peeked at them, covered in faux fur-lined leggings, "you remember how to do this, right?" She inhaled, relishing the faint smokiness coming from her neighbors' fireplaces. "I need this distraction today," she whispered.

"Here we go!" With a nervous chuckle, she pushed forward. There was no stopping now. Then she quickly twisted around, landed, and continued skating. "Backwards skate! I knew I could still do it." Her feet transported her in reverse across the ice, one skate after the other. Feeling the smile shining on her face, she peered up at the sparkling blue sky.

To her surprise, cheers sounded from the dock. LuAnn Sherrill and Janice Eastman, who were not only her dearest friends, but also business partners, carefully paced toward the edge, their ice skates draped over their shoulders. Above, up the incline from the riverbank, their inn seemed to smile down on them.

"There you are!" Tess hailed as she glided nearer, still backwards. "I didn't know you were watching me." She swooshed to a stop, her blades spraying ice chips.

"You are amazing." Janice's bright eyes gleamed. "I'm impressed."

Tess shrugged. "I didn't know if I'd even be able to find my balance."

LuAnn pulled her hat down over her ears. "You're really making us do this?" A strand of silver hair fluttered into her eyes. She tucked it back into the hat, shaking her head in mock reproach.

"Aw, come on," Tess cajoled. "The Ohio River only freezes once in a blue moon—we have to try, plus, your body will remember what to do. Muscle memory—that's what the experts call it. It's true. I read about it on the Internet." She grinned mischievously. "It worked for me. Even backwards."

"You really want me to do this?" With an exaggerated sigh, LuAnn plopped down on the edge of the dock, then yowled. "It's cold!"

Janice tightened her coat and perched next to LuAnn. "Whoo! That is cold."

"No time to fret over cold backsides," Tess said. "Hurry and get those skates laced up."

"Okay. I'll give it a try." LuAnn carefully hopped down onto the ice. "You coming, Janice?"

"I will...but I want to admit something first."

LuAnn pushed off to join Tess, and they studied Janice like moms waiting for a child's confession.

"Let's hear it," Tess said.

"I've never skated before!"

"What?" both Tess and LuAnn blurted.

"Don't judge!" Janice pleaded.

Tess joined them. "How is that possible? Never mind, we'll help you." She gripped Janice's left arm while LuAnn clutched the other, then, with a little yelp, Janice hopped down.

Janice's broad smile warmed Tess's heart. She was grateful for a distraction today. Her friends refreshed her spirit.

"I always made an excuse to stay home when the kids went skating," Janice continued. "Cooked soup, made hot chocolate, cookies—for the skaters when they returned." She sighed. "But truth be told, I was just too flat-out scared to try and learn."

"Well, this is a brave new day for you, my friend," LuAnn exclaimed. "And this is one more fear we are here to help you conquer."

One step at a time, Tess and LuAnn taught their friend to glide over the ice.

"I should've known this was so much fun...and nothing to be afraid of. This time the treats will have to be provided by Winnie and her new kitchen help. She's a welcome addition, since Taylor's still gone and Constance moved to Canton." Janice's blade etched a steady line in the ice. "Kylie seems like a sweet girl."

Tess gently lifted Janice's arm from hers. "Do you want to try on your own?"

LuAnn tilted her head. "I bet you can."

Without an answer, Janice sailed across the ice as if she'd been skating for years. "I'm doing it!"

Tess and LuAnn eyed each other.

"I would say so!" Tess sped up to reach her.

LuAnn, still a little wobbly, grabbed Tess's arm. "I'm not so sure."

A frown shaded Janice's face. "You're not sure about what?"

"I mean about the new kitchen help."

"Oh. Phew."

"That girl…I don't mean to be unkind," LuAnn said. "But…"

Tess chuckled. "You are so nice, Lu. I know where you're going with this. She's not the, uh, brightest bulb, is she?"

"Well." LuAnn eased closer to Tess and Janice, and they fell in sync with each other as they made their way along the river. "Let's just say this morning I caught her putting sugar in the salt shakers."

"Oh no!" Tess came to a stop, chuckling.

Janice bumped into her. Almost losing her balance, she grabbed Tess's coat. "Sorry!" She nearly rolled over Tess's back, then managed to straighten. "I don't know how to stop yet."

They recovered, then strode forward.

After a few strides, Janice lowered her head and peered over her glasses at the two others. "Kylie will get there. She just needs some more time."

"Of course." Tess slid ahead, then returned. "I was just imagining our guests salting their soup with sugar."

"Yeah, me too." LuAnn chuckled softly.

"Skating is so fun. I never knew!"

"It really is." LuAnn slid the opposite direction. "We should advertise skating as one of the inn's excursions this year."

Tess leapt at the idea. "Yes! We could rent skates and blankets."

"And offer thermoses of hot chocolate!" Janice added.

"Let's do it!" Tess slid away from the others. "I do love skating." The thought triggered a pang, but she dismissed it and sped ahead. "Watch this!" She increased her speed. "Jeffrey taught me."

As Jeffrey's name slipped past her lips, memories flooded her thoughts, flashes of skating adventures with him. She couldn't halt them.

On their first date, forty years ago, he'd taught her how to skate. She'd fallen so many times he held her hands like the Olympic couple skaters, just to steady her. Well, not only for that reason. Even from that first date, she'd felt comfortable with him, relished his touch. She basked in the comfort she'd felt with his arms around her, guiding her, like he always did.

Then another memory came. A year after that first date, he took her skating again. As she slid to him, he faltered, lost his balance, and fell. She couldn't believe he'd fallen. But she soon realized it had been no accident. With those blue eyes drenched in love, he took one knee and produced a box. As he opened it, Tess gasped at the diamond's sparkles. "Yes." Of course she'd said yes.

These memories lasted for mere moments as Tess continued to rush forward.

"You're going too fast!" LuAnn called.

Tess had been setting up to show off a mini-jump, but the distraction of her memories threw her off. Her legs continued reaching for the jump, but her mind wasn't in it, and with an awkward, twisted tumble, she crashed down onto the ice.

"Tess!" Janice blurted as she and LuAnn skated to her and knelt.

"Oh, girl." LuAnn held her hand. "Where does it hurt?"

Tess rubbed her hip. Already she knew a bruise would soon appear. What was she thinking, trying a jump? "I'm sorry." She ventured a chuckle. "I guess I'm not as agile as I used to be. I'm fine, though. Don't worry."

LuAnn and Janice stared at her. They weren't buying the cool front Tess was selling.

She exhaled and observed her visible breath until it disappeared, then shifted her gaze to the two still gaping at her. As embarrassed as she was, her friends' concern meant the world to her. Who else would she rather fall on her backside in the middle of a frozen river with? No one. Finally, she stretched her legs out in front of her.

"I was thinking about Jeffrey. It's the anniversary of our first date...and engagement. He asked me to marry him on the ice."

Janice's eyes crinkled with compassion. "I'm so sorry. Anniversaries can be hard. I knew yours was coming. I forgot."

Tess exchanged a glance with Janice. Janice's husband had also died. Her friend really did understand how painful anniversaries could be. And it had been nearly a year since LuAnn's mom's funeral. She'd experienced this type of pain too, and Tess and Janice would be there to listen and support. Tess shifted. For some reason, this year's anniversary seemed different to her—not as painful. Maybe she was healing from Jeffrey's death, just a bit. Maybe the inn had brought joy back into her life. Maybe she had a whole lot to be thankful for after all.

"It's okay, really. Anniversaries are hard, but wonderful too. I treasure my memories with Jeffrey. I loved being married to him." And maybe, someday, she'd be ready to move on.

Could she? She wasn't too sure, but right now, she had other things on her mind. She pulled herself to a standing position.

"Your ankle is okay?" LuAnn asked. "You didn't re-injure where it was sprained, did you?"

"No, it's fine." Tess slid forward. "All right, ladies." She returned to them. "We should get back to the inn. We can't leave Winnie without us for too long, even though she's got Kylie with her."

"Thorn's there too. I saw him come in this morning. He's working on fixing Winnie's old radio. She loves that old relic."

"Yeah, ever since Marcus dug it out of storage for her, she's been playing those World War II songs her mother sang."

Winnie had become one of Tess's favorite people since coming to the inn. Not only had her cooking given the soup café the best reputation in town, she also served the clients with gracious hospitality and demanded the highest standards of herself and her cooking. Tess wondered how Kylie was handling Winnie's expectations. Standards were good for the young woman, and helping a young person learn responsibility could only be positive—at least she hoped so.

The three women exited the ice and trekked toward the inn. Up ahead, Tess noticed a car pulling into the parking lot near the front entrance.

Not wanting to tramp their snowy boots over the inn's hardwood floor, they clomped through deep snow toward the back entrance. After sloughing off her winter wear, Tess thought she heard a car out front. With a peek, she spotted a vehicle pulling into the inn's parking lot.

"That must be our new guest." LuAnn moved next to her. "I thought she was going to arrive earlier."

"Our new guest?" Janice joined them. "I'm glad she made it before dark. I'll double-check her room. You two want to check her in?"

Nodding in unison, Tess and LuAnn made their way across the parlor to the reception area. Janice hiked up the stairs, then, as the door's bell jingled, Tess and LuAnn took their places behind the desk.

A woman with chin-length, straight brown hair strode in pulling a suitcase behind her. "Hello." Her tone was business-like but pleasant. Un-strapping a satchel from her shoulder, she lifted her chin and reached out her hand. "I'm Bonnie Bradshaw. I have a reservation."

"Welcome to Wayfarers Inn," Tess said as she shook her hand. She couldn't remember the last time a guest greeted her so formally. This woman seemed to have a purpose more than checking out the quaint historical town.

LuAnn glanced down at the reservation book she had already opened, then pointed. "Yes. I have you right here."

Ms. Bradshaw's shoulders slumped slightly. "I'm glad to have made it." She offered her driver's license without being asked.

"We are too." LuAnn wrote down the information from the license.

"It was a long, snowy drive from New York." She smiled when LuAnn gave the card back. "I hope you don't mind. I'm here to do a radio story about judges from the Civil War."

LuAnn's eyes sparkled like they always did when someone mentioned history. "What? What about..."

"Civil War judges?" Tess asked. "How would that topic be connected with Marietta?"

Bonnie leaned forward. "I'm actually pretty excited about this story. My great-great-great-great-grandfather was a judge in New York—where our family still lives. It was a free state, you know. But because of the Fugitive Slave Act—do you know what that is?"

LuAnn nodded. "It was an Act, upheld by the Supreme Court, that gave slave catchers the right to enter free states and recapture slaves to bring them back to their owners in the South."

"More like kidnap," Bonnie said. "But that's right." Her eyes shone approval.

"Show off," Tess murmured with a grin.

"Anyway, Grampa Graves resided over the district court that either gave permission or denial to the slave catchers. They had to have the correct documents, etc. I'm going to be researching that process as I work on the story."

"How interesting to have someone like that in your family history," Tess said.

"Yes. We've always been proud of our abolitionist history—apparently Grandma Graves was also a bit of an activist." She replaced the satchel over her shoulder. "Is my room..." she pointed toward the stairs.

"Of course." LuAnn chuckled. "I was so captivated by your story ... I'll call someone to help you."

In a moment, Thorn arrived and Janice appeared at the same time, giving a thumbs-up about the room's readiness.

Thorn nodded toward the suitcase. "You need help with that?"

"I really could have carried it myself." Bonnie threw Thorn a grateful glance. "But I do appreciate the help. It's heavy, isn't it?"

Thorn pretended to struggle to pick it up, but then grinned. "Not too bad."

Bonnie smiled at the three women.

As Bonnie started to follow Thorn toward the stairs, Tess realized she hadn't answered their question. "Uh, excuse me, Ms. Bradshaw."

"Call me Bonnie."

"Oh, thanks. What connection did your grandfather have with Marietta?"

"Right." She paused. "He stayed at this inn when it was called the, uh..."

"Riverfront House." Tess finished her sentence, her mind spinning. An abolitionist judge from the Civil War time stayed here? Did he know about the Underground Railroad stop, and if he did, maybe he even helped some of their "parcels." She liked hearing about those who aided the slaves fleeing for their freedom.

"Yes. And, well, he died on his return trip home, not far from here. They say it was from a heart attack, but there are rumors of foul play."

Tess peered at LuAnn and Janice. Many mysterious incidents had happened surrounding the inn since they bought it, but nothing like this.

"Foul play?" Janice must have been thinking the same as Tess.

"I'm hoping to find some answers about that as well," Bonnie continued before heading toward the stairs.

"Let us know if there's anything we can do to help," Tess called after her.

Bonnie disappeared up the stairs.

"Something new to learn about the inn's history." LuAnn tucked her hair behind her ear.

"And so mysterious," Janice added. "He died after staying here?"

"We should introduce her to Maybelline," LuAnn continued. "I wonder if she knows anything about this judge."

Before Tess could respond, a bloodcurdling scream sounded from outside.